A PASSIONATE INTERLUDE
UNDER THE SUMMER SUN . . .

"I *am* a servant and a very good one, too!"

Lord Peter seized one of her hands and examined it. "That hand never did a day's work, my dear."

Cassie tried to pull her hand away but he hung onto it fast. She suddenly realized she was sitting in the middle of the cornfield with this lord, that he was a strong and masculine man with a very steady disturbing gaze, and her hand trembled in his.

He put an arm about her shoulders and smiled down at her. She could feel the warmth and strength of that arm through the thin muslin of her dress.

"D-don't," she pleaded as his face drew closer, blotting out the sun.

"One kiss for a summer's day," he murmured. His lips closed on hers, gentle and sweet. He was amazed at the wave of passion that engulfed him, at the freshness and tenderness of those lips. He bent her back into the corn, raised his head and said huskily, "Why! You are enchanting!"

—From "The Summer of Discontent"
by Marion Chesney

Summertime Splendor

Marion Chesney Cynthia Bailey-Pratt
Sarah Eagle Melinda Pryce

JOVE BOOKS, NEW YORK

SUMMERTIME SPLENDOR

A Jove Book / published by arrangement with
the authors

PRINTING HISTORY
Jove edition / July 1992

ISBN: 0-515-10877-4

Jove Books are published by The Berkley Publishing Group,
200 Madison Avenue, New York, New York 10016.
The name "JOVE" and the "J" logo
are trademarks belonging to Jove Publications, Inc.

PRINTED IN THE UNITED STATES OF AMERICA

10 9 8 7 6 5 4 3 2 1

CONTENTS

ABOUT THE AUTHORS

MARION CHESNEY ("The Summer of Discontent") is one of the most popular and prolific authors of Regency Romance including writing such series as "The Six Sisters" and "A House for the Season." Ms. Chesney lives in London with her husband and son. This is her first story for Berkley.

CYNTHIA BAILEY-PRATT ("Lady Fair") is the author of *The Temporary Bride, Gentleman's Folly*, and the soon-to-be-released Regency *Queen of Hearts*. She's currently restoring her farmhouse in Maryland where she lives with her husband and two fat cats.

SARAH EAGLE ("A Summer's Folly") is the author of two Jove Regency romances, *The Reluctant Suitor* and *The Marriage Gamble*. Her story "A Christmas Spirit," appeared in *A Regency Holiday*. She also writes for Harlequin as Sarah Hawkes and for Meteor as Sally Falcon. She lives and works in Little Rock, Arkansas.

MELINDA PRYCE ("Tides of Love") was nominated as one of the best new Regency writers by *Romantic Times*. She is the author of *Thief of Hearts, A Love to Treasure*, and *Suddenly a Lady*. Ms. Pryce has a husband, five kids, and is working toward a brown belt in Aikido.

THE SUMMER
of
DISCONTENT

Marion Chesney

At FIRST IT LOOKED AS IF IT WAS GOING TO BE THE USUAL English summer, chill winds and driving rain. But then, at the end of June, the sun shone down and one lazy hot day began to follow the next.

Bramfield Park, home of the Earl of Wychhaven and his family, should therefore have been a place of sunshine and calm, undisturbed by any ripple of the realities of life that plagued most of the rest of Regency England. After all, the earl was armored in great wealth and lineage, and he had one of the most beautiful daughters in England.

But discontent prowled the cool, handsome rooms of his stately home and added lines to the face of his countess. For the beauty of the family, Sophia, had appeared in London at yet another Season, and, horror of horrors, she had not "taken." In other words, she was back at Bramfield Park without one single proposal of marriage.

Her parents could not understand it. They were a fastidious couple, both elegant and mannered. Their home reflected their exquisite taste, and, to them, Sophia was everything that pleased the eye: tall and statuesque, graceful, thick glossy brown hair, a darling of a straight nose, a rosebud of a mouth, and versed in all the arts to entrap a man from the flutter of a fan to white arms plucking the harp in the drawing room.

Perhaps if it had just been the London Season that had been the theater of Sophia's failure, they could have borne it. But they had taken her to Brighton in the wake of the

Prince Regent. Sophia had even danced at the Royal Pavilion. But no suitors had arrived at the Wychhavens' expen-
sively rented house on the Steyne.

Uncle Wilbur, the earl's brother, had said that they might
try puffing off their other daughter, Cassandra, but this was
treated as yet another sign of old Wilbur's dotage.

If Sophia had failed so miserably, how could such as
Cassandra succeed?

Cassandra—Cassie to her friends and family—was a sad
disappointment to her stylish parents. She was small and
slight in stature, clumsy and coltish, and worst of all, she
had red hair. Not auburn, pure flaming, unadulterated red.
Red hair was associated with the Scotch race and therefore
unfashionable. Had not the great Duke of Wellington shaved
his son's eyebrows because they were red?

So as the days passed and the heat increased and the
various relatives and houseguests of the Wychhavens began
to wilt, Cassie escaped more and more into the countryside.
She disliked her sister, Sophia, and occasionally felt quite
guilty about that dislike even though Sophia had earned it.
Sophia could be very cruel and was always taunting Cassie
about her lack of looks.

Then one day a stone dropped into the stagnant pond of
Bramfield Park.

The earl had received a letter from Lord Peter Courtney.
Lord Peter, like the earl, was a great art collector, and he
was returning to England from the Grand Tour. He had
gone on the tour immediately after leaving the army and
had not graced society for many years. He was reported to
be thirty-two.

In his letter Lord Peter had expressed a wish to see the
earl's collection. The earl promptly wrote back, saying they
would be delighted to receive him, and then he and his
countess fell into an orgy of plans for making a match for
Sophia with Lord Peter.

Into the animated discussion of those plans cut the dry
voice of one of their guests, Mr. Jensen. "I have heard

Courtney is a cold fish," he declared. "Got ice water running in his veins."

"Nonsense," said the earl. "He has written a charming letter. I understand him to be a fastidious man of great intelligence."

Mr. Jensen stifled a yawn. "Wasn't that just what I was saying? A cold fish."

Cassie dreaded Lord Peter's arrival. She felt she had enough chilly, fastidious people in her life without a possible brother-in-law joining their ranks.

So on the day when Lord Peter was due to arrive, Cassie went down to the kitchens and persuaded the French chef to give her a basket of cakes to take to Miss Stevens.

Miss Tabitha Stevens was a spinster who lived in a neat cottage outside the village of Bramfield. She had a tiny little income from a family trust and lived in genteel poverty. She had never adjusted to her true financial state, and thus pretended to have a whole cottage full of servants by shouting orders to imaginary footmen and maids. All she had left was her dignity. An odd friendship had been formed between the hoydenish Cassie and the genteel spinster. Cassie knew what it was to be unloved. She was sorry for Miss Stevens and supported that lady's fiction that she, Miss Stevens, was in fact a great lady who was merely staying in a little country cottage for amusement.

Cassie with her basket over her arm wandered slowly along the green lanes that led down to the village. In some places the hedges were so high that they arched over the road, forming green tunnels of welcome gloom from the heat of the sun. As no one bothered about Cassie, no one had warned her to carry a parasol on all occasions, and so her face was lightly tanned. She was wearing a high-waisted muslin gown, cut down to fit from one of Sophia's rejects—her parents employing all the parsimonious ways of the aristocracy—and a wide-brimmed straw hat. She walked out of the coolness of one particular tunnel and into the fierce heat of the sun. A cornfield stretched away to one side, and to the other lay a field of flax, the tiny blue flowers interspersed with the scarlet of poppies. She stopped for a long while, gazing at that carpet of blue and red flowers in delight. It seemed a finer sight to her than any painting or piece of statuary in her home.

She paused until the thought that the cakes might spoil in the heat made her hurry on at last.

Miss Stevens's cottage was a Tudor one: pretty from the outside and yet so dark and inconvenient to live in.

The garden was a riot of all the flowers Miss Stevens loved. Roses hung heavy with scent over the low doorway. In the little pocket-size garden delphiniums like blue sentinels stood guard over snapdragons, astors, dahlias, and tobacco flowers.

Cassie knocked at the door. "James!" came the sharp voice of Miss Stevens from within. "Answer that!"

Cassie waited patiently for her friend to cease calling to a nonexistent footman.

Finally the door swung open and Miss Stevens stood there. "Why, Cassie!" Usually Miss Stevens was a stickler for the formalities, but somehow Cassie had always been just Cassie to her. "I do not know where that lazy footman of mine has got to. Come in, my dear."

She led the way into a small, dark, low-beamed parlor. The furniture was of the locally made cottage variety. Chintz curtains fluttered at the open windows. There were no carpets on the floor apart from a brightly colored hearthrug that Miss Stevens had hooked herself, but the old boards were polished to a high shine. Cassie appreciatively breathed in the familiar scent of roses and beeswax and lavender and settled down in a comfortable chair after handing over the basket.

Miss Stevens tried not to show how truly grateful she was, for she loved cakes and could hardly ever afford even to make any. She called, "Lucy, take this to the kitchen." But of course, the maid, Lucy, never appeared.

"Drat the lazy girl," said Miss Stevens. "I shall get her to bring us some tea."

She bustled out.

Cassie sighed with pleasure and took off her hat and dropped it on the floor. The cottage was cool and pleasant. From behind the cottage came the lazy clucking of Miss Stevens's six hens. Miss Stevens came in, carrying a tray with a pot of tea, two old-fashioned cups without handles, and some of the cakes.

She was a small, middle-aged woman with a face like an anxious sheep. Her white hair was tightly curled on her head. She was wearing a very pretty, rather girlish muslin gown, Cassie having filched it for her out of Sophia's extensive wardrobe, knowing that the spinster did not have suitable clothes for such unusually warm weather.

"So," said Miss Stevens, pouring tea, "tell me what is happening."

"Hope rises again for Sophia. A certain Lord Peter Courtney is arriving."

Miss Stevens frowned in concentration. "Courtney? Courtney? Ah, youngest son of the Duke of Cadshire." Miss Stevens studied the social columns in newspapers given to her by Cassie. "Returned from the Grand Tour. Unmarried. Was a major in the forty-fifth."

"And I gather," said Cassie, "a cold, prissy fish of a man."

"Oh, dear, but he was a soldier brave, Cassie, riding into battle in the teeth of danger. I can see him now. His horse rearing and plunging as the cannonballs tear past him. 'Onward!' he cries!"

"Alas, Miss Stevens, he is a collector like papa, and that is the reason for his visit. Papa hopes he will add Sophia to his collection." She made a face. "She would do very well, you must admit, if she kept her nasty mouth closed."

"Cassie!"

"Well, she was being catty again today about my hair. Besides, why should the army make a difference? Old Lord

Todhampton came to stay last year, and he spent years and years in battles, yet he wears stays and a tremendous amount of paint and clatters about everywhere on his high heels. I can picture this Lord Peter, sort of cold and grayish, quite small and very fussy."

The older woman refused to listen. "Perhaps he will be dashing and handsome. Perhaps this is your beau at last, Cassie. I think it so odd of your parents not to give you a Season."

"I think they will . . . next year," she said hopefully, not really believing her words. "Mama was talking about either Bath or Tunbridge Wells, and Papa said it might be an idea to ship me out to old Aunt Philadelphia in Calcutta. He said army men far from home always fall in love with anything in a skirt."

"Monstrous!" exclaimed Miss Stevens, in between nibbles at a cake. "Mmmm. This is *so* divine. Gives me an unusual feeling of sin. Yes, I think your parents are quite unnatural. Have you still got that governess? The clever one?"

"Miss Jamieson? No. Sophia took against her, so off she went. That was our fourth and last governess."

"What was up with her?"

"She liked me," said Cassie seriously. "I tried to warn her, you know, that Sophia must have all the attention. But she did not listen, so off went Miss Jamieson and was promptly snapped up by Lady Cheam, who had been trying to lure her away this age."

There came the sound of carriage wheels and horses' hooves in the distance. "Who will that be?" asked Cassie. "The baker?"

"No, he makes his rounds on Thursday morning. The fish man?" Miss Stevens tilted her head on one side. "More than one horse. I wonder . . . Oh, dear, whoever it is, they are stopping here."

Miss Stevens ran to the window. A traveling coach stood outside with a crest on the door panel. A tall man was climbing out. He called up to the coachman, "It is damnably hot and I need some fresh air. I shall ask here for directions." And the coachman answered, "Yes, my lord."

"My lord!" screeched Miss Stevens. "And he is coming *here!* I cannot answer the door myself like a *peasant.*"

Cassie grinned. "I'll do it for you. Where's the stuff?"

"Upstairs. In the chest of drawers in my bedroom."

The year before when Miss Stevens had received a visit from a haughty relative, Cassie had acted as her maid. The "stuff" was a maid's cap and apron and a brown wig.

Cassie put everything on at lightning speed and ran down and opened the door. A tall handsome man with eyes as cold as ice stood looking down at her. "Is your mistress at home?"

Cassie silently held out her hand. He took out a card case, extracted an embossed card, and held it out to her. Cassie curtsied and took it into Miss Stevens. "Oh, Lor—" squeaked Cassie, reading the card. "It's him. Courtney." There was no time to say any more, for Lord Peter appeared in the doorway.

"Lord Peter Courtney," announced Cassie in a shaky voice.

Miss Stevens rose to her feet. "So charmed," she lilted. "Pray accept some refreshment. I am Miss Stevens of the Surrey Stevens."

He bowed. "You are most kind, but I simply want directions to Bramfield Park."

"Oh, dear, you won't stay? Bramfield Park is two miles along the road. You will come to the West Lodge. It has a red-tiled roof, most unusual in these parts. Of course, my little cottage orné has thatch. A quaint sophistry, do you not think?"

He gave a frosty smile.

"But if you must be on your way . . ." With a certain air of pride, Miss Stevens rang a small brass bell on the table.

Cassie promptly reappeared. Miss Stevens said grandly, "Show Lord Peter out, Lucy."

Lord Peter turned as he entered the garden and looked

at the maid. "What is Bramfield Park like?" he asked and then immediately wondered why he had chosen to question the maid and not the mistress.

"Terribly boring," said Cassie cheerfully. "Like a museum." She decided all in that moment that even such a horror as her sister did not deserve to be allied to this cold and intimidating man. He was holding his hat in his hand, and his thick black hair gleamed in the sunshine. He had black eyebrows as well, thin and supercilious. His eyes were winter-gray and hooded by heavy lids. He was slim but powerfully built with a small waist, well-muscled thighs, and broad shoulders. The thighs on whom Cassie's wide-eyed gaze fell were shown in all their strength by a pair of thin leather breeches, which fitted him like a second skin. "Of course," went on Cassie, as he had not moved, "they are expecting you to propose to Lady Sophia."

"Why should I do that, you impertinent baggage?"

"Because you are a collector, like the earl, and they do so hope you will collect Sophia, for she did not take at her last Season. You are their Last Hope."

He looked at her narrowly, his eyes scanning the thin, tanned face and the clever hazel eyes. "Are you usually so forward?" he demanded.

Cassie blushed and hung her head. He drew out a sovereign and handed it to her. "Buy yourself a new wig, my chuck."

"Why?" demanded Cassie, stepping back a pace.

"Because the monstrosity you are wearing is too small and your red hair is showing under it. Why hide it? I like red hair."

Cassie felt so hot with mortification, she thought she would collapse in a puddle at his feet.

He gave a laugh and jerked her into his arms and kissed her full on the mouth. And then he released her, and still laughing, he walked away.

Cassie turned and ran back into the cottage, scrubbing her mouth with her apron.

"I was watching from the window!" exclaimed Miss Stevens. "He *kissed* you!" She clasped her hands together and gazed at Cassie earnestly. "And so handsome, too. He has fallen in love with you. I can see it all. And when he realizes that you are not a lowly maid but the daughter of the house, he will cry, 'Be mine!'"

"No, he will not," said Cassie, wondering whether to laugh or cry. "He thought he was bussing a pert maid. Anyway, he gave me a whole sovereign." She put it on the table. "You had best share it out among your real servants."

Miss Stevens wanted to be honest, to cry out that she had no servants. But a whole sovereign! She thought of all the food and coals that would buy and kept silent.

Cassie crept back into Bramfield Park by the servants' entrance and made her way up the back stairs to her room. She rang the bell and told the maid that she was feeling unwell and would like a tray in her room, rather than joining the family for dinner.

Then she pulled a chair up to the open window and settled down with a book.

At half past six the door to her room opened and Sophia walked in. "Why are you sitting there in that terrible old gown?" she demanded.

"Because I am sick unto death, sister dear," said Cassie calmly. "You will need to enchant Lord Peter all on your own."

"You are not ill," Sophia said disdainfully. "You cannot bear once more to be cast in the shade by my beauty."

"I don't care what you think," said Cassie. "Go away, Sophia, you give me the headache. What's Lord Peter like?"

"I have not seen him yet. Mama decided I should be presented in the drawing room before dinner. I have a new Attitude. Do you know that statue by the console table?"

"Yes."

"Well, Mama says I am to stand beside it in the same attitude." Sophia threw back her head, put one hand out as if to ward off something, and put an arm across her forehead.

"Vastly fetching," commented Cassie. "Do you know whom that statue is supposed to represent?"

"Yes," lied Sophia.

"Brave you." Cassie picked up her book and began to read.

But no sooner had the stately Sophia stalked out than Cassie's eyes began to dance. The statue represented the Rape of Leda by Zeus, who had transformed himself into a swan. The swan bit had been broken off in transit and only the horrified Leda remained.

This she had to see.

She went down the back stairs and then through a door on the first landing to a passage that ran behind the walls of the drawing room. It was supposed to have been used by the Cavaliers escaping from the Roundheads during the Civil War. But two years before, Cassie had placed a ladder at a point behind the wall of the drawing room, for she had discovered that a painting of an ancestor high over the fire-place had a device where the painted eyes of the portrait could be drawn back on threads, allowing a good view of what was happening in the room below. She assumed some Cavalier had thought up the device to be able to hide and yet get an idea of what was going on in the house.

She looked down into the drawing room. Lord Peter had not arrived, but Sophia was being placed in position for her Attitude. Attitudes were much adopted by young society ladies of the Regency. An Attitude was supposed to—usually—represent some historical or classical figure.

Then Lord Peter arrived. He bowed to various members of the company. Then Cassie heard her father say, "And our greatest treasure, our daughter Sophia."

"Very fine," she heard Lord Peter remark. "The statue is . . . ?"

"Leda," said the countess.

His eyes began to dance. "Where is the swan?"

"Honk! Honk!" said Cassie gleefully from behind the portrait.

Lord Peter quickly covered his face with his handkerchief. "Too much snuff," he mumbled.

"What was that honking noise?" demanded Sophia, abandoning her pose.

"I am afraid it was I," said Lord Peter, though he had no idea where the diverting noise had come from. "I was blowing my nose. I do apologize. Will you walk with me, Lady Sophia?"

She inclined her head gracefully.

"That is a fine portrait up there," said Lord Peter, coming to a stop in front of the fireplace.

"I have never really looked at it," commented Sophia. "Some ancestor. Not worth much."

Lord Peter looked up into Cassie's eyes, and she saw to her horror that he had quite deliberately winked. She darted down the ladder and then fled to her room.

Unfortunately, there seemed to be no end to the good weather. The heat at last invaded the large, cool, stately rooms of Bramfield Park, and flies buzzed furiously over the gallipots in the corners. Not a breath of air moved the long curtains. Chairs and tables were moved out onto the long terrace at the back of the house for the guests. Lord Peter found himself restless and bored. For once, the pleasure of looking at beautiful things, so necessary to his soul after the long years of battles, did not soothe his senses.

Sophia was placed in his way everywhere he went. And she was such tiresome company. She was so obsessed with her own beauty that she appeared to see no reason to make any interesting conversation at all. At first he was surprised that such a beauty and such an heiress had not been snapped up, but as he got to know her more, he became aware of a coldness in her which was repelling. Sophia, he decided, did not like anyone in the whole wide world except herself and regarded the rest of the human race, including himself, with a thinly veiled contempt.

He was occasionally puzzled by the continuing non-appearance of the younger daughter, but decided she was still probably consigned to the schoolroom. He assumed she was some naughty child who had hidden behind that portrait in the drawing room to spy on the company. But he didn't have time to think about this, as the Wychhavens were making great plans for a ball to be held in his honor. He wished there were some way he could make his escape. The place was a bore. The only thing that had amused him so far had been that odd little maid at the cottage in the village.

He decided to pay Miss Stevens a visit, setting out walking early one morning so as to be free from his host, who would no doubt have roused Sophia from her bed to accompany him if he knew his plans.

He hesitated a little before pushing open the gate to Miss Stevens's garden. It *was* still fairly early, eight o'clock, but he heard a clatter of dishes coming from the house. At least the maid would be awake.

He knocked on the door.

There was a long silence. A curtain at an upstairs window under the heavy eyebrows of the thatch twitched and the white blur of a face looked down.

Then, "James! Answer the door!" came Miss Stevens's frantic call. There was a long silence. "Well, then, Lucy, where are you, girl?" called Miss Stevens.

Another long silence, and then the door was at last opened.

"Oh, Lord Peter, do step in," said Miss Stevens. "I do not know what has happened to servants these days."

He followed her into the parlor, ducking his head under the low beams.

"Some refreshment, my lord?"

"No, I thank you. Where is your maid?"

"I remember now," said Miss Stevens. "I sent her to the village to buy some . . . some bread."

"An interesting child and with the accents of a lady. Where did you find her?"

"She was sent to me from the orphanage," said Miss Stevens, her ever-fertile imagination coming to her rescue. "Yes, I, too, was amazed at the clarity of her speech and the delicacy of her manners. Of course"—Miss Stevens looked mysterious—"breeding will out."

"Do you mean she is of good birth?"

"Very high birth, my lord. She is the daughter of . . . Ah, but I must not reveal his name."

"Lucy is the by-blow of some lord?"

Miss Stevens colored delicately. "I wish there were some other way of putting it, but . . . yes."

"But how did she come to affect the manners of a lady? Contrary to romantic belief, the daughter of an aristocrat brought up in an orphanage would look and sound exactly like any brat from an orphanage."

"She was not there very long." Miss Stevens looked at the clock, as if for inspiration. "This lord—you must forgive me for not giving you his name—brought Lucy up as his own daughter, governesses and all that." Miss Stevens waved an airy hand. "But he married a cruel and beautiful lady. 'Get that creature gone from hence!' she cried."

He leaned forward and looked at her intently. "I am sure it was a snowy night."

Miss Stevens returned his look with a limpid gaze. "How did you guess? It was two winters ago and the snow was falling fast. 'Get you to the orphanage, where you belong!' cried this cruel lady, her beautiful rouged lips curling in a sinister smile as she pushed poor Lucy out into the snow. Lucy was wearing only a thin muslin dress. She was nigh dead with cold when she stumbled into the orphanage. For long days and nights her life hung in the balance. But she was befriended by Mrs. Griggs, a fine woman of strong religious principles who was married to one of the governors.

A careful application of chicken soup brought her back to life. I myself make very good chicken soup."

There was a long silence. Laughter bubbled up inside Lord Peter, and he felt he must make his escape soon before he laughed in her face. But some imp prompted him to say, "I am amazed the orphanage took her in just like that. I mean, such things have to be arranged, and orphanages are full to overflowing as it is. She looked strong enough. Would not the workhouse have been a more suitable place?"

"Not the workhouse," whispered Miss Stevens, looking so afraid that for one mad moment he almost believed her story. But then he saw the careful darns on her old gown, for Miss Stevens was dressed ready for her morning chores, and the trembling at the corner of the spinster's mouth, and he realized that Miss Stevens herself lived in dread of the workhouse. He guessed that apart from the mysterious Lucy, she did not really have any servants at all.

He rose to his feet. "A most fascinating story, Miss Stevens," he said. "No, do not try to call your servants. I will find my own way out. I shudder to think that one of my class should be the cause of such distress." He dug in his pocket and pulled out a rouleau of guineas. "Perhaps this will help to give the girl a dowry."

"My lord, I cannot possibly accept—"

"But it is for Lucy, and I am sure she will be glad of it."

He bowed and left, leaving the stunned Miss Stevens staring at the guineas.

The morning was fine and the air still held a certain amount of freshness. He decided to take a look at the village.

It consisted of a long straggling row of houses and shops with an inn at one end and a squat church at the other. He searched along the row of shops until he found the bakers. No Lucy.

Suddenly bored again and disappointed but reluctant to

return to Bramfield Park, he walked on through the village.
There was a small shady wood to the right of the road as
he walked beyond the village to the far side, away from
Bramfield Park. The morning was becoming hot, and the
shade of the trees looked inviting. And then, as he looked
into the wood and along the narrow path that traversed it,
he saw a flash of red.

Red hair. He plunged along the path. It twisted and turned
through the wood, and he began to run. And then, at the far
edge of the wood where it bordered a cornfield, he saw the
girl, her slim figure moving easily and quickly.

"Lucy!" he called.

She stopped and looked back and then took to her heels
and ran straight into the cornfield. He ran after her out
of the dark coolness of the wood and plunged in among
the cornstalks, seeing always that hatless red head bobbing
above the stalks ahead of him. He caught up with her in
the middle of the field. She stopped suddenly, realizing she
could not escape him.

He took out his handkerchief and mopped his brow.
"I'faith," he cried, "you run like the wind, girl! There is
no need to have fear of me. I wish you no harm."

"Now, how was I to know that?" said Cassie reasonably. "Goodness, I'm tired." She sat down in the corn and
grinned up at him. "I am not used to racing so early in the
morning."

He took off his coat and placed it on the ground and sat
down beside her.

"We are crushing Farmer Warby's corn," pointed out
Cassie.

"Only a little of it. Miss Stevens told me a very interesting story about you."

"Oh, really?" Cassie gave him a sidelong look. "Which
one?"

He laughed. "What an odd thing to say! She told
me of your illegitimate birth and how your father, Lord
Thingummy, married a cruel and beautiful woman who

turned you out one night and made you walk to the orphanage."

"Was it snowing?" asked Lucy, a gurgle of laughter in her voice.

"Can't you remember?"

"Of course I can and of course it was."

"Then if you were brought up as a lady, it must be hard for you to be a maid of all work."

"I survive." Cassie plucked at an ear of corn.

The sun was glinting on her shining red hair. It was thick and hanging in a tangle of curls down her back. Her face was small and elfin, and he noticed when she lowered her eyes that her lashes were ridiculously long.

"Would it surprise you," he said, "if I told you that I did not believe one word of Miss Stevens's story?"

"Not at all. You who are so rich and secure in the world cannot know of the miseries that befall a poor bastard child." Her eyes were wide and serious.

"You are not trying to tell me that all that farago of nonsense is true?"

Cassie looked so hurt that he began to wonder if that famous actress, Mrs. Siddons, might not have a rival at last.

"I remember it well," she said in a low voice. "It was bitter cold. I pleaded and begged, but she threw me out just the same. I thought I would die of the cold, but I have a strong constitution."

"Miss Stevens said you nearly died, that your life hung in the balance."

"Which it did," said Cassie. "But I rallied, which all goes to show that I do have a strong constitution. Talk of other things. How do you find Bramfield Park?"

"A trifle dull."

"And are you going to propose to Sophia?"

"Surely Lady Sophia to you, citizen, or are you of a radical persuasion?"

"Are you going to marry her?"

"She *is* very beautiful. She has a sister, has she not? Cassandra? I have not seen her. Is she a child?"

"I would not ask about poor Cassandra. She is . . . deformed. That is why she is never introduced to the guests."

"Is this deformity so terrible?"

"She is a hunchback, not so bad, but horrible for her parents, who like everything about them to be beautiful."

"Why is it, my sweeting, that I do not believe a word you say?"

Cassie looked away. "Perhaps you are not in the way of conversing with servants."

"And why is it that I am sure you are not a servant? That Miss Stevens is an indigent gentlewoman without any servants?"

"I *am* a servant and a very good one, too!"

He seized one of her hands and examined it. "That hand never did a day's work, Lucy."

Cassie tried to pull her hand away, but he hung on to it fast. She suddenly realized she was sitting in the middle of the cornfield with this lord, that he was a strong and masculine man with a very steady, disturbing gaze, and her hand trembled in his.

He put an arm about her shoulders and smiled down at her. She could feel the warmth and strength of that arm through the thin muslin of her dress.

"D-don't," she pleaded as his face drew closer, blotting out the sun.

"One kiss for a summer's day," he murmured. His lips closed on hers, gentle and sweet. He was amazed at the wave of passion that engulfed him, at the freshness and tenderness of those lips. He bent her back into the corn, raised his head, and said huskily, "Why, you are enchanting!"

For one moment she stared up at him, her eyes wide, hearing the light breeze ripple through the corn and the birds singing from the woods, and then she wriggled like an eel from under him and jumped to her feet. "You disgusting *old* man!" she shouted, and then she was off and running.

He stayed where he was, shocked. How old was this Lucy? Eighteen? Perhaps nineteen? But to be called old and in tones of such loathing. Suddenly, he felt as old as she had damned him. And just as disgusting.

Cassie ran hard all the way to Miss Stevens's cottage and arrived panting and disheveled. Miss Stevens was in the back garden, watering her vegetables.

"Why, Cassie!" she exclaimed. "What is the matter? You must have something cold to drink. James!"

It said a lot for Cassie's kind heart that she did not scream out that there was no James, had never been a James, or a Lucy, or a Jane, or a page called Ben, or any of the other retinue of servants that Miss Stevens claimed to have.

"You told Lord Peter that I was a bastard child," said Cassie. "He followed me, he chased me, and he kissed me, and God alone knows what else he would have done had I not escaped."

"Oh, my dear, tell him who you really are. He behaved wickedly, yes. But he thought he was dealing with a servant. When he knows you are the earl's daughter, he will marry you."

"No, he will not marry me," said Cassie, exasperated. "And I have no time for men, lords or otherwise, who think they can have their way with servant girls. Do you know what would happen if he ever found out about me? He would go to papa and report that his daughter was running wild in the countryside, pretending to be a peasant, and your maid. I would be confined to my room on bread and water. Do you remember when I slipped out to go to the village ball and papa descended and found me dancing reels with the peasants? One month of bread and water was what I got for that—*and no books*. Think what he would do to me if he ever learned of this! Worse than anything, I called Lord Peter a disgusting old man."

"Cassie!" shrieked Miss Stevens. She dropped the pail of water she was holding. "He is one of the most handsome men I have ever seen. Did you remark his legs? I have never seen a finer pair."

"Anyway, if he calls again, tell him that your lips are sealed as concerns my history," said Cassie, who did not want to think of Lord Peter's physical charms, legs or otherwise. "I was hard put to follow your tale of wicked beautiful women and the snow."

"One woman, Cassie," Miss Stevens looked miserable. "I thought I had done rather well. Come into the house and let us have some tea."

Cassie sat dejectedly in the parlor listening to Miss Stevens in the kitchen berating a nonexistent maid. Miss Stevens came in carrying a tray and saying, "I really must speak strongly to that girl. She becomes lazier by the minute." Then the spinster's eye fell on the rouleau of guineas.

"Cassie, dear. Those guineas are for you."

"What? Why . . . ?"

"Lord Peter left them. He said they would provide you with a dowry. Do you think I ought to return the money to him?"

"That will engender more questions. Use the money yourself, Miss Stevens. I do not need it."

Miss Stevens bent over the teapot to hide her confusion and gratitude. She need not dread the winter ahead. She would be able to afford wood and coal. She could even buy a new gown!

"Cassie," she said tentatively when she had recovered, "I think Lord Peter is a very fine man."

"I should not have been so rude to him," said Cassie ruefully, "but he does frighten me. There is something very predatory about him."

"There is always something predatory about a man in love," said Miss Stevens.

"Do you not mean in lust?"

"Really, Cassie, I know what I am talking about. I remember when Sir James Torrington was much taken with me at the hunt ball."

"Did he kiss you?"

"Oh, no, but he danced with me twice, and he helped me to jelly at supper *and his hand shook.*"

"And what became of him?"

"I had no dowry"—Miss Stevens sighed—"and so like all the others, he cooled off."

Cassie crept down to the secret passage just before dinner. The guests and family were assembled. Lord Peter, she noticed ruefully, did look extremely handsome. He was talking to her father. "Am I never to meet your other daughter?" he was asking. Cassie clutched the top of the ladder.

"She is an odd little thing," said the earl. "Not very sociable. Not like our Sophia." He turned and gazed fondly on his elder daughter, who promptly struck an Attitude, supposed to be Penelope awaiting the return of Odysseus. One white hand shielded her brow as she gazed out to sea while the other white hand warded off suitors.

"Is she still in the schoolroom?"

"Cassie? No, she is eighteen but looks like a child. We do not have high hopes for her."

"Why?" asked Lord Peter. "Has she a hunched back or a squint?"

"You jest, my lord, you jest. There is the dinner bell."

Lord Peter stood his ground. "Perhaps you would do me the honor of presenting me to your daughter, Cassandra, at dinner tomorrow night."

"Of course, if that is your wish," said the earl, and then the guests moved off toward the dining room.

Now what was she going to do? thought Cassie. Not only did she not want to meet Lord Peter again, she had promised Miss Stevens.

For Miss Stevens, who had become more and more elated at the sight of Lord Peter's guineas, had invited Cassie to dinner on the following evening, and Cassie had accepted.

Then she had an idea. She went up to the schoolroom and

rummaged around in a cupboard until she found a tube of red paint and a paintbrush.

She went to her bedroom and sat down at the toilet table after placing a branch of candles on it and then carefully began to paint red spots all over her face.

The footman who arrived half an hour later carrying Cassie's dinner on a tray nearly dropped it at the sight of her. He ran downstairs and told the butler, who ponderously bent over the earl at the dinner table and informed him his daughter had broken out in spots.

"Sophia? Not a blemish on her," said the earl, who only ever thought of his elder daughter.

The butler bent his head again.

Lord Peter heard him exclaim. "Cassandra! Oh, send for the physician immediately."

Upstairs, Cassie now carefully arranged in bed, awaited the arrival of the doctor. He arrived an hour later. His name was Dr. Ferguson, a dour and taciturn Scot. He examined Cassie, studied the spots, and then went over to the toilet table and soaked a cloth in water, and returning to the bed, wiped her left cheek and then looked grimly down at the wet paint on the cloth.

"Oh, dear," said Cassie, "you've found me out."

"Wasting ma guid time like this. What's the game?"

For some reason Cassie decided to be nearly honest. "Miss Stevens has come into a little money. She invited me to dinner tomorrow night. She . . . she is lonely, as you know, and does not have much fun. Papa is going to insist I join them for dinner tomorrow night, and I know Miss Stevens will even now have begun the preparations. I . . . I could not bear to disappoint her."

The doctor frowned down at her and then suddenly began to pack his implements back into his bag.

Lady Wychhaven entered the room at that moment, and Cassie quickly covered up the clean cheek with her hand and looked appealingly at the doctor.

"What is wrong?" asked Lady Wychhaven.

"Lady Cassandra has eaten something that has given her an allergy. Of course, it might be the chicken pox. I think she should be confined to her room for a week and not given verra much to eat."

"Very well, Dr. Ferguson. Does she have a fever?"

"Yes, my lady, but not verra high. But she can move about. Do not let the servants near her in case the infection spreads. Leave her meals outside her door. You will find she is capable of getting them herself."

"An infection! Good heavens, imagine if Sophia should become marked! Go to sleep, Cassie, and do please keep to your room. Think of Sophia."

The next afternoon Lord Peter was informed slyly by the earl that Sophia was in the rose garden. So Lord Peter took refuge in the library with a book behind a screen in the corner beside the window that led out onto the terrace.

He had suggested earlier to the countess that he might pay a visit to her sick daughter as he had once had the chicken pox and was not likely to get it again, but the countess had treated this kind idea with horror. What if he carried the infection on his *boots* from the sickroom! she had shrieked just as if Lord Peter had announced his intention of jumping on Cassandra. What if poor Sophia got spots? His mind kept drifting away from the printed lines in front of him. He was in his undress, wrapped in a silk banyan, and had no intention of putting on a starched cravat, waistcoat, coat, and breeches until the dressing bell sounded later for dinner. It was just too hot. If Sophia liked to posture about the rose garden in the burning heat, then she was welcome to her own company.

Then he heard voices from the terrace and drew his chair back behind the shelter of the curtain so that he would not be seen.

"It is a vast pity that Lady Cassandra is ill, Mr. Braithwaite," came Mr. Jensen's voice. "She is remarkably bright and lively, and I must confess I find the company here dull."

"I have never seen her," came Mr. Braithwaite's voice. "Is she a fright? I am told she has none of her sister's beauty."

"Lady Cassandra is an attractive waif. They are ashamed of her because she has red hair."

"Then they should dye it," said Mr. Braithwaite. "Lady Torrance was a famous beauty in my youth. Men stood up in their carriages to get a better look when she drove past. No one knew her hair was dyed and yet it was. Its natural color was brilliant red."

"I do not think her parents have enough interest in her," said Mr. Jensen, "to do anything about her one way or t'other. Care for a game of billiards?"

Their voices faded. Lord Peter put his book in his lap. There could not be two girls in the neighborhood with red hair, surely.

He was still speculating idly about this daughter, Cassandra, as his valet helped him to dress for dinner. His room faced the back of the house, that being where the grandest guest apartments were. He was looking out the window as he was adjusting his cravat when he saw a slight figure walking through the shrubbery. He caught a glint of red hair shining under a frivolous bonnet covered with silk flowers.

He dismissed his valet and then made his way out. He saw a footman bearing a decanter and wineglasses to one of the other guest's rooms and asked him, "Which is Lady Cassandra's room?"

He was informed it was on the floor above, directly above his own. He told the servant he could find his own way.

He hesitated outside Lady Cassandra's door. There was a note pinned to it. "I do not wish dinner. Please do not disturb me at all."

He cautiously opened the door. There was a still figure lying on the bed. He was about to retreat when a light breeze moved the curtains and a shaft of sunlight struck the bed, lighting up the head of the figure. He gave a stifled exclamation and went closer. He reached out a tentative hand and then gently drew down the bedclothes. There was a dummy lying on the bed made out of two pillows, a nightdress, the top of a wig stand, and an improvised wig of red wool.

Lord Peter went down to his own quarters and informed his valet that he was to tell the company that he was indisposed. Then, with a feeling of freedom he had not experienced since he was a boy, he made his way out of the house and down the drive, very quickly, expecting any moment that the earl would send some servant after him to call him back.

"Don't answer it," urged Cassie some time later as she and Miss Stevens were preparing to sit down to dinner. Miss Stevens had gone to a lot of trouble and felt very grand having dinner at the new late hour of seven o'clock, just like they did in London. The knocking at the door which had disturbed them became more peremptory.

"It cannot be a tradesman," said Miss Stevens. "A tradesman would call at the kitchen door. The vicar perhaps?"

And then they looked at each other in alarm as they heard the door being opened, and then the next moment Lord Peter had walked into the parlor.

Miss Stevens rose to her feet, flustered and nervous. "My lord, what an unusual hour to call. We were just sitting down to dinner. Perhaps you would care to join us . . . ?!"

"Delighted," he said. "You are most kind."

"Perhaps I should explain why dear Ca—dear Lucy is joining me at table. You see, as I have already told you, she is a lady by birth, and as I did not expect company . . ."

"Think nothing of it."

"Now I must get James and Jane and tell them we have a guest."

Miss Stevens bustled out.

"Do sit down, my lord," said Cassie. "This is a very low-ceilinged room, and I do not like you towering over me. How did you know I would be here?"

"Because you work here, do you not? Besides, I have taken a liking to Miss Stevens."

Cassie rose and went to the dresser and took out cutlery and began to lay an extra place at the round table in the middle of the parlor. "I think," she said, "you are come to torment me. Miss Stevens is not exactly in funds, and you are stretching her meager resources by dropping in for dinner like this."

"I will make it up to her," he said. His eyes teased her. "Did you get your dowry?"

Cassie hesitated. She wanted to say she did not want it, but Miss Stevens must already have spent part of it on this wretched dinner. "Thank you," she forced herself to say.

"Of course, to me it was not much, but it will perhaps secure some tradesman for you as a husband, some very *small* tradesman."

"The butcher, Mr. Evans, is under five feet in height, but alas, he is married."

"I meant someone not too prosperous."

"Did you now? I would never have guessed that."

Miss Stevens entered then with the first course and fictitious tales of what had happened to her servants. To Cassie's infinite relief, Lord Peter set himself to please, telling them of the countries he had visited on the Grand Tour and of the paintings, statues, and objects d'art he had brought back with him. His tales of Venice in particular fascinated both ladies, Cassie dreamily imagining the glory of a sunny city where the streets were canals. For his part, Lord Peter found the simple dinner excellent. Thrifty Miss Stevens had not spent too much on luxuries. The meal consisted of green pea soup, roast forequarter of lamb with mint sauce, peas, and new potatoes, followed by gooseberry pudding and strawberry tartlets.

When the meal was over, Miss Stevens surprised Cassie by rising and saying they would leave Lord Peter to his wine.

"Now what?" asked Cassie as they stood in the back garden where neat rows of lettuce glimmered palely in the dusk and bats fluttered overhead, wheeling in circles as if they were toys being held by children on strings.

"The night is warm," said Miss Stevens. "It is cooler here, Cassie, than in the drawing room."

"Miss Stevens, I do not wish to upset you, but you don't *have* a drawing room, and that he will find out when he comes in search of us."

Miss Stevens looked blank as she always did when caught out in one of her lies.

"Never mind," said Cassie gently. "He can find us here. It was a lovely dinner, Miss Stevens, much better than anything I could get at home."

"He is pursuing you, Cassie."

"He is amusing himself, Miss Stevens. If he had an interest in billiards, say, he would not find diversion in chasing a housemaid. I wonder if he still thinks I am a housemaid. I hope he did not see me leaving the castle and follow me."

"I am sure he would have said something to that effect if he had." Miss Stevens gently took Cassie's arm. "Do you not think he is very fine? He would make you an excellent husband, Cassie."

"Lord Peter is too old, too cold, and altogether too terrifying," said Cassie.

"But do you not sometimes dream of a beau, my dear?"

Lord Peter, who had just entered the garden in time to hear the last question, stood listening.

He heard Cassie give a wistful little sigh and then he heard her say, "Of course, Miss Stevens. I dream of someone young and handsome and full of life and fun, someone who does not particularly care for beautiful things, someone who would find *me* beautiful, red hair and all. Such as

Lord Peter has no interest in me. He wants some beautiful creature who will supply him with beautiful sons and who will be as stately and cold as he is himself."

Lord Peter quietly retreated into the house. He sat down once more at the table and picked up his half full wineglass. Was that really how he appeared? Did such as Cassie know what it was like not really to have enjoyed any youth at all, to have been at war since age sixteen, leaving him with a craving for stillness and peace?

When Cassie and Miss Stevens eventually came in search of him, he promptly rose to his feet and bowed over Miss Stevens's hand, thanked her for a splendid dinner, and said he must take his leave.

He looked so somber and grim that Miss Stevens felt uncomfortable and wondered whether her cooking had given him indigestion.

Lord Peter strode back to Bramfield Park under a full moon. The air was full of scents of summer, wild roses mixed with the tangy smell of wild garlic. A fox slid across the road in front of him. It was a night made for love and romance, a night for wandering through the country lanes with someone you loved.

Strange, he had not thought of love for a long time. All those yearnings he had had in his early youth, he had considered long gone. As he approached Bramfield Park, he pictured the elegance of its rooms, the dullness of the conversation, which no amount of beautiful objects could compensate for, and then he thought of his own home in Wiltshire, of its cool, elegant, *lifeless* rooms, and felt quite bleak. He had been so anxious to escape from Bramfield Park, to bring his visit to an end, but to escape to what? And then there was the ball to come. He knew that despite every appearance to the contrary, the Wychhavens expected him to announce his engagement to Sophia at the ball. He suspected that Sophia with her overweening conceit had helped to give her parents this impression. And would Lady Cassandra grace the ball? Would she find that handsome young man of her dreams, and while he propelled the chilly statue that was Sophia through the steps of some dance, would he have to witness the spectacle of a Cassandra who was blissfully happy?

He decided he was becoming maudlin.

He marched up to his room and allowed his valet to prepare him for bed. He banished all thoughts of Lucy or Cassandra or whoever the hell she was firmly from his mind, closed his eyes, and ordered himself to fall asleep.

But early the next day he rode into the village and told the surprised tradespeople of Bramfield that Miss Stevens was to have credit on all goods until the end of the year and that all bills were to be sent to him.

After a few days of being confined to her room pretending to be ill, Cassie grew weary of the game, now that there was no need for it. She made her way early one morning to Miss Stevens's cottage and found that lady in raptures because she had discovered that she had unlimited credit in the village shops until Christmas, thanks to Lord Peter's generosity.

"So you see," said Miss Stevens, "it means I can now afford a real maid." Miss Stevens was too happy to explain away her previous fictional servants. "Little Lucy Dasset would be glad of the training, and her parents say they would not expect me to pay her much more than meal and board. I shall have a real Lucy! And she starts today."

Glad of Miss Stevens's good luck but feeling strangely restless, Cassie finally left and walked through the village, heading for the woods at the other end. She strolled slowly along the path through the woods, hoping that she might hear a call behind her, hear a light quick footstep, but there was nothing but green silence. The day was so hot that even the birds had ceased to sing. She walked for a long time that day, even returning to Miss Stevens's cottage for tea, but there was no sign of Lord Peter.

Despite herself, she was drawn again to spying on the

drawing room that evening. This time Lord Peter appeared to be paying a great deal of attention to Sophia. But why, wondered Cassandra bleakly, did she feel so lost and alone?

Again the next day Cassandra wandered off through the fields and meadows, ending up at Miss Stevens's cottage, but there was no sign of any tall figure pursuing her. She returned wearily to Bramfield Park, using the front door, just as her mother was crossing the hall.

"Cassie!" exclaimed the countess. "This is the outside of enough. You are, I gather, fully recovered. The dressing bell has just gone. Come upstairs with me. You will present yourself to the company, and high time, too."

Cassie sat miserably while the lady's maid looked out a suitable gown under the countess's supervision. She twitched nervously while the maid did up her hair. Lord Peter would make a joke of it, of that she was sure, about how she had been acting as Miss Stevens's housemaid. Her parents would laugh, and then her father would see to it that she was locked up for at least a month.

With a feeling of going to the scaffold, Cassandra at last walked downstairs, head held high, train of her white dinner gown looped over one arm.

Lord Peter was walking around the drawing room with Sophia on his arm in that way the upper classes had of taking promenades in their rooms as if extensive gardens and the whole wide countryside did not exist. He flicked an uninterested glance in Cassandra's direction and went on talking to Sophia. When would he tell them? wondered Cassie. Probably at dinner so as to be surrounded by the largest audience possible.

Mr. Jensen came up to her, followed by Cassie's uncle Wilbur. "Glad to see you are recovered," said Mr. Jensen.

"Hot, hey?" wheezed Uncle Wilbur. "But the weather will break soon, mark my words. Do you know what has caused all this unnatural heat, Cassie?"

Cassie shook her head, uncomfortably aware that Lord Peter's eyes were now on her.

"Balloons, that's what. Interfering with the elements. Damaging the clouds. Frightening them off. Unnatural, that's what it is, like coaches going at thirty miles an hour. Thirty miles an hour! Demme, enough to cause damage to the brain."

"You are looking amazingly pretty this evening, Lady Cassandra," said Mr. Jensen, pointedly interrupting Uncle Wilbur's diatribe. "And for someone recently risen from sickbed, you have a healthy tan."

"Oh, dear." Cassie gave a nervous laugh. Would this evening never end? "Most unfashionable."

"Pooh! Suits you," said Mr. Jensen.

Lord Peter eyed them coldly. Mr. Jensen was forty if he was a day, with a thin white face and graying hair, but Cassandra seemed quite enamored of him. He did not know that Cassie was desperately hanging on Mr. Jensen's every word to try to ward off from her mind thoughts of the exposure to come.

The dinner bell rang and they all filed in, two by two, like overdressed, overheated animals going into the ark, thought Cassie. She was escorted by Mr. Jensen. Frightened at the inevitable unmasking of her folly, Cassie tripped and stumbled on her way to the dining room. Lord Peter escorted Sophia, who was, of course, placed next to him at dinner.

The long French windows of the dining room were open. The dining room was on the ground floor, a *very* modern innovation. But no breeze moved the curtains, and the line of wax candles down the center of the table burned brightly, their flames tall and unwavering.

Mr. Jensen was entertaining Cassie with scandalous anecdotes about what had happened during the London Season. Although Cassie had been *at* the Season, she had not been part of it. The only ball she'd attended was held in her parents' town house, in Sophia's honor.

While Mr. Jensen was talking, Cassie glanced down the long table to where her sister sat and noticed that

Sophia was unusually animated. Her cheeks were delicately flushed, and she was endeavoring to flirt with Lord Peter. Why, her sister was a little in love with him, marveled Cassie, and then thought sadly that they deserved each other.

Cassie, however, began to relax and think herself safe. Lord Peter had not cried out at the sight of her, had not told the company that she had been pretending to be a servant. And then during a lull in the conversation, she heard his voice say with dreadful clarity to her mother, "Do you know a Miss Stevens?"

Before the countess could reply, Sophia tittered and said, "That mad old spinster! She is so poor, she cannot even afford one servant, and so she pretends to have many. It is better than a play to hear her calling to footmen and maids who do not exist."

"You horrify me!" exclaimed Lord Peter. "Miss Stevens is a distant relative of mine. I had no idea she had been so badly neglected by the family. I must make her an allowance directly. She should have said something. I am very fond of Miss Stevens."

Cassie stared down the table at him, and he shot her one brief mocking look.

"Sophia was just teasing," said the countess hurriedly. "Were you not, my pet?"

"Oh, indeed, Mama. You must not take me seriously, my lord. I quite dote on Miss Stevens."

"In that case, I will pluck up my courage and ask a very great favor. Would it be too much of an impertinence to ask that Miss Stevens be sent an invitation to your ball, Lady Wychhaven?"

"I shall send a footman over with one this very evening," said the countess.

"That will not be necessary. I will ride over with it myself tomorrow."

The conversation then became general, and Cassie sat, stunned. He had not said one word about her masquerade.

"Do you know Miss Stevens?" she heard Mr. Jensen ask.

"Yes, yes," said Cassie. "She is a dear friend of mine."

"Then I shall look forward to meeting her."

Cassie bit her lip. She leaned over to Uncle Wilbur. "I wonder if Lord Peter realizes the fluster into which she will be thrown. She will long to go, but she will need a suitable gown, and then she will have to walk all the way to Bramfield Park, for she cannot afford a carriage." Cassie knew that Miss Stevens, thanks to Lord Peter's rouleau of guineas, could afford to hire some sort of gig from the inn, but also knew that Miss Stevens was treated as some sort of joke by everyone in the village and would probably have to submit to the insolence of some local driver on her road to Bramfield Park.

Uncle Wilbur, who was sitting on the other side of Cassie, said suddenly, "I could take a carriage down and fetch her. And as to her gown? Is she fat?"

"No, not at all," said Cassie.

"Then take something of Sophia's."

"That would not answer." Cassie wrinkled her brow. "If Sophia recognized that gown, she would make such a scene."

"Then one of your own?"

"Even if Sophia knew it was one of mine, she would still make a scene. It only lacks a week until the ball, too short a time, surely, to get something made."

"The nearest biggest town is Barminster," said Uncle Wilbur. "Could take her there to the dressmakers, Mr. Glossop. These dressmakers are often left with gowns that the lady who ordered cannot pay for. I have it! I shall say I want an outing, take one of the carriages, and escort Miss Stevens to Barminster."

"Good idea!" exclaimed Mr. Jensen. "We'll all go."

"I do not think we should mention either Sophia's remark, which prompted Lord Peter's rejoinder," said Cassie cautiously, "or that he claimed to be related to her. I am sure he is no relation of hers, but any mention of her relatives throws Miss Stevens into confusion. She is always so sad that they hardly come to see her and that they keep her on such short commons that she is barely able to afford coals for the winter. Let her think it was mama herself who decided to invite her."

Lord Peter looked over. Now, what were that odd three so happy and elated about? wondered Lord Peter crossly. He compared Sophia's looks, unoriginally, to a summer's day, and that young lady rapped his hand with her fan and flirted her eyelashes at him, but Cassie did not even look down the table.

"I had better go tonight and warn her," Cassie was saying.

"We will all go," said Uncle Wilbur. "After dinner. No harm in just saying we want to take the air."

Lord Peter noticed that when the countess rose to lead the ladies to the drawing room so as to leave the gentlemen to their wine, Uncle Wilbur and Mr. Jensen rose, too, and followed them out.

He was so engrossed in wondering what that pair was up to—and if it had anything to do with Cassie—that he did not notice that the earl was now sitting next to him and asking, "Is it too much to hope for an announcement to an engagement at the ball?"

"I beg your pardon?" Lord Peter said automatically. Were they plotting something? And why was that Jensen fellow always hanging about? He was old enough to be Lady Cassandra's father.

"To put it bluntly," said the earl. "Are you going to marry my daughter?"

"Yes, yes," said Lord Peter, who had not heard a word.

"You have made me the happiest of men."

Lord Peter heard that. He looked at the earl in alarm.

"I have?"

"Of course. Do you wish me to announce your engagement at the ball? Or do you wish to do it yourself?"

Lord Peter cursed Cassie in his soul for having distracted him so badly that he had unwittingly given his assent to an engagement.

"I shall announce it myself," he said, thinking rapidly. "But you must promise to keep it a secret from your wife and daughters."

"If that is your wish." The earl looked disappointed.

Damn that witch Cassandra, thought Lord Peter bitterly. I should have exposed her.

He was to damn her even more bitterly when they joined the ladies and he found Cassie absent.

"Where is your sister?" he asked Sophia.

"Uncle Wilbur wanted to take the air," said Sophia, "and Cassie and Mr. Jensen went with him. Poor little Cassie. Such an odd child. And such unfortunate hair."

"I cannot understand this dislike of red hair," remarked Lord Peter testily. "It is damned as Scotch, and yet red hair is traditionally British. Caligula never invaded Britain but pretended he had by taking some tall Gauls, dying their hair red, and parading them as British prisoners of war."

Sophia had not the faintest idea who Caligula was or had been, and so she hid her face with her fan and peeped over the top of it at him in what she was firmly convinced was a killing manner.

Miss Stevens sat openmouthed in bewilderment, facing Uncle Wilbur and Mr. Jensen and listening to Cassie telling her she was to go to the ball and how they were going to try to find a gown for her.

"Oh! Oh! Oh!" She kept giving little shrieks of amazement.

"I do not think I can go through with it," she said when Cassie had finished. "So much to think of. And . . . and . . . I would need to walk because you know . . ." She looked at Cassie miserably.

"Bring the carriage down and escort you meself," said Uncle Wilbur suddenly.

Miss Stevens's faded blue eyes looked at the spry white-haired figure of Uncle Wilbur with dawning surprise and gratification. "I should not . . . but yes, sir, in that case, I could face *dragons*. We must have something to celebrate." She rang the bell. "Lucy!"

And for the first time ever, a real servant appeared, a small shy girl, neatly dressed in a print frock and apron.

"Fetch the elderberry wine," said Miss Stevens grandly, and Lucy bobbed a curtsy and went off to bring it.

They fell to discussing the dress Miss Stevens should wear. Uncle Wilbur became quite skittish after several glasses of elderberry wine and said transparent muslin was the thing, and to Cassie's amazement Miss Stevens blushed and giggled like a young girl.

At last it was agreed they should all go to Barminster on the following day and that Cassie, Uncle Wilbur, and Mr. Jensen would call for her at eleven in the morning.

At ten in the morning Miss Stevens was so excited about the forthcoming expedition that she was dressed in her best to go out; the youthful gown that Cassie had given her, a straw bonnet ornamented with silk flowers, a rather faded gold silk pelisse trimmed with cotton lace, and a parasol.

She sat rigidly in a chair in her little parlor, wondering whether they would actually come. It all seemed too much excitement to arrive in the life of one lonely spinster all at once.

And then she heard the sound of horses' hooves and stared in amazement at the clock. But it could not be them. Much too early.

But she heard the garden gate creak a few moments later and then, a few moments after that, a brisk rap at the door. Lucy, Miss Stevens knew, was out in the back garden hanging out the wash. Too unnerved to go through her usual rigmarole of calling on imaginary footmen, she answered the door herself and looked up at the tall figure of Lord Peter Courtney.

"My lord," she gasped. "I was not expecting you."

He smiled down at her in a way that made Miss Stevens wonder why on earth Cassie was not head over heels in love with this man.

"It will only take a little of your time," he said. "May we go inside?"

Miss Stevens sat down nervously facing him. "I am come," he began, "because of a lie I told at dinner last night. I asked the countess if she knew you, and for some mad reason I claimed that you were a distant relative of mine."

"Oh, Lord Peter, I am most gratified."

"The delicacy of the situation is this. I cannot have a relative, supposed or otherwise, living in circumstances that I gather are not particularly comfortable."

Tears appeared in Miss Stevens's eyes. "I try so hard, my lord, to keep up appearances. I had not thought the poverty of my situation so evident."

"I am sure to most people you appear a lady of means, Miss Stevens," he said, reassuring her. "But I am also sure such a kind and good lady like yourself would not humiliate me by refusing my offer."

Miss Stevens dried her eyes with a lace-edged cambric handkerchief and looked at him in a dazed way. "Offer?" she echoed.

"I would like to settle a sum on you, just a little, three hundred pounds a year." Lord Peter could have made it very much more, but he shrewdly suspected that any grand sum would be turned down flat.

Miss Stevens turned from mortified red to shocked white. She put a trembling hand up to her heart. "Three hundred pounds."

"A trifling sum, I admit. Do please say yes. Think of Cassie—Lady Cassandra. She is very fond of you and would be pleased to see you living in some comfort."

Miss Stevens thought of three hundred pounds, of warmth and comfort, of security, of the fact that he had already ordered the tradesmen to send their bills to him right up until Christmas. She fell to her knees and raised her clasped hands up to him. "You are a saint," she whispered.

Alarmed, Lord Peter raised her to her feet. "Enough, Miss Stevens. It means so little to me, I assure you." He helped her to a chair and picked up a fan from a table and fanned her.

When she had recovered somewhat, Miss Stevens looked up at him. "Are you doing this for Cassie?"

His face hardened. He recalled Cassie calling him old and disgusting. "I have no interest in that hoyden," he said curtly. "Well, I am glad that is settled, Miss Stevens. I must bid you good day."

Flustered, she followed him to the door, begging him to stay and take some refreshment, but he merely smiled and said she would be hearing from his bankers and left.

Miss Stevens sat down again and forced herself to be calm. She was firmly convinced that all Lord Peter's interest in her had been caused by Cassie. How wonderful it would be, thought Miss Stevens, if Cassie should snatch the prize from under Sophia's haughty nose.

She sat so long buried in thought that she did not at first realize the party to take her to Barminster had arrived and were impatiently waiting outside until her little maid came running in to tell her.

The weather was still hot and fine, and so Uncle Wilbur had managed to get hold of an open carriage, which he was driving himself, looking like a relic of the last century in splendid chintz coat, ruffled shirt, long silk waistcoat, knee breeches, and three-cornered hat.

In her excitement Miss Stevens fell into the carriage and was helped up into her seat by Cassie and Mr. Jensen, who listened amazed to the torrent of gratitude pouring from the spinster's lips about "dear" Lord Peter and how he was a veritable saint.

When she had finished, Mr. Jensen looked slyly at Cassie. "There's something here you have not told us,

Lady Cassandra. I could have sworn last night was the first time you had met our illustrious guest. So how is it that Lord Peter suddenly claims Miss Stevens here as a relative?"

"Because she is," said Cassie, flashing Miss Stevens a warning look.

With all the ease of the lonely and imaginative, Miss Stevens began to lie fluently. "Yes, indeed, I had quite forgot. I am a very *distant* relative, of course, and with my nearer relatives being so indifferent to me, I had forgot about the faraway ones. You could have knocked me over with a feather when I learned of the connection."

The carriage had reached a straight stretch of road, and Uncle Wilbur called, "Hold on tightly. Going to spring 'em," and off they hurtled at a great rate while Miss Stevens hung on to her bonnet and wondered whether it might be possible to die from sheer happiness.

Barminster was a fairly large town on the coast which had started life as a fishing village, but then had been made fashionably popular at the end of the last century by the vogue for sea bathing. It had not yet had the honor of a visit from the Prince Regent, but one of the royal dukes had bathed there and also some foreign prince from a country no one had ever heard of. It attracted a great number of the new rising middle class, who were anxious to ape their betters and who were possessed of a rigid snobbery that outdid any pecking order in the ranks of the aristocracy and gentry. The old Pelican Inn on the waterfront had been converted into a hotel to meet the new demand, and it was there that Uncle Wilbur took them to refresh themselves with tea and cakes before walking through the narrow lanes to where Mr. Glossop had his dressmaking salon, Mr. Glossop having risen too high in the world to call his premises a shop.

Uncle Wilbur explained the situation to the dressmaker while Miss Stevens stood shyly by, wishing she were younger and prettier and more worthy of all this attention.

"I do have a ball gown," said Mr. Glossop, "made to order for a certain lady. But, fan me ye winds, if she did not decamp and leave me with it. It will fit madam's figure excellent well." He snapped his fingers, and two young male assistants as rouged and pomaded as their master jumped to attention. "Fetch the gold silk," he ordered.

Soon the dress was spread out before Miss Stevens for inspection. It was high-waisted in the current fashion, and the bodice and hem were thickly embroidered with gold thread and seed pearls. There was a gold silk turban to go with it with a fall of gold gauze hanging down the back.

"Try it on," urged Cassie.

Miss Stevens was led off. Cassie looked out the window at the stretch of blue sea beyond. She wondered what had prompted Lord Peter's generosity. Could it possibly have anything to do with her? She found herself remembering the feel of his hands and the warmth of his mouth. She felt Mr. Jensen's eyes on her and blushed as red as her hair.

Miss Stevens came back and stood nervously before them. "Perfect," said Uncle Wilbur, and the others agreed. The rich gown gave her dignity. The assistants leapt about the shop with long mirrors, which they wheeled this way and that so that Miss Stevens could see herself all round.

She took a deep breath. "I shall take it, Mr. Glossop. How much?"

Mr. Glossop wrote the price on a slip of paper and handed it to her. "Oh!" shrieked Miss Stevens in distress. "So much! I couldn't possibly . . . Dear me, I'm wearing it. I must get it off before anything happens."

Uncle Wilbur twitched the slip of paper from the spinster's nerveless fingers, raised his quizzing glass, and examined it. "A bagatelle," he said with a shrug. "We'll take it, Mr. Glossop. My present, Miss Stevens, but I expect a dance, y'know."

"I couldn't . . . I mustn't . . ." wailed Miss Stevens. "Four hundred pounds for a mere gown in a provincial town. It's *wicked*."

"Take it," urged Cassie.

"It is a reduced price," said Mr. Glossop. "The thread is

real gold—and the pearls! May I be cast into the deepest pit if I do not tell the truth. May savage horses stamp on me. May the fiends from the nether regions stick me with pitchforks if I tell a lie. Those pearls are genuine, from the Indies, brought up from the depths of the ocean in the brown fingers of divers who risked their lives so that you, madam, may look beautiful. My stars and garters, part of my soul is in that gown."

"Which is just about the only reason she shouldn't buy it," murmured Mr. Jensen.

"Oh, fiddlesticks," grumbled Uncle Wilbur. "I want to get out of here. You, Miss Stevens, take it off, then you, Mr. Glossop, wrap it up. We'll take it with us."

The dress was duly carried back to the inn, where Uncle Wilbur ordered champagne and told Miss Stevens the only way to cope with that tiresome gratitude of hers was to drown it. And Miss Stevens, who seemed to be shedding years by the minute, giggled and drank glass for glass with Wilbur.

Enlivened by champagne, Uncle Wilbur then announced that he would hire a boat and take them out on the bay. And so, all of them slightly tipsy, they boarded a rowing boat and cruised over the still glassy waters, Uncle Wilbur rowing with surprising strength.

The boat trip was accounted such a success that they returned to the hotel for buttered shrimps and more champagne, and it was decided that they should take a gentle walk along the beach and then have dinner before returning home.

The guests that evening remarked that Lord Peter Courtney was out of sorts and barely said a word at the dinner table. Sophia looked as beautiful as ever and smug, too. For her father had confided to her that Lord Peter meant to propose to her at the ball. All previous failures had fled from Sophia's vain mind. She was not in the least surprised that Lord Peter should wish to marry her. She considered him to be a very lucky man.

Lord Peter's gloomy gaze kept drifting down to those three empty seats at the other end of the table. He wondered where they were.

When the ladies retired to the drawing room, he said he had a headache and rose to go to his room. As he was crossing the hall, he heard the sound of singing and laughter.

The hall door was standing open. Up the drive came an open carriage driven by Uncle Wilbur, who was singing "Sweet Lass of Richmond Hill" at the top of his voice. Cassie, flushed and laughing helplessly, was leaning against Mr. Jensen, who had an arm around her shoulders. The carriage swung round in front of the entrance. Mr. Jensen jumped down and helped Cassie to alight. He bent his head and kissed her hand.

Lord Peter turned on his heel and marched up the stairs. Damn her!

Cassie finally found the courage to seek out Lord Peter on the day of the ball, finally running him to earth in the library. He put down the book he had been reading and rose to his feet. "Well, Lady Cassandra?" he demanded frostily.

"I came to thank you for your generosity to Miss Stevens," she said.

"It was the least I could do," he replied in chilly accents. "Anything else?"

"I also wanted to thank you for not betraying me."

"I could hardly do that," said Lord Peter. "I do not wish to tell all and sundry that I am in the habit of kissing serving wenches. What more, Lady Cassandra?"

"Nothing," she mumbled and turned on her heel, collided with a column bearing a bust of Plato, and sent it smashing to the ground. Plato, now minus his nose, rolled across the floor and lay at Lord Peter's feet and stared up at him with blind eyes.

Cassie gave a choked sound and ran from the room.

Hatless, she sped out of the house and through the grounds, not stopping until she had reached the coolness of the woods on the other side of the village. A little way into the woods there was an old crab apple tree with wide spreading branches. She climbed up and lay down in a fork of the tree and stared blindly up at the leaves. He despised her. He had only been generous to Miss Stevens out of duty, a duty caused by his lie.

To suit her miserable mood, black clouds were piling up against the sun. The air was very still with a waiting feel about it, as if every parched blade of grass and tree were holding its breath until the blessed rainwater should fall again. Why had she called him old and disgusting? Because he had frightened her, she thought. The effect he had on her senses was alarming. He filled her mind with wanton dreams, dreams that Cassie had been schooled to believe that no lady could possibly have. Ladies, as everyone knew in polite society, were incapable of either lust or passion.

She closed her eyes to shut out the memory of his lips against hers and drifted off to sleep. But in her dreams, he came to her and he folded his arms around her and kissed her deeply, so deeply that her body began to burn and yearn.

None of these feelings showed on her sleeping face, and Lord Peter stood there, looking down at her. He had gone in search of her. He felt he had been rude and cruel. He wondered, as he looked at her, why it was that Sophia should be hailed the beauty of the family and this redheaded witch ignored. Her skin was golden, and the glory of her hair burned like a flame.

She was lying cradled in the low fork of the apple tree, her face on a level with his own. He bent his head and kissed her full on the lips, letting out a stifled exclamation as the lips under his burned with a fierce passion, for Cassie was kissing him in her dreams. She wound her arms around his neck, and he lifted her from the tree and laid her gently on the warm grass on the ground beneath. Cassie's lithe body moved sinuously against his own—and then her eyes opened.

She struggled feebly against him, but he continued to kiss her, long, drugged sweet kisses. One huge drop of rain plopped down and then another. There was a tremendous flash of lightning and then a terrific crash of thunder. They were rolling passionately entwined on the ground as the heavens opened and a torrent descended on them.

He got to his feet and picked her up and carried her deeper into the wood, then set her on her feet under the spreading branches of an oak tree.

"Now look at us." Cassie laughed. "It will take ages to wash and arrange my hair for the ball."

"The ball!" he exclaimed. "The deuce. That's where I am supposed to propose to your sister, Sophia." He had taken out a handkerchief and was mopping his face with it as he spoke. When he put the handkerchief back in his pocket and looked around, bewildered, she had gone.

He ran through the woods, looking for her, finally ending up at Miss Stevens's cottage. But no matter how loud he hammered on the door, no one answered.

Inside, Cassie sat on the floor with her head on Miss Stevens's lap.

"There, there," said Miss Stevens, stroking Cassie's wet hair. "Do not cry any more. What beasts men are! To kiss you and then tell you he was to wed your sister! I simply do not understand it."

"It's because he thinks I am a wanton," said Cassie, sobbing. "I do not want to go to that ball."

"I think you should go. Get it over with," counseled Miss Stevens. "I have a feeling the minute you hear him announce that engagement to Sophia, then you will lose all desire for him."

"I hate him!"

"Then show your indifference. You can look very charming, Cassie. You could even outshine your sister if you put your mind to it. Gentlemen *like* you, or so your uncle and

Mr. Jensen told me. Mr. Jensen also told me he was present at that ball for Sophia in London during the Season and that all the men clustered around *you*. You must go."

Cassie rose to her feet. "You are right. I should go and look my best and show him I do not care a rap. And I must be there to see you in your new gown."

"I have been thinking about that gown," said Miss Stevens slowly. "I have never before questioned the order of things, for, as you know, Cassie, God puts us in our appointed stations. But four hundred pounds for a ball gown! That would keep a poor family comfortably off for years."

"Then wear the gown and sell it back to Mr. Glossop and give the money to the poor," said Cassie. "We shall both look our very best tonight, Miss Stevens, and may Lord Peter Courtney rot in hell."

"Language!" shrieked Miss Stevens.

The countess looked in surprise at her younger daughter, for Cassie had just demanded the Wychhaven pearls. "Perhaps Sophia may want them," said the countess, "and everything must be done for Sophia. This is *her* night."

"It is always *her* everything," retorted Cassie. "But just for this one ball, I plan to look my best, and I want the pearls."

"Well, then, you shall have them. But do wear some sort of headdress to cover that hair of yours."

With a pang Cassie remembered Lord Peter saying he liked red hair. "I shall wear my hair as I see fit, Mama. Now . . . the pearls."

The countess told her maid to fetch the pearls. When they were put into her hands, Cassie fingered the cool weight of the necklace and bracelet and then gave her mother a steely look. "I would like the pearl tiara as well."

"But that is too much!" exclaimed her mother. "Much too much for a young girl who has not yet made her come-out."

"And never will," said Cassie, "if it is left to my loving

parents. Did you never think, Mama, that I might feel *hurt* by always being left in the background?"

"But Sophia is the eldest and must be married first. Your turn will come."

"I have heard you," said Cassie bitterly. " 'I suppose we must do something with little Cassie. Tunbridge Wells or Bath, or perhaps ship her out to India where she might catch the eye of some female-starved officer.' " She held out her hand. "The pearl tiara."

"We always try to do what is best for you," said the countess huffily. "You are jealous of Sophia, and you are trying to put a damper on this great occasion . . ."

"The tiara, Mama!"

"Oh, very well. Betty, fetch the thing and give it to Lady Cassandra."

Cassie retreated triumphantly to her room. She shared a lady's maid with Sophia, so she knew that usually meant she would need to dress herself, the maid being kept dancing attendance on Sophia until the very last minute.

She took out the simple white muslin ball gown she was expected to wear. And as she looked at it, she remembered that Sophia had a gauze overdress edged with pearls.

She went along to Sophia's room and hesitated outside the dressing room door. Sophia's petulant voice was raised in anger as she berated the maid for having overheated the curling tongs.

Cassie went next door and let herself quietly into Sophia's bedroom and went straight to the huge press and opened it up. She scrabbled quickly among the piles of clothes until she seized the overdress and scampered off to her own room with it over her arm.

She sat down at her toilet table in her shift and carefully began to arrange her newly washed hair in one of the latest Roman styles. She heard the rumble of carriages as guests arrived at the house. She heard Sophia's voice and her mother's answering one as they walked along the passage and down the stairs to take their places beside the earl to receive the guests. A lump rose in Cassie's throat as she realized that her mother and father would barely notice her absence if she did not attend. The lady's maid came scurrying in, apologizing for having left Cassie to her own devices.

She helped Cassie into her ball gown and then the over-dress. Then Cassie sat down at the toilet table once more, and the maid lifted the fairylike pearl-and-silver tiara and placed it on Cassie's flaming curls.

"Why, Lady Cassandra," said the maid, "you look like a princess. But you must hurry. You are already late."

Cassie grinned. "I plan to make an entrance."

The first dance was over. Miss Stevens, sitting beside Uncle Wilbur, said anxiously, "I wonder where Cassie is."

Lord Peter promenaded on the arm of the countess and wondered the same thing. And then, just as he was passing Mr. Jensen, who was standing with a group of men, he heard exclamations and saw that they were all staring up at the staircase.

"Oh, my stars," whispered Miss Stevens. "Cassie!"

She came slowly down the staircase, her head held high, the gauze of the overdress floating about her slim body. She looked magnificent.

"Excuse me," said Lord Peter and went to meet Cassie at the foot of the stairs. But Mr. Jensen was there before him. Cassie smiled up at him. Lord Peter turned on his heel and strode off.

Cassie danced the next dance with Mr. Jensen and the following one with a young man from the neighboring county. She laughed and talked, but all the while she noticed Lord Peter, noticed him dancing with Sophia and wondered in a bleak way which would break first, her face because it was so stiff from trying to smile, or her poor heart.

The next dance was the waltz, and suddenly Lord Peter was there at Cassie's side, telling all her other courtiers that this dance was promised to him.

For the first few steps she stumbled blindly over his feet until he pressed his hand hard into the small of her back and said in a low voice, "I love you, Cassie."

She stumbled again and whispered fiercely. "You want to amuse yourself with me while you marry my sister."

"That was a misunderstanding. I want to marry you, my darling. *That* is why I could not tell your father I was not going to announce an engagement at this ball. In my heart I must have known all along that I wanted you as my wife—yes, from the first moment I met you when you were wearing that ridiculous wig."

How gracefully her steps now followed his. Sophia watched her little sister with angry eyes, suddenly recognizing that overdress as her own and wanting to tear it off Cassie's back.

"You have not answered me, Cassie," said Lord Peter. "Will you marry me?"

"If you are sure you want to." Cassie looked shyly up at him. "I am very clumsy and gauche. Will you not fear for all your works of art?"

"I don't give a damn if you break the lot so long as you will be mine."

"Oh." Cassie sighed with pleasure. "I feel like Miss Stevens, about to faint with delight."

Sophia marched straight up to her father after the waltz was finished. "Get Courtney to make that announcement now," she hissed. "Cassie is making a fool of me. Look at the way she hangs on his arm!"

She watched as her father crossed the ballroom and said something to Lord Peter, saw both men walk to the raised platform where the orchestra sat, saw the earl say something to the conductor. There was a roll of drums, and all the guests turned and faced the earl, who was standing with his hands raised.

"Lord Peter Courtney has something very special to say."

"Come, my precious," said Lady Wychhaven to Sophia. "This is a proud moment."

Sophia shrugged. "A proud moment for Lord Peter, Mama," she corrected.

Lord Peter looked down at the guests, a commanding figure in black evening dress. He held out his hand to Cassie, who slowly walked forward and took it.

"What is that silly wigeon doing?" demanded Sophia.

"My lords, ladies, and gentlemen," said Lord Peter, "it gives me great pleasure to announce my engagement to Lady Cassandra."

"Thank God!" cried Miss Stevens, clutching hold of Uncle Wilbur. "Oh, thank God."

Sophia's normal icy calm cracked. "You've made a mistake, you fool!" she cried, advancing on the rostrum. "You're supposed to be engaged to me!"

Lord Peter looked down at her. "Control yourself, Lady Sophia, and wish your sister well."

Sophia turned this way and that, noticing all the watching eyes, and then she turned and stumbled blindly from the room.

"That was bad of you, Lord Peter," said the earl. "You gave me your word that Sophia was to be your bride."

"I unfortunately led you to believe so," said Lord Peter, "for which I am truly sorry. But the shock might do Lady Sophia some good. You have spoilt her so badly, you have made her nigh unmarriageable. Wish Cassandra well. In my opinion, she is the real beauty of the family."

The earl scratched his head in bewilderment. "Well, there is no accounting for taste," he said and went off to comfort Sophia.

Cassie could find it in her heart to be deeply worried about her sister's humiliation and was prepared to have the rest of the evening ruined by that worry. But Sophia soon reappeared, as glacially beautiful as ever. Her parents had told her that Lord Peter was an eccentric, and that she had had a lucky escape. They told her that all the men at the ball were in love with her, and Sophia gradually began to believe them until bit by bit the armour of her colossal vanity was restored. So Cassie drifted through the rest of the evening in a daze of happiness.

Toward the end of the ball Lord Peter led her out onto the terrace. The rain had stopped, and a full moon was riding high in the sky. She trembled as he took her in his arms and kissed her fiercely and then said, "How soon can we be married?"

"As soon as possible," said Cassie. "You have brought about happy endings, to me, and to Miss Stevens."

"I think Miss Stevens may yet surprise us with another happy ending. Look there!"

Across a path of moonlight on the lawns strolled Miss Stevens with Uncle Wilbur. His old voice reached their listening ears. "I never thought I would want to get married again, Tabitha, until I met you."

"He means Miss Stevens!" cried Cassie. "What a happy night."

"Except, I think, for your friend Mr. Jensen."

"He felicitated me on our forthcoming marriage and said he already knew we were in love. Would I be very bold if I asked you to kiss me again?"

"Yes, my wanton. Come here to me!"

A month later they were married, Sophia refusing to be bridesmaid because she heard Miss Stevens was to be maid of honor. There was a slight flurry as the nervous bride entered the church and tripped over her wedding gown. Cassie was suffering from bridal nerves and had begun to think Lord Peter did not really want her.

But as he turned at the altar and looked at her, no longer cold and stern but with a face altered with love, Cassie lost all her fears, and nothing spoiled that perfect wedding service except for the noisy and sentimental crying of Miss Stevens, who was to be married herself in the following month.

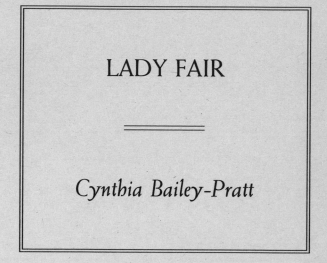

LADY FAIR

Cynthia Bailey-Pratt

IF IT HAD NOT BEEN RAINING, MRS. POLKINGTON WOULD not have reacted as she did to the news that the newly arrived earl would open the fair on the king's birthday. But her energies had been gathering for a week, and Mr. Jasper was not as tactful as he might have been.

Across the hall Miranda sat embroidering, frowning in an effort to hold her needle steady despite her stepmother's continual roaring. Though she had lived with the second Mrs. Polkington from the age of eight, Miranda had never quite adjusted to the other's intensity.

"I have given the welcoming speech every year since coming to live in Trenton, Mr. Jasper, as you are perfectly well aware. Although I concede the Earl of Morest is likely to spend more in your shops than my household can, I don't think we need overset a well-founded tradition for mere monetary gain." Mrs. Polkington coughed, a low rumble like that of a volcano announcing an imminent eruption.

"Now, missus, there's no need to be in such a taking. Haven't I made a civil offer to you? What's wrong with judging the stitching? My own daughter's entered with a nice bit of petticoat she done herself. You can make your speech then."

"No. I will open the fair as I have done for the past ten years. That is my final word."

Of course, it wasn't. Mrs. Polkington never spoke above her usual tone, yet Miranda could hear her throughout the house. Though the grocer's chest was broad and deep, the woman's voice drowned his bass as though it were the distant piping of a child's penny whistle. At last Mr. Jasper departed, muttering.

Miranda hated rainy days, wishing her father had chosen to settle in a desert instead of in the heart of England. When the sky had first darkened last week, the maids had remained only because Miranda offered them a half crown each to spend on the Fourth of June. By then, with good fortune, the sun would once more shine, and Mrs. Polkington would be able to pursue her varied interests outside the house.

Hearing her name, Miranda gathered together her silks and entered the morning room. Her stepmother stood before the fire, her large hands resting on her hips. "Ha, child!"

"What did Mr. Jasper want, Mother?"

"I'm surprised you didn't hear, the way he was shouting!"

"Something about the opening speech?" Miranda ventured.

"An outrage! But I gave as good as I got." Mrs. Polkington's square face was still flushed from the fight. "I told him he couldn't overset tradition, no matter how many members of his committee voted on it. Who's to say this earl will even stay in Trenton? He's only renting the Manor. Come the Season and he'll flitter off again, mark my words."

"Yes, Mother," Miranda said, rethreading her needle.

"Let me see what you are doing." Mrs. Polkington took the hoop, turning her head to one side to look at it, rather like a great bird deciding if an object was worthwhile to peck. "You should have used rose pink for the hearts of the flowers. I suggest you pull it all out and start over."

"But I—"

"Else for the rest of your life," Mrs. Polkington went on, giving Miranda her work back, "when you look at this hanging on the wall, you'll wish you had. Look how well you did these handkerchiefs for me. You do excellently when you take my advice."

Miranda, who had indeed used rose-pink silk, merely nodded and placed the hoop in her workbasket. "Thank you. I shall make you more this year. With your monogram, perhaps."

Although the village of Trenton popularly believed that young Miranda Polkington could not call her soul her own, Miranda herself rather liked the woman her father had married. It was a daily challenge to keep up with her, quite different from the dreamy life she had led after her own mother's death.

Miranda's father had been a mild man who might spend half the day doddering about looking for lost spectacles or trying to remember what he had done with a half-read book. The new Mrs. Polkington had straightened out the house in three days, and Miranda knew her father had been happily bossed until the day of his death last year.

Only sometimes did it come home to Miranda that her father had absorbed the majority of Mrs. Polkington's energies. Now that he was gone, Miranda came under the scrutiny previously focused upon him.

Mrs. Polkington sneezed. The fire dimmed and then rallied. "Drat," she said, fumbling in the bodice of her dress for one of her handkerchiefs.

"Mother, you went into the garden, didn't you?"

"No," she said firmly and then sneezed twice more. When the windows ceased rattling, she confessed, "Well, I slipped out only to tell Whitman he should come to dig the garden. He was with that eldest Bolton girl. Carrying on, as usual."

"You've probably brought your cold on again. Didn't you wear your pattens?"

"I was only outside for one moment. Just down to the cottage and back." Already the great voice was hoarsening.

Miranda sighed. She had nursed Mrs. Polkington through a bout of cold two weeks ago. "I'll send for a hot brick."

"But I can't be ill again," Mrs. Polkington said in real distress. "The fair is in five days. If I can't make the opening speech, they may never let me give it again."

Miranda made no sign that she now realized why the older woman was making such a fuss over this minor honor. "If you go back to bed now and rest . . . really rest . . . we'll drive it off," she said reassuringly.

Mrs. Polkington's flannel nightrail would have made three for Miranda. Yet, with a lace-frilled cap on her head hiding the short gray hair, and the coverlet drawn up, she seemed rather fragile and definitely sorry for herself. "But I hate being sick. It's so . . . so . . ." She sneezed and then finished. "So demoralizing."

"I shan't say I told you so, Mother, but I warned you that you should have spent another few days in bed the last time."

"You know they were holding the meeting about the Town Hall roof, and I had to be there to lend them courage. I hope they're happy now. Mrs. Phipps said yesterday in church that the rain is coming through by the gallon and has soaked all the carpets." Her eyelids closed.

As Miranda slipped out, she saw her stepmother's lips curve up in a smile. No doubt she was imagining the consternation of those who had not wanted to spend money on the roof. Mrs. Polkington had been vindicated again.

Unfortunately, Mr. Jasper and his cronies might defeat her yet over the question of the welcoming speech. Miranda had been aware for some months of the undercurrent of discontent with the ten-year-old tradition Mrs. Polkington relied on. Asked originally as a measure of respect for her new husband, Mrs. Polkington had simply assumed the invitation stood for every year. Not even the vicar could dislodge this notion.

Then, as Mrs. Polkington began to contribute to, and then to run, various village efforts, from the flower arrangements in the vestry to the selection of the school's books, it was soon discovered that she could be both obstinate and

impervious to tactful hints regarding her tendency to be a
trifle overbearing. Even when the suggestion came from
Miranda, Mrs. Polkington did not understand. She thought
she was a help, as indeed she sometimes was. But more
often, people's hackles rose when abruptly told they were
behaving like fools.

Only Mrs. Polkington's chance comment allowed
Miranda to see her stepmother's true motives. She had
to be the center of all eyes for fear she'd be shoved
aside as inconsequential. Miranda could scarcely believe
so noticeable a woman could be prey to such a fear, yet Mrs.
Polkington apparently feared obscurity even more than the
active dislike of her neighbors. And a titled single gentleman
was certainly more interesting than the widow of a minor
scholar.

For a moment Miranda berated herself for not realizing
Mrs. Polkington's feelings sooner. She regretted that sometimes she had felt hemmed in and overwhelmed by her
stepmother's voracious interest in and resultant comments
on every facet of her life. Miranda felt she must do something to atone for her exasperation.

Catching sight of the oiled umbrella hanging on the newel
post, Miranda made her decision. Though slight and pale,
she had not known a day's illness since recovering from
the whooping cough at age six. A walk across wet fields
would not harm her.

As she walked, huddled in her pelisse against the brisk
wind that blew the storm clouds away, Miranda rehearsed
the plea she would make to the earl. If he could be persuaded to refuse to make the speech, the merchants' committee would have to fall back on Mrs. Polkington.

Tradition did count for something, after all, even if everyone was sick to death of the "Hearty England Shall Never Fail" speech. Miranda had a sneaking suspicion that
her stepmother saw herself on these occasions as Queen
Elizabeth addressing the sailors after they'd fought the
Armada.

Above her, great shafts of light fell from the sky, brightening the raindrops that still bowed down green leaves and tender buds. Miranda paused inside the cattle gate to furl her umbrella. Tilting back her head, she let the sun fall on her face beneath the curving brim of her straw bonnet. "Heavenly," she said with a sigh, and then made a sudden clutch as the bonnet slid backward on her smooth hair. After retying the satin ribbons, she made to walk on.

"Pliz, miss, to stay where you are!"

Miranda jumped. She'd believed she was all alone in an empty landscape. Turning her head cautiously, she saw no one but could not believe she'd imagined the voice. She stepped resolutely forward.

"Pliz, miss, to stay?"

Startled anew, Miranda gaped at the short, black-haired man in blue velvet livery who had apparently popped up from nowhere, like an emissary from Oberon. He grinned at her, showing innumerable teeth and vanished again into the threshing leaves.

Miranda thought that perhaps there was a wild bull loose in the pasture. In all the years Miranda had lived in Trenton, this field had never been used for any but milch cows, though the new earl might have changed that. Miranda began to back slowly toward the gate, but a voice called out, "Dammit, René, tell that girl to stay where she is!"

The voice was English and gruff. The figure in blue livery stood up on the gentle slope of the hill above the pasture and shouted, "Stay! Stay!"

Miranda felt like a disobedient hound. "Why should I?" she muttered, but did not move.

"Put your hand on the gate, can't you?" demanded the English voice. She saw him wave at her from the top of the hill.

"Indeed I shall," Miranda answered and pushed the gate open. She was through it as soon as space would permit and walking quickly down the lane back the way she'd come.

But her narrow skirt only allowed her limbs the short-est stride, inhibiting her from walking quickly, unless she longed for a fall in the mud. The man caught up with her before she'd gone very far. "What is wrong with you?" he asked, catching her just before she stumbled.

"Wrong with *me*?" she squeaked in return, freeing herself with a jerk. He might be tall and well made, with a narrow, tanned face ruined not at all by the slash of greenish paint across the bridge of his long aristocratic nose, but that gave him no right to speak as though she were at fault.

"Wrong with me?" she said even more indignantly. "I'm not the one who is handing out orders to perfect strangers. I'm not the one who sends his servant leaping out of the underbrush like a jack-in-the-box, nearly scaring me out of my wits. I'm not—"

"All right," he said, holding up a long hand decorated with daubs of yellow and blue. "I apologize for René's alarming you. Don't take on so."

Catching her breath, Miranda noticed the brushes sticking out from between the breast of his shirt and his waistcoat. He wore no coat over his white linen.

"Are you an artist?" she asked, finding that his hazel eyes were flecked with gray. They regarded her with an almost impersonal judgment, flicking over her drab pelisse and unsteady bonnet. He frowned.

"Yes, I—"

Embarrassed because she knew she was blushing, Miranda said, "Be that as it may, you had no right to shout at me."

"I'm sorry." He hesitated and then went on. "I wasn't thinking of you as a person, you see."

"Oh, that *is* an apology," Miranda muttered, noticing mud on the hem of her pelisse.

"If you don't let me explain, I think I shall lose my temper." He did not seem to mean it, though Miranda caught a gleam in his eyes beneath a hanging lock of black hair that might have been anger, or perhaps only amusement.

If it was the last, he had good reason to laugh at her. She was suddenly aware that her brown ribbons were again untied and that her bonnet was sliding farther back from her brow. Snatching at it, she placed it more correctly on her head, retying the bow with great firmness beneath her chin.

It was undignified of her, she decided, to be so angry when she'd only been startled by his abruptness. "Were you painting me? Did you want me in your painting?"

"Yes, exactly. When you entered the field, you happened to be in precisely the best spot to complement the scene. So you see, when you moved, I spoke as though you were a figure model instead of a stranger. I apologize, but I was thinking only of the work."

"May I see it?" That was very bold of her, and she blushed anew. "If you don't mind, I mean."

"As a matter of fact, I don't like people to look at my work. My sister showed something of mine to a famous artist several years ago, and I'm afraid he wasn't terribly impressed by my skills."

"Oh, I don't know anything about art," Miranda said. "I can't even manage watercolors. They always run."

He was definitely amused now. "I'll make you an offer. You stand where I tell you, and when I'm finished, I'll show you the picture."

"All right. But only if it won't take very long. I'm on my way to the Manor."

"Not long. I'm showing the scene from high up, so you're actually only a dot of color on the landscape. You'll see."

He spent a moment more beside her, placing her hand on the gate. He touched her as though she were a stick of wood or an animal, like a horse. She did not, however, feel like a stick or a horse. His hands were very warm, and she seemed to feel the impression of them long after he'd taken them away. She suddenly realized that they were all alone, except for the grinning figure of the servant on the hill above.

"Now, stand just like that for five minutes." He retreated some steps, turned, and squinted at her. Brushing the lock of hair from his eyes with an absent motion, a gesture which, from the flecks of paint in his hair, she took to be habitual, he clambered up the hill.

Miranda dropped her eyes from the sight of his lean body in tight buckskins pushing its way up the slope. He must be a stranger to the area, she thought. A traveling artist, going where he pleased. She knew this must be true, for she'd never heard of anyone with artistic leanings in Trenton. Mrs. Polkington would have been sure to find out all about any dabbling in art, even if only in somebody's most secret dream.

Miranda also knew that no man in the least familiar with Trenton would have dared be alone with Mrs. Polkington's stepdaughter. The prospect of being linked matrimonially, even at a distant remove, with that lady had driven off any suitor who might have otherwise been intrigued by Miranda's pale golden hair and petite figure.

Before long Miranda's limbs had turned to lead. The promised five minutes seemed to stretch into a decade at least before the man came back. She noticed that his boots were darkened by the wet grass. "That's excellent. Come on up."

He had picked the best spot for depicting the surrounding countryside. Reaching the top, Miranda caught her breath and then said, "I used to come up here when I was a girl. The Shaws were living at the Manor then. They had two daughters whom I'd often visit. I love it up here."

Miranda realized she was still holding the hand he'd extended to her when she'd needed help climbing the sloping hillside. She dropped it now, her cheeks reddened beneath the white-lined brim of her hat, and looked brightly around her, hoping he hadn't noticed.

An easel and three-legged stool crowned the top of the hill. She approached, then looked at him for permission. "Go ahead," he said. "But as I warned you, I'm no Romney."

"Romney did portraits."

"So you do know something about art."

"Good heavens, everyone knows that much." Turning to the easel, she smiled. Her pleasure was not feigned, even though she knew his eyes were still upon her.

Before her on the canvas the great shadows of the passing clouds swept the square fields, changing their colors from pale green to nearly black. Amongst the clouds the sun showered the world with gold. The track that led to her home, and past it to the village, seemed a road untraveled, disappearing into a mysterious tunnel of trees. The white gate barred the road. A small figure dressed in red, whom Miranda took for herself, stood with her hand upon it as though about to enter.

"It's marvelous," she said with pleasure unfeigned. "If praise from the ignorant isn't an insult."

"Believe me," he said, turning away to swirl a brush in a jar of clear liquid. "I'll take what praise I can get."

"But there's one thing that puzzles me. My pelisse isn't red." She glanced down at it and found it still a plain tan.

"No, but it should be. The contrast with the overall greenness, you know. I'll put in some red flowers to pick up the hue and bring it into greater prominence."

"Oh, I see. I like it very much. I'm sorry I was so rude before." She snatched again at her falling bonnet. If he hadn't been so tall, she wouldn't have had to tilt her head back so far to look into his face.

"If that bothers you so, why don't you take it off? It's much too big for you, anyway. It makes your face look like a kitten's. One with huge ears."

"It was a gift." Their conversation had become much too personal. Miranda remembered that he was a stranger to her, and her feet were wet. "I shan't take up any more of your time, sir. Thank you for painting me. I feel quite immortal now."

"Don't go. Look. René's bringing up the basket. Have a sip of something as a reward for holding so still. Lemonade?

Champagne, perhaps? It's a difficult walk to the Manor from here; all uphill."

Miranda looked around. The servant struggled up with a large wicker basket. After putting it down with an audible sigh, he brought out a napkin-swaddled bottle and held it up, grinning cheerfully at her.

Miranda was aware of a great thirst, though whether it was for drink or for more of the artist's company she could not say. But, though she hesitated, she said at last, "I must go. I left my mother sick in bed, and there are only the maids to see to her. I've been too long away already."

"Oh, your mother. Have I met her?"

"I don't know. She's Mrs. Polkington."

He took a step back. "*You're* the daughter of that dreadful woman?"

"Stepdaughter. And she's not dreadful!"

"I went to Oxford, my girl, where they taught me the meaning of many words. And for *dreadful* they simply said, 'Mrs. Polkington, of Trenton.' She was up at the Manor this morning, shouting at me."

"At the Manor? This morning?"

"Yes, of course. Streaming with wet and telling me what I can and cannot do. My sister was quite upset by her, and she's not well."

For a moment Miranda was struck by the fact that her stepmother had lied when she'd said she'd merely stepped down the road this morning in the rain. The long walk to the Manor would have brought on a cold even if Mrs. Polkington had not already been suffering from the remnants of a previous illness. It was only after Miranda considered this that she realized what else she'd just learned.

"But then, you must be the Earl of Morest!" Miranda was aghast. How rude she had been, how impossibly forward and . . . and . . . rude! Oh, her stepmother must never know, or she'd never hear the last of it.

"Yes, I am. Why do you look like that?"

Flustered, Miranda dipped him a curtsy. "I am sorry, Lord Morest. I had no notion."

"Well, how should you? I left my ermine and coronet at home, and, as my sister often tells me, I have no very noble appearance." He held up his hands. "Especially while painting. But come, don't run off just because my father was an earl."

From behind her Miranda heard the pop of a drawn cork. "I cannot stay. My mother took cold when she came to see you, and I must go back to her. I only came . . ."

"Yes?"

"Must you give the speech this Saturday?"

For a moment he seemed to want to say no. Then, slowly, he nodded. "I must. It is quite against my inclination, you understand. The thought of addressing a large group of people leaves me numb, but my sister has her heart quite set on my speaking, and so I'm afraid I cannot escape the duty."

"I see. Yes, I suppose you must please your sister." Miranda studied his face; the square forehead and straight mouth did not seem to indicate a weak nature, but perhaps physiognomy could not be relied upon.

"You are free," the earl said, studying his day's work, "to go up and try to convince Evelyn that your stepmother would be a more fit person for the task. But after Mrs. Polkington's behavior this morning, I don't think Evelyn will listen. She certainly never listens to me." He took up his brush and moved it lightly over the canvas.

"Thank you. I shall try."

As soon as she was gone, Nathaniel put down the brush. He had meant to work on until daylight faded, but now he had not the heart to continue. René came up to him, holding out a glass filled with bubbles. The earl drained the wine and looked rather grimly on his servant.

René had only three expressions. He either grinned or appeared so somber as to seem sullen. Nathaniel had glimpsed a third look only when a maid had passed through the room while René sat for one of the many character sketches his master had done of him. Nathaniel had always been fascinated by portraiture, which at its highest, consisted not of capturing likeness but of defining the subject's soul. He had never yet been able to reach this height.

Leaning down, Nathaniel picked up an extra canvas from the foot of the easel. Seating himself on the stool, he propped the blank on his knee. He drew the too-large bonnet easily enough. The smooth and sunny hair, with its severe center part, formed beneath it as though Miss Polkington sat before him. Even the heart shape of her face appeared without too much effort. Only when he tried to visualize one of the myriad expressions that had crossed her young face did his hand fail to obey.

Which to choose? The look of scorn, when she thought him a weakling? That was strongest in his memory but was so soon replaced by a glance of pity that it would not remain fixed enough to put down. Then there was her merriment and innocent pleasure in the day, his work, and his presence. He had felt that, but how to convey it? Then the embarrassment that had won over joy and turned at once to shyness upon the discovery that he was more than a wandering artist. And the anger sparking in her eye when he'd first come down the hill to ask her to stand still.

Nathaniel looked at the half-begun portrait in crayons. There was nothing for it. He would have to see her again. Perhaps if he studied her long enough, he could capture a single one of the shifting emotions that had crossed her face. A face, he now realized, as lovely as any he'd ever seen among the throngs of women thrown at the head of an unmarried earl. The only face he'd ever found interesting enough to paint more than once.

Lady Evelyn usually received visitors while lying on a chaise, her cheeks flushed as with hectic activity and an Indian shawl covering her lower limbs. Her hair was combed back above her pale forehead, and dark curls clustered at her temples. A book lay on the carpet as though dropped from a too-frail hand. Miranda felt pity for her and wondered that Lord Morest could not rule such an invalid. But perhaps he was too kind not to humor a sick sister.

"How do you do, Miss Polkington?" Her voice was so weak that Miranda looked at once to the grim maid still in the room, afraid that the excitement of a visit might be too much for her ladyship.

The maid, however, remained impassive. Miranda stumbled through her answer. "Very well, indeed. And you?" Oh, dear, perhaps that was not tactful.

With a graceful gesture Lady Evelyn indicated her couch. "Let us not speak of so dreary a subject. I am delighted to have at last the pleasure of a visit with you. I have already met your charming mother. How wonderful it must be to live with such an energetic individual. I, alas, was full of life once."

"Yes, Mother certainly is—"

"I hope, Miss Polkington, that you never know what it is to suffer."

She could not think of an answer to that. "Oh! Ah . . ."

"Grayson, bring in tea for our visitor. I'm afraid I'm very dull today and so cannot entertain you. I hope a morsel of tea and cake might tempt you to stay. I so rarely get to spend any time with a charming creature like yourself, Miss Polkington. Pray don't flutter off too soon."

"No, I shan't." The southern exposure of the little room made it very warm. Lady Evelyn had not invited Miranda to remove her pelisse.

"If it were left to me, I should never come to the country. I adore London and would spend all my time there, were it not for my brother's insistence on living rurally. He does grant me the occasional Season. . . . I don't wish to imply that my wishes are of no regard to him. . . ."

The lady's voice droned on. Miranda supposed, charitably, that Lady Evelyn had nothing else to think on during her long days cooped up in the house. Why did she not have her couch removed to the marble terrace that ran around the rear of the Manor? Miranda had often played there in the past with the Shaw girls and knew it to be sheltered from the weather while allowing a vista of the distant hills. Ignorant of the nature of Lady Evelyn's illness, she thought that perhaps the doctors had forbidden fresh air. She tried to ignore the stuffy atmosphere and pay attention to her hostess.

"And, as I said at the time, one cannot have everything one wishes for. It would be quite bad for one to be given entirely over to pleasure. The duchess was most kind. She said, looking at me, you understand, that some of us deserve more enjoyment than we get. But I do not complain." As Lady Evelyn drew breath, a knock sounded at the door. She sat more upright on her couch. Miranda thought she saw a gleam of appetite come into the heavy-lidded eyes.

"That will be our tea. Pray open the door for Grayson. Her hands are sure to be full." As Miranda got up, Lady Evelyn said, "When I am alone, I scarcely touch a mouthful. A piece of toast. Tea . . . hardly tea. Just hot water with a slight amber cast—Nathaniel!"

Miranda stood back to let the earl enter. He had removed the brushes from the bosom of his shirt and put on his coat. The dark blue superfine emphasized his height, and for a moment Miranda was startled anew by his attractiveness. Then she saw, though he had washed his hands, that the paint speckles still adorned his black hair. She could not help but smile.

Lord Morest bowed to Miranda, then crossed the floor to take his sister's limp hand, conveying it to his lips. "You're looking well today, Evelyn."

"You must thank my charming guest for that. Miss Polkington, allow me to make you known to my brother, the Earl of Morest."

Miranda opened her lips to say they'd already met when she became aware that Lord Morest was bowing. "I am very glad to meet you, Miss Polkington."

"Thank you, Lord Morest. I—"

"She came to ask you not to speak at the fair, Nathaniel. It seems that is her mother's prerogative."

As Miranda had not yet put forward the reason for her visit, she frowned in surprise at Lady Evelyn's words. For the first time Miranda saw Lady Evelyn smile. It came to her what a singularly acid expression the invalid could have.

"Of course," Lady Evelyn said, "she quite understands that you have a duty to speak, which cannot be forgotten. I have just been explaining that to her. Ah, *that* will be our tea. Open the door, Nathaniel. Grayson, another cup for his lordship."

Miranda tried to remember whether she'd ever read in a lady's magazine how to call one's hostess a liar without giving offense. The subject had never seemed to come up in any of the "Advice to Young Ladies" columns Mrs. Polkington gave her to read after church.

The maid put the tray down by the window. "Might I trouble you to pour out, Miss Polkington?" Lady Evelyn said with a yawn.

Miranda said, "Certainly." She conveyed a cup to her ladyship first and then went back to help Lord Morest.

She thought he looked weary as he took the cup from her hands. With a smile she offered him a plate of small sandwiches, which had been artfully cut into diamonds and rectangles. "You must be hungry," she said.

His sister's voice answered for him. "Oh, not the cucumber, dear. You must be careful!" Lord Morest's hand hovered over the plate and then he shook his head in refusal, his face slightly reddened.

"My brother, Miss Polkington, is a typical man. He will eat those few things that he should not." Lady Evelyn half laughed, half sighed. "It is odd, don't you think, that *I* can eat cucumber sandwiches when so many other delicious foods are denied me."

Miranda rose and carried the plate to her hostess. "Then you must have them."

"Oh, thank you. And if you might just replenish my cup?"

Miranda was still hungry by the time she made her excuses to leave. She knew Lord Morest had eaten none of the sandwiches, and she'd observed him tasting only one plain biscuit. Her own tea had consisted of tea alone. Unless the maid was sneaking cakes and sandwiches into her underclothing, Miranda could only think that her hostess had somehow devoured everything all by herself. A strange feat for an invalid, especially for one who talked unceasingly throughout the hour Miranda stayed at the Manor.

Lady Evelyn was most reluctant to let her go. Only after Miranda's repeated insistence on returning home to her ill mother did Lady Evelyn sigh and leave off pressing her to stay. She overruled Lord Morest's suggestion that he order the carriage to take Miranda home. She said, "Let the poor girl walk while she is able. I'm certain I should give anything to . . . well, I'm sure the ground is hardly damp at all."

Lord Morest followed Miranda to the door. "Nathaniel," called his sister. "I am most anxious to see your morning's work. Don't delay too long. I shall want my *siesta* soon."

Walking through the long hall, Miranda was aware of the tall gentleman beside her, though her eyes were fixed upon the maid's back. What an easy stride he had! Her own steps were staccato on the marble floor while his came down much less frequently. Despite the constraint of her skirt, she found herself trying to match her stride to his and nearly mowed down the maid when the woman stopped.

"Excuse me," Miranda murmured.

The maid opened the front door and waited, her lips pursed.

"That will be all, Grayson," Lord Morest said. The maid stared at him. "Go to your mistress, Grayson." After a moment the maid curtsied and disappeared.

The air in the hall was cold after the stuffy warmth of Lady Evelyn's chamber. A fresh breeze blew through the open door. Miranda stepped outside, knowing that Lord Morest still followed her. She was pleased by this but a little nervous too. He had not been so silent on the hillside. She wished he might speak freely as he had then, but now wanted him to speak of her.

"Miss Polkington?"

"Yes," she said, turning. Her bonnet had slipped back again, but she did not correct it. The sunlight lit her hair. Miranda was conscious of this, and conscious, too, that his eyes lingered on its silver-gilt smoothness. He smiled and she blushed as if he had read her thoughts. "Yes," she said again, more coolly.

"May I paint you?" Impossible to mistake her pleasure in being asked. Many people had asked him to paint them, his sister in particular being most insistent, but their eyes shifted and their mouths hung open in their eagerness. Miranda Polkington simply became lit from within as though a candle shone out for a moment in a midnight street. But then the light was veiled.

"No, I don't think so. My mother wouldn't approve, I fear."

"If I did not speak on Saturday, would she approve of my painting you?"

Miranda put out her hand. It did not quite touch his sleeve. "You truly misjudge her, Lord Morest. She is not a hard woman, nor a mercenary one. She has always been so kind to me. It is simply that she disapproves of young girls putting themselves forward. For myself, I should like to be painted . . . by you. But I must abide by her wishes."

"Need she know?"

Miranda bit her lip, yet could not entirely repress a smile. "Now you misjudge me. I must go."

"I'll walk with you."

Just then the maid reappeared. "My lady is asking for you, my lord. Shall I tell her you are coming?"

Miranda walked quickly away, not looking back until she'd reached the shelter of some trees at the bend in the drive. He'd gone in, as she knew he must. She now understood his reluctance to act against his sister's wishes. Miranda quite forgot her earlier stirring of pity for Lady Evelyn and transferred the feeling to her own stepmother. Mrs. Polkington would simply have to accept her defeat over the speech. Her usual methods would not avail her against so subtle a woman. Even as she thought it, Miranda knew such meekness was not likely.

Mrs. Polkington only stirred for a few moments that night. She frettishly refused more than a sip of soup, complaining the cook had put in too much fennel. Nor did she wish to have her hot forehead bathed with eau de cologne. "Don't fuss so, Miranda. Always fussing . . ."

Miranda decided to let her stepmother sleep. Her fever did not seem severe, compared to her previous bout with the ague. Waking up in the night, Miranda was comforted by the rumbling snores coming through the wall their bedchambers shared.

The next morning Mrs. Polkington was ravenous. "Haven't we any more eggs? I shall have to give the hens hot mash. And send the girl for extra bacon; not this streaky kind that has no meat. Now, Miranda, what did you do yesterday? I asked for you several times, but Nichols said you'd gone out. I don't mind that you left the house without telling me, but I was ill and there was not a soul in the house except for Nichols, who, you'll not repeat this, I think is a trifle dim."

As Mrs. Polkington did not trouble to moderate her tone whenever she expressed this opinion, Miranda was certain Nichols knew all about it. But it would be pointless to try to argue Mrs. Polkington out of her convictions.

Miranda only said, "I did leave for a little while, Mother, but you were well attended. Cook, as you know, nursed her brother before his death."

"An unsuccessful effort, to say the least. But I don't scold you, dearest. I simply wondered where you went." Mrs. Polkington leaned forward over the leavings of her breakfast, quite dipping her bosom in the greasy plate.

Miranda had intended telling her stepmother about her meeting with the Earl of Morest and his sister. Once when awakened, she'd passed the time before falling back to sleep in framing a description of her visit, in case her patient required amusement. Now, catching sight of Mrs. Polkington's bright and eager eye, Miranda had nothing to say. "Oh, I walked about the fields. The sun came out for quite two hours."

"You were gone two hours? Whom did you meet?"

"No one."

"No one? Not in two hours? Where on earth did you wander? Did no one pass you or stop to speak?"

"No, as I told you. I felt I should take exercise. It has been raining for the better part of a week, you know."

"Don't be pert, miss. In which direction did you go?"

"Toward . . . toward the Manor."

Mrs. Polkington dropped her gaze. "Indeed, that is a pleasant walk." She inhaled and sighed, a great gust of air. "I believe I shall not have a cold after all. You were right to send me at once to bed. Take this tray. I shall get up now."

"I think you should rest one more day, Mother, lest—"

"No, no. The sun has come out. I shall walk to the village. Has that girl gone for the bacon yet? Call to her, Miranda, and tell her not to go. You and I shall walk in together and confront the butcher. Mr. Phipps is very influential. If his wife can get him to agree that I should give the welcoming speech, it would be a powerful vote against the earl. I took the opportunity to talk with her, and I may say she shares my point of view entirely. I should have gone to see him yesterday."

"I wonder . . . I wonder what the earl is like?" Miranda

felt deceitful pretending she'd never seen him. But she consoled herself by remembering that Mrs. Polkington had not said *she'd* been to the Manor yesterday morning, either. Besides, Miranda felt a great longing to discuss Nathaniel, Earl of Morest, with someone, even her stepmother.

Mrs. Polkington said, "Didn't I mention I met him? Well, not to say 'met.' I passed him on the street. He's a plain sort of man. Quite ordinary. Nothing to recommend him but his title, I fancy. Are you ever going to take this tray away, Miranda?"

She did as she was bid. "Would you call him plain? Someone told me he was quite handsome."

"Who told you that? Probably that minx Louisa Tremble." Mrs. Polkington was obviously storing away her conjecture to be brought forth as fact in some later conversation.

To save Louisa's reputation, Miranda said, "I disremember who it was exactly. One of the clerks, I think."

"You should know better than to gossip with those silly boys at Manton's. They always presume on the acquaintance. You must keep close to my side at the fair, Miranda, lest one of them tries to speak with you."

"Yes, Mother."

So this year's fair was to be the same as all the others. Miranda had known it would not be different. She would remain by Mrs. Polkington as she walked sedately about the Common, accepting the greetings and congratulations of her neighbors. Miranda's friends would spend five or ten minutes with her before going off to enjoy themselves on the swings, the roundabout, and Pitch and Toss. She would hear their laughter until dusk, which Mrs. Polkington decreed as the time to leave. Afterward, she would listen to the rattling bangs of the fireworks and would sometimes catch a glimpse of red or gold fire from her window.

Mrs. Polkington walked as though in time to a march no one else could hear. They kept a barouche but rarely used it. Stopping in at the bakery, they found Mr. and Mrs.

Phipps in a state of near exaltation.

"Pink, pink, pink!" the baker shouted as they entered. "Pink with white roses and tracery." He came forward, clapping his hands together in glee. "We've not enough marshmallow, nor lemon, neither. I'll ride at once." He reached for his coat and put it on over his apron. Turning to the door, he perceived the ladies. "Good day, Mrs. Polkington! I cannot stay to talk."

"If I may have one moment—"

"No, I must fly at once to Scarborough. I shall buy more currants, too, if any are to be found," he added, over his shoulder. He went out, the service bell jangling overhead.

"Mrs. Phipps? Are you there?"

"Coming, coming." The baker's wife had cheeks as plump and round as muffin tops. "Did you ever see a man so mad and merry?"

"He seemed very excited," Miranda said.

"It's her ladyship. Decided to give a ball, she has. The very night of the fair. My husband's gone distracted, what with the cakes and sweets she's ordered. They've no pastry hand of their own at the Manor, not that many can match my Thomas. If I were to tell you of the offers he's received to go into private service, well, we'd stand here a time, indeed."

"A ball?" Mrs. Polkington's mouth opened into a square as though she were about to scream. Then she snapped it shut. "I congratulate you. Can you have everything done by Saturday?"

"We'll do it, just as my Thomas told her ladyship. And we won't be the only ones to work hard. All her goods are being ordered local. Mr. Jasper's boy was just in for some bread. All the green goods are to come from his shop. And her ladyship's ordered all the decorations from Manton's. Oh, it's a to-do, rightly so." The baker's wife snapped her fingers. "Fine sugar! I'd best remind him."

Surrounded by the warm, sweet smells of the bakery, Miranda saw defeat come into her stepmother's eyes. "I can't fight this," the older woman whispered. "The earl will spend a fortune in Trenton. My custom is nothing compared to it."

Trying to comfort her, Miranda patted the other's hand. "Perhaps they won't care for that."

"Of course they will. Don't be more of a fool than you can help! They're merchants—what else do they care for but profit?"

As her stepmother paced restlessly past the array of sticky buns, Miranda thought of the myriad kindnesses offered her by the men and women who ran the shops. Sweets handed secretively over the backs of pews, a bit of ribbon to tie up a doll's unruly locks, patient listening to her imperfect recital of shopping lists, and the friendship of their families. But Mrs. Polkington had been, or had tried to be, her second mother, and so Miranda looked sympathetic.

"There's nothing for it now but to try to put a good face on the thing. I only hope Lady Evelyn has the grace to send us an invitation, considering how she's plotted to ruin my speech."

"Do you think it was deliberate?"

"Deliberate! I imagine she laid awake last night planning this ball, and the first thought in her mind was how to undermine me. Come along, Miranda."

Nathaniel had just drawn rein across the street. He liked visiting the Old Coat alehouse after a hard morning's painting. Though Lady Evelyn maintained he took no interest in his tenants, he did enjoy listening to the talk of the idle men who could be found there at all hours.

Looking around before dismounting, he saw the ladies come out of the bakery. Nathaniel noticed Miranda as he averted his eyes from Mrs. Polkington's thick ankles, revealed as she lifted her skirt to keep it from the mud. There was nothing wrong with Miranda's ankles.

"Good morning, Mrs. Polkington," he called.

Her bonneted head swiveled toward him, and he saw her mouth tighten as though pulled together by strings. "You stay here, Miranda," he heard her say as she set off toward him.

The girl did not move. But Nathaniel felt she wanted to come to him. The desire to cross the street was plain in every line of her body. He could see her face, uplifted and admiring. He wanted to raise his hand and summon her forward. Would she disobey her stepmother for him? Though they had known each other but an hour, Nathaniel dared to hope she might.

But here was Mrs. Polkington in the way. Forestalling her torrent of complaints, he said, "Won't you introduce me to your young friend?"

"She is my stepdaughter. Hardly worthy of your notice, Lord Morest. About this speech . . ."

"May I meet her?" He saw Miranda step forward even before Mrs. Polkington called her name. Though she had been pleased and excited at first, with each step her expression altered until she was as vapid as a doll. It was as though he watched champagne turning flat.

"Miranda, the earl has expressed a wish to meet you."

"Good day, Lord Morest." Her voice, so merry on the hill, was toneless, and her blue eyes were as dull as the buttons on a mourning suit.

"How do you do, Miss Polkington. I hope my sister is to have the pleasure of seeing you at her ball."

With a harrumph, the elder lady broke in. "We do not keep late hours, Lord Morest. These excitements are not suitable for a young girl."

"Then perhaps we will see you there, Mrs. Polkington. I promised myself the pleasure of a dance with you." For one instant a spark of life came into Miranda's face as her small lips twitched irrepressibly.

Something of her amusement must have been reflected in his own expression, for Mrs. Polkington turned at once to her stepdaughter. With alarm Nathaniel saw the spark die as suddenly as though blown out. "Run along to Manton's, Miranda, and match that silk. They will be all day about it as it is."

"All right, Mother. Good day, Lord Morest." She dipped him a curtsy, her eyes veiled. He could not help but watch as she walked away, though he felt it was dangerous to pay too much notice to her. Fortunately, at that moment, Mrs. Polkington glimpsed someone deep in the shelter of the alehouse porch.

"Ned Whitman, why haven't you dug my roots yet?"

"Eh, missus, my back's been all crooked up with rheumatism this past fortnight."

"You're well enough to lift that beer to your lips. And to get half the girls in the parish with child." A low chuckle from the other idlers did not stop Mrs. Polkington from enlarging on this theme. "Yes, though you're not willing to support them. My garden had better be dug tomorrow, or I'll summon the parish officers."

Nathaniel dismounted. Miranda had gone in to the drapers. He could not be sure, but he flattered himself that she turned to look at him just before entering the shop. As he tied the reins to the ring-post, Mrs. Polkington said, "Now, Lord Morest, about that speech—"

"It's much too warm to talk about that here, ma'am. Come inside with me, and we'll discuss it over ale."

Scandalized, as he'd known she would be, and embarrassed by the soft sound of laughter now turned against her, Mrs. Polkington said, "I will not!"

He lifted his hands helplessly. "Well, then . . ."

"This is all of a piece with your sister's behavior. I am sorry for her. To have to bribe the merchants of this town to give to you an honor that is rightfully mine!"

"What do you mean, bribe?"

"Do you deny that she deliberately planned this ball to persuade the merchants of the value of her custom? It is beyond any barefaced effrontery of which I have ever heard persons of your class indulging in! It's an outrage, and so I shall always maintain." Mrs. Polkington seemed ready to begin a condemnation of the entire nobility when Miranda waved to her stepmother from down the street, calling her.

Nathaniel's eyes went at once to Miranda. He could distinguish none of her features save the slimness of her figure in a tight pelisse. He could not help but smile, ignoring the glance Mrs. Polkington sent him as she set off to find out what Miranda wanted, a glance that should have withered him in his Hessians.

A youngish man, dressed with some care in the remains of a gentleman's coat, rather than a laborer's smock, and with the foppish touch of a colored neckerchief about his sunburned throat, came out of the alehouse with a foaming tankard in his hand.

"Yer lordship?" he said, offering it. "The prime minister himself would need a drink after talkin' with her. Nothing like argufying with a woman to give a man a thirst. I should know." He sniffed reminiscently.

Nathaniel handed the tankard back to Ned Whitman and fumbled in his pocket for the price of it. "Nay, nay, yer lordship. I'm not so down I can't offer a drink to a man who needs one. You can stand me the same at the fair, if you'll be there."

"As you heard, I'm to give the first speech of the day."

"Aye, I've heard. And glad I am of it, too. That woman always says the same thing, over and over. We've all heard enough of it."

From the sheltered porch behind him, a voice said, "Now, then, I always take to it when she stamps her foot on poor old Boney-parte." A chorus of voices rose from beneath the covered overhang, some supporting one critic's viewpoint, and some supporting the other. There was no heat in the discussion. Nathaniel felt that no one was saying anything that had not been said before.

He had not, until now, realized that so much popular interest was taken in the giving of the speech. He had thought only his sister, Mrs. Polkington, and the more prosperous merchants had thought much about the matter.

In his imagination he had seen himself making a few extemporaneous remarks to no more than a dozen people. He now understood that this speech of his would be discussed and examined all through the long summer to come, and might even remain a topic of interest until next year. He felt a nervous clutch in the pit of his stomach. How he wished Lady Evelyn had not persuaded him into renting in this corner of England. In the North, where Morest was, the only expression of loyalty to the king on his birthday was a silent prayer during church service and, possibly, an extra toast drunk during dinner. And in London, though there was a great outpouring of emotion on the Fourth of June, no one ever asked him to address a few words to the populace. He'd never even spoken in the House of Lords, not being a party man.

As soon as Miranda and Mrs. Polkington set out for home, the older woman asked, "Did you think the earl attractive?"

"Well, I suppose . . ."

"Come, come! Don't hedge, Miranda. It's a simple enough question."

"He seems pleasant enough," Miranda said, thinking of how her stepmother had been dwarfed compared to the earl, confidently astride his large horse. She recalled the spread of his thighs and his upright trunk. Knowing she should not have noticed these things, she felt heat come into her cheeks. Nevertheless, she added, gathering courage, "I did not think it could be the earl you were speaking to, at first. Did you not say he was a plain man?"

"Ah, so you do think him handsome! Let me tell you, my girl, if you knew the stories I've heard, you'd not think so. A rake, a libertine, a flirt! The upper classes have no morals to speak of, so you be wary."

The earl had not seemed that sort of man to Miranda, though she knew she had not experience enough of the world to tell a rake from a parson without prior information. All the same, she believed her stepmother now no more than when Mrs. Polkington had spoken of the earl's appearance, though it would not do to say so. "He can hardly find anything to amuse him in me."

"You don't know men as I do. Remember, I've been married twice and you are but a green girl. Eighteen has no judgment."

"Yes, Mother."

"I have been thinking." Mrs. Polkington went on in a less emphatic style. "Soon we shall have to make a trip to Margate or Bournemouth. It is too late to make arrangements for this year, but next year is a definite possibility."

"I hope you are not so pulled down by this illness that you feel the need for a sea bathe."

"We shall not go for me, you silly child. The journey will be for you. That is where the young men are to be found."

"Young men?"

"For you to marry, Miranda. Don't you ever want to set up your own housekeeping? Not too far from me, I hope. Why, if you are fortunate enough to find some man or other with means, you might rent the Manor after Lord Morest and his sister leave it. You're passably pretty, you know. And if I can find two husbands with my face, imagine the luck you'll have with yours."

Miranda could not restrain a smile at this fair assessment of Mrs. Polkington's looks. But why had she brought up this plan now? Usually, her ideas were not put forward until the hour of their occurrence. Had it something to do with the earl?

Miranda did not see the earl again until Saturday morning, the morning of the fair. She did, however, hear him frequently spoken of. Miranda had never given gossip much of a hearing, knowing she would learn everything from Mrs. Polkington in time. Now she listened eagerly to shopkeepers' wives, passing laborers, and those among her friends who visited.

"From what I saw of him, I thought him most pleasant in his appearance," Louisa Tremble said, taking another biscuit.

"But so grim," added her bosom-bow, Catherine Andress. "Why, he looked positively thunderous at last evening's Poetry Recital. I thought perhaps the selection did not please him."

"Why?" asked Miranda. "What was read?"

"Cowper, I think, or was it Milton?" When appealed to, Louisa shook her head. The other girls smiled. They knew she only went to the regular Tuesday evening programs to gaze upon John Woodfall, the curate. He was fond of reading brisk, manly verse, though Louisa was exerting great efforts to make him recite love poetry.

"Well," Catherine said, "I'm not sure if it was Cowper's verse or simply his translations of Milton's, but when the earl came in halfway through, he looked about, frowned, and sat down noisily in the front row. I noticed, though, that he could not refrain from glancing around quite as though he were looking for someone." Catherine was betrothed to a younger son of a baronet, who lived at some distance, and so felt she could take note of other men without being labeled a flirt.

"Yes, and Mrs. Sedgewick, who sat beside him, said he could not keep still from one moment to the next. You should have been there, Miranda. I'm sure you would have been interested." A note of pity crept into Louisa's voice. *She* would not sit at home, not for a thousand step-mothers.

"My stepmother did not think I should go. Her cold is still troubling her." Miranda thought how her two friends' eyes would widen if she told of her meeting on Monday with the earl and his kind request to paint her. She felt warm remembering the admiration in his eyes when he'd asked her.

"Yes, everyone noticed Mrs. Polkington was not there. I declare, it is the first occasion she's missed since coming to Trenton. Where is she today?"

"She has walked out to see Mrs. Carstairs, whose family has just increased."

"Again!" the two girls said. From there the conversation wandered into other matters and did not return to the earl before the girls left.

Miranda, however, had been given much material for thought. For a moment she flattered herself that it had been she Lord Morest had looked for at the Poetry Recital. Then she shook the thought away. For the rest of the afternoon, no matter how busy she kept herself, the memory of his kindness and admiration when they'd met on the hill continually returned to her.

The next day Ned Whitman arrived to dig the garden. After receiving his orders from Mrs. Polkington, he went out to the rear of the house with his spade, found a spot where the warm spring sun was shaded, and lay down for a brief nap before beginning. Miranda found him there, when she brought him a sweating mug of small beer. At her soft cough Whitman jumped up. "Don't go scaring a man that way, miss."

"I'm sorry I startled you. Here. I imagine you're very hot and thirsty after working so hard." She politely ignored the virgin state of the garden and handed him the drink. It seemed incredible to her that he could drain the entire mug without pausing for breath, but indeed, it was a long time before Ned raised his head.

"Thank you, miss. That was the act of a proper lady, as I said to his lordship just yesterday."

"Yesterday?"

"As ever was. I met him just yon side of yer wall, there. He was walkin' up and down. I stopped and greeted him, taking the liberty as we met now and again in the Old Coat. A drop of ale eases my rheumatism a treat," Whitman added with a sideways glance at Miss Polkington. As she made no move toward the house with the mug, he went on speaking. "He asked me whose house this was, though in my own mind, miss, I think he knew."

"What time was this?"

"Not far off sunrise, miss."

"Sunrise?" Miranda wondered how long the earl had been walking up and down in front of her house. He must be anxious indeed to paint her portrait. She wished she'd known at the time he was there, though she could not have gone out to him. Not without Mrs. Polkington hearing her. Then she thought to ask, "What were you doing here?"

"Comin' to dig this garden as yer mother told me to. 'Course, when his lordship offered me a bit o'breakfast at the Manor, I couldn't say no, t'wouldn't a been polite. Then, half the day gone, wasn't no use to come by here again. I'll get that done today, never mind."

With a glance at the house Miranda said, "You'd better. My stepmother—"

"'Nough said, miss. Yer the daughter of yer father, right enough. A finer gentleman never lived, as I told his lordship. Always openhanded, whether it was a doctor's bill or a stoup of stout." Seeing that Miss Miranda had not caught his second hint, either, Whitman philosophically shouldered his spade and went to work. After half an hour, though, the younger maid brought him a second mug and the opportunity for an hour's pleasing diversion.

Friday the weather turned cloudy again. If the downpours of the previous weeks were to recommence, the fair could not be held tomorrow. Mrs. Polkington forgot her depression and spent the day happily inquiring into the running of the kitchen. The cook gave notice. Miranda did her best to soothe her. Fortunately for domestic felicity, the moon came out at twilight. The clouds parted, and Saturday dawned fair and clear.

Miranda took more than her usual care in dressing herself that morning, allowing a few curls to come forward onto her cheek. Mrs. Polkington did not approve. "You will be mistaken for a gypsy if you wear it like that. Go back upstairs and make yourself respectable. And I can't say I quite like this tying up of young girls' sleeves with ribbons."

Miranda held her breath.

"But as it is the fashion, I cannot quarrel with it. Do you think, though, that lavender would be more becoming to you than blue? Blue makes your eyes so big, you look quite startled."

"I would not like anyone to think I am just coming out of mourning, Mother."

"No, there is that. Hurry up, now, and fix your hair. And I'm not at all sure but you should wear your high-necked spencer. That dress is really too revealing for the day; I can't imagine what I was about in letting you make it up."

Miranda did not argue, nor she did bring the heavy spencer down. It would not have fitted correctly over the falling lace collar of her day dress, or so she told herself. She muttered, "It isn't low. I can scarcely see my throat."

Yet, knowing that her stepmother would comment if she did not have something warm with her, Miranda took out from the bureau the wide silk and wool scarf that had been her father's last gift to her. Checking in the mirror, she tucked up the offensive curls. She pushed her bonnet back into place on her head, tying the bow more securely.

"Are you ready, Mother?" she asked as she came down.

"I? Certainly." Mrs. Polkington raised her chin. "I, at least, am correct." Miranda could not but agree. Her stepmother was muffled up in a woolen day dress, tight to her impressive shape, with a high-ruffled collar, long sleeves, and a woolen shawl flung like the cloak of a gladiator over her shoulder. Even in the coolness of the hall her cheeks were nearly purple from the heat of her attire.

Long before they reached the Common, they could hear music, a thin, distant piping. Miranda began to walk faster, drawing even with and then passing Mrs. Polkington. She felt a jerk on her arm and looked down to see the handle of a parasol attached to the crook of her elbow. "We are not running a race, Miranda. Kindly walk beside me. There

are the Reverend and Mrs. Halliday. What will they think
of you, charging on this way?"

Though Miranda walked more sedately, bowing at the
vicar and his wife, she could still hear the music. Gypsies
and vagabond players always found their way to Trenton's
fair, though she'd never seen one of their performances.
Sometimes, as she stood patiently beside her stepmother,
she could hear them declaring the wonders to be found
within their brightly striped tents.

Not since she was eight years old had she seen the Punch
and Judy show, though the laughter caused by the pup-
pets could be heard all over the Common. Miranda could
remember crying the first year her stepmother had come,
because she missed Mr. Punch so. Mrs. Polkington had
tried to teach her that nicely brought up girls never wanted
to see vulgar things, but part of Miranda still longed for a
papier-mâché fool.

A week ago the Common had been empty of all save
a few young trees. Now it was transformed. A temporary
city had grown up. Temporary, but thriving nevertheless.
Even trees had been brought in, roots encased in large
balls tied with string, to separate one section of the fair
from another.

Miranda saw a banner above a yew lane proclaiming, THE
KING! GOD BLESS HIM! As they passed beneath it, many
people echoed the sentiment. Miranda and Mrs. Polkington
were no different. Despite the rumors of a recurrence of
George III's bout with madness, the citizens of Trenton
still loved their king.

Mrs. Polkington's patriotism was quickly forgotten.
Standing on the edge of a large rectangle filling with
people, she whispered as though to herself, "There's
the platform. The earl is already there. Look! He's
shaking hands with Jasper. I shouldn't, if I were
an earl."

"Yes, I see him." Miranda tried now not to stare. Though
today he was properly dressed, she saw him wearing a

paint-spattered waistcoat while the wind molded his shirt-
sleeves to his strong arms. Looking down at the green grass,
she knew it was foolish to remember the earl as he was then.
There could never be anything between them. Even if, by
some miraculous chance, he were interested in her, Lady
Evelyn would have already chosen some woman suitable
to be a peer's wife.

"Can't you stand still? Remember your ladylike repose!"

It wasn't enough to be ladylike. Lord Morest would only
marry a Lady with a capital L. A countess or a duchess in
her own right, perhaps. Lady Evelyn would see to that.
Better to forget how he had looked at her.

Schooling her features as she knew well how to do,
Miranda raised her head to study the men on the platform.
Mr. Phipps seemed to be stifling in his stiff stock. Mr.
Jasper was obviously pleased with himself, for he stroked
the gold watch he held in his hand, the sign and portent of
his accumulated wealth. The vicar was just now climbing
up, bowing on the steps to address a last word to his wife.
And Lord Morest . . . he turned and met her eyes. His smile
reached in and stole her heart.

There was no need to point to herself, asking if it was she
he meant. He was not looking past her at someone else. He
smiled at her and at no other. Miranda felt her cheeks flare.
Her breath all but stopped. Yet, she had no will to drop her
gaze, to free herself from the power she felt reaching out to
her. She stared and stared until the portly form of the grocer
stepped between herself and Lord Morest.

"My friends," Mr. Jasper began. There were good-natured
if rough jests from the laboring men and tousled women at
the back of the crowd. Mrs. Polkington took Miranda's arm
and drew her farther away from them.

The grocer raised his hands for silence. "My friends . . ."
he began again.

Mrs. Polkington said loudly, "I'm certain Mr. Jasper has
dipped into his own treacle barrel and will now sprinkle it
all over Lord Morest."

"I have the great honor . . . noble gentleman and goodly sister . . . regret she is unwell today . . . best of England . . ."

After ten years of Mrs. Polkington's speech, Miranda had developed a talent for only catching one word in five. Even though the grocer spoke about the man she'd just fallen in love with, Miranda knew she would hear none of the things she most wanted to know about him. Had he always wanted to paint? What had his nurse called him when he was a child? Who was the first girl he'd ever kissed? Had he ever been in love? Was he in love now?

She looked at Lord Morest again. He bowed to the flutter of applause from the crowd. Belatedly Miranda put her hands together. He touched the brim of his hat to her, and Miranda clapped more enthusiastically.

"Pray silence for his lordship," Mrs. Polkington said more loudly still. Miranda looked at her, surprised at the sharpness of her stepmother's voice.

Lord Morest said, "This kingdom of Britain is founded upon three things. Firstly, a strong army and navy."

Mrs. Polkington rolled up her eyes, but her "Harrumph!" was lost in the hurrahs of the crowd.

"Secondly, upon a principle of government by law, rather than by the force of that army or navy. And thirdly, this country is founded upon love between monarch and people, which supports that government of law and which is stronger than any military force ever to take the field."

Letting fly with an explosive cough, Mrs. Polkington flourished a large spotted handkerchief, which she pulled from her reticule. "I beg your pardon," she said as curious heads swiveled in her direction.

Taking no notice, Lord Morest went on. "As you know, the king is not well. Yet I know, even in his illness, he thinks upon this bond between himself and his people. I hope to establish such a bond between myself and the citizens of Trenton. With that hope, I have been persuaded by my sister to purchase the Manor and make it my secondary seat. The lands in which I hold my title must remain my primary seat, of course, but I find no peace there to compare with that I find in the healthful air and charming companionship of Trenton."

Miranda did not want to be vain, but it definitely seemed as though he addressed her in that last sentence. The crowd, however, took it to themselves and cheered his lordship three times. Mrs. Polkington shut her lips tight and glared fiercely at those people she knew.

"Chief among my pleasure here has been my frequent discourses with a lady known to you all. I am sure you are as eager as I to hear her speak a few words upon this auspicious occasion. Mrs. Patrick Ames Polkington!"

For a moment there was silence. Then Miranda, ignoring the astonished gulpings of the woman by her side, began to applaud. Lord Morest joined in at once. The merchants on the dais gazed at one another in frustrated amazement, and then they, too, clapped their hands. In twos and threes the crowd began to join in.

For once forgetting her duty to Miranda, Mrs. Polkington ascended to the platform to a fanfare of raucous cheering. People from all over the fair came running over to see the excitement. Never had Mrs. Polkington spoken to a larger group.

Before the ovation died, however, Miranda found Lord Morest beside her. His lips were moving, but she could hear nothing. He spoke again. She shook her head. He frowned. Bowing shortly, Lord Morest walked away.

Realizing he thought she'd answered "no" to the question he'd asked, Miranda followed after him. She paused to glance back at the platform. Her stepmother absorbed the applause, one foot thrust out before the other. If she'd been wearing a waistcoat, she surely would have had her thumbs in the armholes.

Once Miranda was out of the yew-sided courtyard, the sound died noticeably, though still loud. She hustled along, sometimes knocking into people and stopping to apologize, but always keeping Lord Morest's well-tailored back in view. He stopped before a beer vendor.

"Lord Morest," Miranda said, reaching out a hesitant hand.

His face as he looked on her was cold, but there still lived in his eyes the expression that had startled her before. "Yes, Miss Polkington?" he said, folding his arms.

"I did not hear you before, the noise was so great. What is it you said?"

Nathaniel smiled. Miranda marveled at how a simple change of expression could turn him instantly from a stranger to the man she loved. "I asked if you would go around the fair with me."

Miranda knew it would not be long before Mrs. Polkington came looking for her. No matter how many flourishes she added, her speech never lasted longer than twenty minutes. Could she trade twenty minutes of freedom for the days of commentary and questions she would have to undergo? "I would be pleased to, Lord Morest."

"Your beer, my lord," said the vendor.

"Never mind." Nathaniel put a coin on the board. Holding out his arm, he led Miranda away. "I saw a handbill yesterday for a Scottish Giant. Ned Whitman says he's very good. What did you think of him last year?"

"Last year?" The muscle beneath her hand was far more interesting than any giant. "Oh, I heard he was good."

"Heard?"

"Usually I remain by my stepmother. She does not find giants very appealing. Lord Morest," she said, stopping. "Let me thank you for what you did for her. I know she will be grateful. This means so much to her."

"And to you, I hope. It was for you, I think, that I did it. It seemed the best compromise for both our problems. My sister will be pleased I delivered some address to the mob, and your stepmother will not now be driven from the limelight. Now, about that Giant. And I've heard there's to be a skeletonic man. Thinnest man in Latvia, the handbill said."

The gaudily striped tent smelled of must inside. The sun shone through the canvas, turning Miranda's white dress red and blue. The same man who had sold them their tickets mounted to the stage. He made a face at the small number of people seated on the crude benches. Most of the day's visitors were still listening to Mrs. Polkington take away Napoleon's character.

"Ladies and gentlemen, you has the honor to be among a very select, and extremely small, group of people to see these wonders of the 'uman form. First, let me present Griselda, the woman no corset could hold." The barker flung out his hand, and onto the stage walked a woman. She was perhaps a trifle above the common weight but was by no means as impressive as Mrs. Polkington.

Lord Morest said, "She is certainly of remarkable size."

The barker claimed their attention once more. "Next we has her 'usband. They met during our recent tour of Europe, and it was true love. Just exactly the case with them two, there in the front."

The others in the tent chuckled. Miranda blushed in the darkness and moved away from Lord Morest on the bench. She had no notion of how she'd come to sit so close to him.

"He probably says that at every performance, if anybody looks the least like a couple," Lord Morest whispered.

"I take great pleasure in presenting to you, McGowan, the Scottish Giant." Out onto the makeshift stage walked a man, only an inch or two taller than the barker. A farmer and his wife got up and left the tent, allowing a brief flash of sunlight to illuminate the interior.

"Never mind, never mind," said the barker. "I gets to keep fourpence regardless. Now, for the rest of you, I want to say that the people in Scotland are as we know very short." He waved his hand about four feet above the ground. "So when I sees this fellow, I thinks he's a giant. And so he is, in Scotland."

With rude noises several others walked out.

"Now, then, for our latest addition to our little family. Caratacus, the skeletonic man!"

Lord Morest applauded vigorously. Onto the stage walked a man no thinner than Nathaniel himself. If anything, he was a shade heavier. His simple suit of brown linen strained at the seams, as though it had once fit better.

"Now, in Latvia, where old Caratacus was born—that's not his name, by the way, but it's as near as I can come—in Latvia, I say, they don't eat nothing but corn. Nothing but corn, day in and day out. Well, this poor fellow can't stomach the stuff. So he'd et nothing from the time he was two years old. Now, I sees him and I thinks I should bring him to England. And what do you think happens?"

"I've no idea," Miranda said involuntarily.

"Well, I'll tell you, young lady."

"I was afraid of that." Instantly Miranda covered her lips with her hand, afraid of what Lord Morest must think of her bandying words with a common showman. But Nathaniel only laughed and shook his head.

Rapidly the barker said, "This fellow eats our good British roast beef, washing it down with the best porter, and he puts on weight. Pounds and pounds. It's all I can do now to keep him in at night. Thank you for coming to see us. Come back. Bring your friends." All four members of the troupe bowed.

Still laughing, Nathaniel went up to the showman with a coin in his outstretched hand. "Take this, for you'll need it to pay the fine if any authority ever catches sight of this show."

"I've had some very fine gentlemen in 'ere, once or twice. Foreign princes, even." Weighing the coin, he said in surprise, "Thank you, Captain. Thank you, sir."

"What did you give him?" Miranda whispered, then added quickly, "Forgive me, it is none of my affair."

"Why shouldn't you ask? I gave him a guinea. Effrontery like that should be rewarded. Would you like a hot bun?"

He waved away her shy efforts to put a penny on the counter for her refreshment, as he had kept her from paying her own entrance into the show tent. "A penny bun will neither make nor mar me," he said.

"But I can't allow—"

"How much have you in your purse?"

She did not need to look. "Sixpence."

"Is that all you are given to enjoy yourself on? Oh, I forgot, you stay by your stepmother. Sixpence is too much. Very well, I shall keep a careful accounting of what I spend on you, and you shall repay me at the end of the month."

"I am not a child," Miranda said, her pride stung.

Nathaniel's eyes dwelt on her face. "I know you are not," he said in a low, serious tone. Before she knew what he was about, he flicked loose the curls confined by her hat ribbons. "You should always leave these curls free to kiss your cheeks."

Never had the sun beat down so warmly on her. She fell to studying his hands, which were marred by cuts and stains. Not the cultivated hands of a nobleman, yet how she wished she could carry them to her face and press her lips to them. Her breath was fast as he leaned close to her.

"Which would you rather do first? See the tightrope clowns? Visit the menagerie? Gain instruction in married life?"

Miranda looked up to see him laughing down at her. "What was that last?"

"Punch and Judy, of course. They are bound to be here. I've never been to a fair they've missed yet."

On the way they stopped to play Pitch and Toss, landing rings around the necks of fat-bottomed wine bottles. Miranda showed a surprisingly keen eye, though she tended to get flustered whenever Nathaniel watched her. He landed every ring he threw, despite the crooked necks of the bottles. The prize was a gimcrack bracelet of brightly painted tin, the sharp edges turned under.

"I know a lady isn't supposed to accept jewelry from a gentleman until his intentions are made clear, but would you, Miss Polkington, accept this valuable ornament from your humble slave?"

"With the utmost pleasure, my good Lord Morest," she replied, dipping a low curtsy despite the muddy street. She slipped the bracelet on her wrist, feeling that she would keep it forever. When old, she could take it out and admire the loud colors, remembering today.

They walked along in the mode of their great-great-grandparents, her ungloved fingertips on top of his outstretched hand. Though his face was solemn, Miranda could see the twitch of laughter at the edge of his lips. Only when she realized what stares they collected did she snatch her fingers from his as though burned. "I had better return to my stepmother. I am certain she will be looking for me."

"I'm sure she is. But . . . stay anyway?"

She could not bear to refuse. "Where is the puppet theater?"

"Down this way, I believe."

The lane was cool thanks to the transplanted trees. Sunbeams darted through the branches surprised like the birds to find a wood where none had been before. Miranda felt Nathaniel's rough fingers slide into the palm of her hand and grasp it. She dared not look at him until he drew her into his arms.

Her bonnet tumbled to the ground behind her.

Never had she felt another's heartbeat. It raced beneath her hand resting against his chest. Though they were surrounded by sunlight, she felt only his warmth. The sound of the world seemed immeasurably far away. Miranda had not known her arms possessed enough strength to hold Nathaniel close.

Then his lips were against her cheek, and her eyes closed in bliss as he murmured, "When I paint you, it will be with your hair down, like an angel of the earth."

*   *   *

Sitting with his head on her lap, Miranda looked up to find the shadows growing long. The day was all but done. Had they truly spent so much time sitting on the grass, laughing, talking, and kissing? He'd told her the answers to all the things she'd wondered about, and more. Bringing her to talk about herself, he found cause for laughter in the small doings of every day.

Running her fingers through Nathaniel's smooth hair, Miranda knew that she should never have such a perfect day again. She could almost hear what Mrs. Polkington would say when at last she returned home. Miranda made a promise to herself that she would answer no questions, let her stepmother interrogate her as she would. But the thought of Mrs. Polkington's voice was overlaid by the memory of Nathaniel's.

"Why do you let her control your life?" he'd asked.

"Don't you do the same with Lady Evelyn?"

"That's different."

"Why?"

He had drawn in a great breath of air and then let it out. "My mother died when I was twelve. Evelyn is six years older than I. I was a sickly boy, and Mother made Evelyn promise to always look after me. She passed up opportunities to marry to keep that promise."

"Was your father dead, too?"

"No, he didn't die until I was twenty-two. He saw to it that I went to Oxford, but that was the extent of his involvement in my life. He lived in a separate establishment in London."

"Why didn't Evelyn marry when you went away to school? Unless she was already ill."

"Her illness did not begin until after I came home from the army. I saw painting in Spain and France, new and exciting, like nothing in England. When I told Evelyn I was more interested in art than my earldom, she had her first attack." His brow furrowed, and Miranda saw him angry for the first time. It was a useless anger, the same as that she'd often felt within herself.

She said, "I wish I had such a wonderful talent. To escape into something besides yourself must be . . ." She could only shake her head and smile at him. He'd kissed her for the thousandth time, and each kiss made him dearer to her.

The sun gone, Miranda shivered. Dimly she remembered her insight into Lady Evelyn's plans for Nathaniel's future wife. In all the words they'd shared, he'd never spoken of his own dreams of love. Miranda knew in her heart that this day would be like a dream to him, brief and scarcely recalled upon awakening. She hoped she could find strength enough not to intrude herself upon his attention once today was over.

Nathaniel opened his eyes. For a long moment he lay in her arms gazing up at her tender smile. "Will I see you tonight, at this affair of my sister's?"

"I don't know. Even if we are invited, I have nothing to wear to such an elegant party."

"What's wrong with what you have on?" He sat up and stretched out his arms while he yawned. Curving them around her, he hugged her tight.

"Only a man would ask that," Miranda said, gently releasing herself from his embrace. She stood up, revealing the crumpled coat he'd insisted she sit on.

Nathaniel picked it up, beat it against a tree to get rid of any stray grass, and shrugged into it. "Come as you are, and so will I."

"Like that? Lady Evelyn will never allow it."

Nathaniel put his hands on her arms and said with a severe expression, "I am not a slave to my sister's every whim, you know. She hates that I paint, and I paint anyway."

"Yes, that's true."

He smiled and touched her chin with his forefinger. "Please come to the ball. I'll dance every set with you."

"I'll . . . I'll try to get away. Mother isn't happy with Lady Evelyn, you know. She thinks the ball was just an attempt to keep the merchants' committee on your side about the speech."

"I hate to say it, but Mrs. Polkington is probably right."

Holding on to her hand, he bent and swept her bonnet off the ground. He placed it gently on her head and tied the bow. "It's growing dark. I'd better walk you home."

"You mustn't. I shall have so much to explain already, and if she sees me with you . . . I don't even want to think about it."

"Is she such an ogre? I'll come in with you."

"No, Nathaniel. You mustn't. I'll see you at the ball."

"What will you tell her? She'll want to know where you've been."

Miranda blushed in the twilight. "I'll say I was with friends. Miss Tremble, and Miss Andress."

"Lie? You? I don't think you can. If you ever told an untruth to me, I should know it instantly. Your face gives you away every time."

If that was true, he must have seen how much she loved him. Miranda was glad it was dark so he could not see her expression now as she said farewell. "I must go now, Nathaniel."

He conveyed her hands to his lips, one after the other. "Your voice is so sweet when you say my name, I forgive you for wanting to leave me."

"Wanting to?" The disbelief in her tone was so apparent Nathaniel gathered her once more into his arms. With the greatest effort she'd ever known, Miranda moved away. "Good night," she said.

"Not good night, Miranda. Good evening. I'll see you soon."

She left him there, a silhouette against the deepening sky. After she had walked some distance, she noticed that her cheeks were wet. It was all very well for Nathaniel to say he defied his sister when it came to painting. Miranda could only remember how often he'd surrendered to her wishes on other matters. If Nathaniel had said even once that he loved her as she had come to love him, then she might have believed he could be strong enough to resist the years of Lady Evelyn's influence.

Even at her happiest moment, feeling Nathaniel's hands caressing her face and hearing him telling her how beautiful he found her, she knew what pain to expect in the future.

He had announced in his speech that he was purchasing the Manor. That meant he would come often to Trenton, live here at least part of the year. She would see him. He would be kind to her, even after he married. Perhaps sometimes he would remember this June the Fourth and look past his wife for her.

"I cannot go on living here," Miranda said aloud. Hadn't Mrs. Polkington said something about Margate? Perhaps she could be persuaded to make the visit a permanent one. But even as Miranda thought of ways to make Mrs. Polkington amenable to a change, she knew her stepmother would not leave Trenton after this day's work. She'd never be willing to start over again in a seaside town. Just finding the right committees to join might be the work of months.

As for Miranda's other option, finding a man in another town to marry, the idea was repugnant. She loved Nathaniel. There could never be anyone else.

Turning in at the gate, Miranda saw a shadow pass behind the drawn shade of the morning room. Her stepmother was already home. Miranda advanced. To help her be brave, she kept Nathaniel in the forefront of her mind. Let Mrs. Polkington learn that Miranda had spent the day with him, and Nathaniel would find living in Trenton a hell of unsubtle hints and suggestions.

"There you are!" Mrs. Polkington said while Miranda stood in the doorway and stared. Her stepmother wore her best silk tunic, hanging loose over a rich reddish gown. A white satin dress cap, given to Mrs. Polkington on her second wedding, and scarcely ever worn, dangled its golden tassels above one shoulder. "I cannot think what has kept you so long, Miranda. Really, you become more vague every day. Just like your father. Hurry now, child, and dress. Nichols is waiting to help you."

"Dress?"

"For Lady Evelyn's ball, of course."

"But . . . have we an invitation? I thought—"

"She sent one this afternoon. As soon as she heard of my triumph, I fancy. Never mind questions. Hurry. I've had Nichols lay out your Swiss muslin over that pinkish slip. It is the past fashion, but really you look very nearly pretty in it. Now, don't stand here talking, Miranda. Hurry!"

Hardly believing that she was not to be questioned, Miranda acted as her stepmother instructed. Yet, even while alone with her in the barouche, Mrs. Polkington did not raise the subject of Miranda's disappearance. Rather, her monologue dealt with how well her speech had been received.

As they entered, Mrs. Polkington whispered, "Do try to keep your head up, Miranda. The unevenness of those curls is hardly noticeable. Will you look at that Tremble minx? Does she think this is her wedding that she should throw bouquets?"

Looking up at Louisa from the Manor's main stair, Miranda saw her friend flourishing her flowers over the balustrade in a most peculiar manner. A sudden upward surge by the entering guests separated Miranda from Mrs. Polkington, though she could still hear her stepmother's voice. "I, of course, expected no such reaction, Sir Gilbert. But it quite warmed my heart. Oh, that's very good of you. Yes, many people have said I spoke better than last year. Thank you."

There was nothing for it but to climb the stairs alone. No sooner had Miranda reached the top than her arm was seized in a frenzied grip by Louisa, who pulled her into shelter behind a potted palm. "I was so trying to get your attention, Miranda. Listen, you must help me."

"Why, what is it? You seem frightened."

"No, not really. It's just . . . if my mother asks, please tell her I was with you all the afternoon." Her friend bit her lip and looked a little sly. "I know you weren't with your stepmother, because we . . . that is, I looked for you after her speech. I don't think Mother will ask, but if she should, could you tell her that? It isn't fair to ask you to lie, but . . ."

Miranda looked through the fronds before her. She and Louisa seemed to be out of earshot of all the other guests who were pressing forward into the ballroom anyway. "I will do as you ask, Louisa."

"Oh, thank you!" The other girl sighed, further damaging her flowers by squeezing them in ecstatic fingers.

"If you'll do the same for me, should my stepmother ask you where I was."

"Why, Miranda, what were *you* doing this afternoon?"

"That's not fair. I didn't ask where you actually were."

"I wasn't doing anything wrong. Exactly. That is, I went for a walk with John. We lost track of time. Nothing wrong. It's just that, well, you know Mother doesn't approve of him because he's the curate. But he'll be a vicar one day. Lord Morest has promised him a living in the North, as soon as the one in his keeping falls vacant. And then I'll marry him, and Mother can have nothing to say to it." Louisa stamped her lightly shod foot on the marble floor. Though it made no noise, the meaning was clear.

These words reminded Miranda that she had forgotten Lord Morest in loving Nathaniel. Miranda wished her own troubles could be solved by determination and a defiant gesture. She herself had never thrilled to the power of a curate's mellow voice during a spring service. No, she must aim for the highest limit of matrimonial ambition. If only she could be certain Nathaniel wanted more from her than her face on canvas. She sighed and ruefully shook her head.

"Don't tell me you don't approve, Miranda!" Louise Tremble nearly howled.

Realizing her friend had been talking while she mused, Miranda hastened to reassure Louisa. "I shall tell your mother just what you wish. I also suggest we say only that we had a very enjoyable time and that we saw and did everything of which she'd approve."

"You *are* clever, Miranda. That way she can't trip us up over details. Thank you, thank you." Louisa leaned to the side to look around the plant. "I don't see my mother now, or Mrs. Polkington. Let us go in together, then."

Miranda agreed and they linked arms. However, when she wished to sidle into the ballroom along one wall, Louisa paused, caught Miranda's arm fast, and posed in the center of the doorway. Only when heads turned to admire the two pretty girls, one so pale and the other a thriving brunette, did she consent to move forward again. "That's the way to enter a ballroom. It's too bad I shan't make a come-out, but then, I needn't now."

"Are you so sure of John Woodfall?" Miranda asked enviously.

Louisa's nod of sublime confidence needed no addition.

When the Shaw girls had lived at the Manor, Miranda had often played with them in the ballroom, dancing with a set of handsome bolsters for partners. She remembered the blue ceiling, painted to imitate the sky, and the carved and gilded panels around the mirrored walls. Now, instead of a child's humming, violins and a pianoforte played as ladies and gentlemen took their places for a quadrille. Miranda pressed her hands together, suddenly a child again with all her imaginings coming true.

Then she saw Nathaniel standing beside his sister. He, too, had changed his clothes. He now wore an elegant black coat, silvery satin knee breeches, silk hose, and dancing pumps that seemed out of place on his large feet. He looked uncomfortable, tugging at his tight stock. Miranda could not be angry, though he had all but promised to stay as he had been at the fair. He could no more withstand his sister's suggestions than she herself had been able to

choose a new costume, once Mrs. Polkington's wishes had
been made known.

Mrs. Polkington appeared by her side. "You mustn't lurk
here. Come, let us greet our hostess."

Lady Evelyn wore a white gown, suitable to a girl in her
first Season, which played up the flush on her cheeks and
made her dusky hair even more dramatic. She released her
clutch on her brother's arm to fling welcoming hands into
a startled Mrs. Polkington's grasp.

"My dear, dear woman! Such a triumph! I have been
badgering Nathaniel to tell me all about it. As you know,
I was unable to attend. Oh, pooh! Think nothing of it! But
one must conserve one's energies, especially when they are
not so very great. You, I know, must never be ill."

Nathaniel said, bowing, "Good evening, Miss
Polkington."

"Good evening, Lord Morest," Miranda answered with
a correct bend of the knees. She could not help it, she
must look to see his reaction to her finery. Would he smile
when he noticed that she still wore the bright bracelet he'd
given her today? She'd found just courage enough to wear
it, though she'd concealed it from Mrs. Polkington. But his
intense eyes studied only her face. She doubted he even
saw that she had changed her gown.

"Nathaniel," said his sister, recalling his attention. "Have
you done your duty by Lady Makeworth?"

"I don't remember." Holding out his hand, he said, "But
I shall do my duty by Miss Polkington. If she will honor
me?"

The acceptance hovered on Miranda's lips, but Mrs.
Polkington's voice rolled out. "Yes, yes, dance with him,
Miranda. You should seize the chance. Not many earls are
likely to ask you in the future, you know. I never had the
opportunity. You shall have to tell me what it is like."

"On second thought," Nathaniel said, "let us fetch
these lovely ladies some punch. Will you help me, Miss
Polkington?"

"Of course. Would you care for some cake, Mother?"

"You mustn't think I'm so ungenerous, Miss Polkington. Bring your mother some of the dressed crab. It was our mother's recipe. Do you remember, Nathaniel?"

"I'm afraid I was far too young to attend any of Mother's parties." Miranda could tell his smile was false. "Come, Miss Polkington."

She followed him and said, "Your sister seems in a happy mood tonight."

"Yes. Tell me, what did you say to your stepmother when you returned so late?"

"I did not tell her anything; I had not time." Was it that he did not want to be compromised into proposing marriage? "You have nothing to fear, Lord Morest," she said stiffly, walking more toward the refreshment table. "I shall not tell her anything of what I did this afternoon."

In two long strides he was beside her again, drawing her arm through his. "I am glad for your sake that you did not. She would have turned your mind over like old feather ticking."

At the touch of his hand all her fears evaporated. "I don't know why, but I want to keep it all a secret."

"Don't you know why?" His smile intrigued her. But before she could ask him anything, they were among the others, and there was no more chance for private speech.

When they carried their booty back to the older ladies, Mrs. Polkington had but an instant to sip her punch before Lady Evelyn introduced her to an elderly gentleman. Without knowing quite how it happened, Mrs. Polkington was soon dancing with him.

Tasting her thin bread and butter, Lady Evelyn made a face. "Nathaniel, my dear, would you be so good as to procure me a small glass of ratafia? I can't seem to taste anything through this punch. Are you certain you mixed it well?"

"I will find you something else to drink, Evelyn. Miss—"

LADY FAIR   105

"No, no, leave the child with me. I've hardly had a moment to speak to her." Nathaniel hesitated, but then bowed and went off to do his sister's bidding. Lady Evelyn said, "I cannot blame you, Miss Polkington, for not coming to see me again. I am little enough company for a young and lovely girl like yourself. Tell me, how do you find my brother?"

"He . . . he seems to be very good to you, Lady Evelyn."

"Ah, yes. He is a dear. I've told him time and again that he is not responsible for my illness, but he will take the blame for it, no matter what I say."

Nathaniel returned with a tiny glass of the bitter liqueur. "Thank you," Lady Evelyn said as she sipped it. "Now, if it isn't too terribly much trouble, could you find me a chair? You know how standing brings on my aches, silly things that they are. Dear Miranda—I simply can't call you Miss Polkington—do you see my fan anywhere? Could I ask you just to wave yours in my direction a moment? It is terribly warm, but I daren't ask them to throw open the windows lest it bring on my sciatica."

Miranda began to feel a tightening across her shoulders. She felt she would prefer the booming insistence of her stepmother to listening to the thin, demanding whine of Lady Evelyn any longer. Just then she heard Mrs. Polkington say, "You couldn't be more wrong, sir, not in several millennium!"

"Dear Mrs. Polkington, so vibrant and alive!" Lady Evelyn said, as though these were not desirable qualities.

Not even Nathaniel's return, followed by a footman bearing a padded slipper chair, made Miranda feel any better. Nathaniel was trapped by a tyrannical woman, Miranda thought, just as she was trapped. Like flies in a web, the more they tried to free themselves, the more entangled they grew. How Miranda wished for the strength to slash the web, a strength she knew she'd never find.

"Lady Evelyn," Miranda said, "I'm not feeling quite the thing. I think—"

"But you mustn't run away so early. You haven't even told me how you liked the fair." Placing her elbow on her knee, Lady Evelyn leaned forward, a sharp look coming into her selfish eyes.

Aware that Nathaniel stood just behind her, Miranda said, "I enjoyed myself very much, thank you."

"Ah! And with whom did you visit the fair? Your step-mother, as usual? Or, perhaps, with someone else?"

What had Nathaniel told her? "I spent the day with my friend, Miss Tremble. Have you met her?"

"I don't believe so. Unless you mean the charming brunette girl who spent the entire time with John Woodfall? Or so my maid tells me. She's a very religious girl and felt an hour or two in the church would be more beneficial to her soul than a day given entirely over to pleasure." And Lady Evelyn smiled.

Miranda was fairly certain there was a threat concealed under the thin-lipped smile of the other woman. "I . . . I don't know what you mean, Lady Evelyn."

Suddenly Nathaniel's hand was on her shoulder. Miranda's fingers flew at once to cover his in a touch that told more about her feelings for him than a blatant embrace in the center of the ballroom could have done.

"What do you mean, Evelyn?" he asked.

"I? Why, nothing, Nathaniel. I merely wondered what this girl had to look so guilty about. Now I suppose I know." The thin voice took on strength. A few people, bored by the dancing, began to look their way.

Nathaniel said, "This isn't the place for a discussion."

"I agree," his sister said. "Let us go to my chamber. You will wait here, my dear Miss Polkington."

"No, she's coming with us." Lady Evelyn looked startled by this quietly spoken defiance, but she stood up, flicked the train of her skirt over her arm, and stalked away.

Miranda could hear the whispers start as she followed the brother and sister out of the ballroom. Her only consolation was that her stepmother was talking far too loudly to hear the gossip.

As soon as Nathaniel shut the door to the hot and stuffy chamber, Lady Evelyn sprang to the attack, saying, "Don't tell me you've allowed this girl to inveigle her way into your affections. She wouldn't look at you if you weren't an earl. This is just a foolish plot to escape that horrible woman. Don't think I blame you, dear Miss Polkington. I'm sure any life, even that of a common mistress, would have its appeal after living with her."

"Go on," her brother said.

Both women looked at him in surprise. Miranda had some hope he would defend her, but he sat upon a chair as though a judge. Lady Evelyn recovered first.

"I shall go on. I must say I'd been expecting you to behave in this silly manner for quite some time. It's just like you to form an attachment for the first unsuitable girl to come along. When I think of the time and effort I've lavished on you, trying to make you see where your true duty lies! Can't you see that a nobleman has certain responsibilities? It would be a crime for you to marry some nobody . . . and with such a mother! What a happy home life you can expect with Mrs. Polkington visiting. And she'll stay and stay, if I know her type of woman."

"You alone have mentioned marriage," Nathaniel said.

"Thank God you've that much sense. Perhaps we can keep this disgraceful business from becoming known."

He merely nodded in response. Turning toward Miranda, he said, "Your turn. What have you to say?"

"Nothing." Tears burned her eyes as she bowed her head. "Nothing."

"There, you see!" Lady Evelyn proclaimed triumphantly. "Faced with the truth, she is silent."

"I wish *you'd* be silent, Evelyn. Just for a moment. Well, Miranda. You've heard what my sister has said. Is there nothing you wish to add? She's made some serious charges against your character. Do you wish to defend yourself?"

All she wished to do was hurl herself into his arms. She felt that would answer all questions and settle all doubts. With Lady Evelyn in the room, however, she dared not do it. That lady seemed incapable of an act of honest emotion and was all too liable to distort any she witnessed. Miranda could only gaze longingly at Nathaniel. It was as though he were moving far away from her, leaving her forever.

Nathaniel chuckled, and then laughed. Instantly the air in the humid chamber seemed lighter. He got up and crossed to Miranda. Taking her hand, he faced Lady Evelyn. "Sister, I want to apologize. No, hear me out. All my life I've known that you wanted more than anything else to run the estates of Morest. In short, you wanted to be earl. Because I felt sorry for this inequality, I've let you do as you will with your life and mine. I made no objection to your nagging and complaining, even when I should have, when it began to make you ill."

"Nathaniel, how dare you talk to me this way! I've cared for you since—"

"I'm sorry, Evelyn. That bird won't fly. I've taken care of you for the past ten years, giving in to your whims and crochets because it seemed to make you happy. Only recently have I come to see the damage I've done to myself. Miranda proved to me that living with a dragon is always dangerous, even if the dragon means well."

"Are you calling me—"

"I don't want to hurt you, Evelyn, but I think it is time you started living for yourself, instead of trying to control my life. I'll make the Manor over to you. You can run it as you please." He looked down at the girl by his side. "I'm going back to the North, to Morest, where I belong. There's some vistas near there I've always wanted to paint."

Evelyn seemed to have no words left, only gasping cries. But when Nathaniel opened one of the glass-paned doors that led onto the terrace, she said, "Don't open that! You know how damaging the night air is to my lungs."

"Evelyn, that last doctor said there was nothing wrong with you, except that you keep yourself mewed up in stuffy little rooms like this one. Fresh air and exercise was his prescription. I suggest you follow it. As we are going to do now."

A few steps down the walk Nathaniel took Miranda's face between his hands. She breathed in his painterly scent of turpentine and oil, and it seemed like incense. "I haven't told you how very lovely you are," he said. Then he kissed her.

Drawing in a sobbing breath, she said shakily, "I love you."

"A convenient quality in a wife." His arms about her, he laid his cheek against her smooth head. "And even more so in a husband. Will you like being my wife, Miranda?"

She gave him an answer without words. With a boom the stars exploded and rained down. Miranda and Nathaniel looked up. "Oooh," she said. "Fireworks."

Leaning against his body, she watched as another rocket mounted with a loud hiss into the sky. Farther along the terrace other guests emerged to applaud and cheer the blue, gold, and red explosions in honor of the king's birthday. Nathaniel found his appreciation of the pyrotechnics was improved by kissing Miranda with each launch. Then he felt a heavy touch on his shoulder.

"Lord Morest," Mrs. Polkington began. "I demand that you unhand my stepchild at once. What kind of a man takes advantage of a defenseless girl in this shocking fashion?"

"It's all right, Mother," Miranda said. "I have no objections."

"I realize you are innocent, Miranda. But to allow such familiarity . . . unless . . . can it be . . . ?"

"I have the honor to ask for your daughter's hand . . ." the rest of Nathaniel's sentence was lost in the bang of another rocket.

Such paltry noises could not override Mrs. Polkington's voice. "Delightful! How the Phippses' and the Jaspers' eyes will bug out at this! Oh, they shall not condescend to me now! Let me see, we shall have the wedding in August. That will be time enough for bride-clothes and fripperies. We shall have to go to London, Miranda. You must learn to act and dress as befits a countess, you know. I shall draw the guest list tomorrow, and then there are the solicitors we shall need to consult. It is a pity Lady Evelyn is not in better health. All the responsibilities will fall on my shoulders. There are a thousand things to be done."

As she began to enumerate them, she gathered a larger crowd than had been called forth either by the fireworks or her speech of this afternoon. Miranda tugged at Nathaniel's sleeve. "Can't we just slip away as we did this afternoon?" she asked as the final sparks died away in the warm evening air.

"Certainly."

He bowed to Mrs. Polkington, who broke off in midsentence to splutter, "Where . . . where are you going?"

"The Border," Nathaniel threw over his shoulder as he led a laughing Miranda off the terrace.

"Oh, that was too bad of you," she said when she caught her breath. "Did you see her expression?" And she laughed again until she realized she walked on cobbles and that there was a strong smell of horses. "Aren't we returning to the ball?"

"No. Where is that groom?" He shouted and a short form appeared in the stable doorway. "Have the traveling chariot put to, and send someone for my valet."

As the groom ran off, Miranda asked, "Where are you going?"

"As I said, we are going to the Border."

"The Border . . . Scotland?" She could feel her heart beating fast in the base of her throat and she put her fingers to it. "Are you in earnest?"

"Completely. I won't live without you, but neither will I spend the next several months listening to Evelyn and Mrs. Polkington turning this into their wedding instead

of ours. We won't matter in the least. Unless you want
bride-clothes, and half a thousand guests, and all the rest
of it?"

"You mean, if we leave now, we are free to do as we
like?" The idea appealed to her. "Oh, Nathaniel, can we?"

On the road to Scotland, Miranda slept in Nathaniel's
arms. Nichols and René were warned by his glance to make
no noise that might wake her. It took a day and night to
reach Gretna Green, and Miranda stayed cheerful despite
the length of the journey and the knowledge that she'd left
her reputation behind her. When they'd collected the maid
from Mrs. Polkington's house, she'd asked if Miranda was
sure the earl meant to marry her. Miranda had answered,
"I don't know, and I don't care." If he'd asked, he could
have shared her room in the quiet little inn they stopped at
Sunday afternoon.

After their swift wedding they spent a week at that same
inn and knew great happiness. Then they went south again
to London. She met Nathaniel's artist friends, both fellow
nobility painting in austere studios and men living in dark
alleys but whose rooms were full of laughter and light.
There were frequent noisy parties with many people, but
Miranda could not always distinguish which couples were
husband and wife.

About a month after their marriage, Miranda sat in one
of these studios, bouncing the artist's fat baby on her knee.
The child's mother was posed as Terpsichore, the muse
of dancing, while Nathaniel and the artist discussed her
masses. Smiling at the baby, Miranda sighed.

At once Nathaniel said, "You've convinced me, old man,"
and came over to sit beside his bride.

"What is it, sweetheart?" he asked, holding out a forefinger to the infant, who instantly wrapped a chubby fist
around it, giving up the attempt to grab Miranda's bracelet.

"We should go home," Miranda said.

"To Morest?"

"Yes, please, I'm longing to see it. But first, we should go to Trenton. They are our family, Nathaniel."

"You are my only family now, dearest." She leaned against him with a happy sigh. Whenever he looked at her, she could feel her heart melting within her bosom. Nothing in life had ever given her greater joy than to spend every day in his company.

"But you are right," he said. "We'll go to Trenton."

Their chariot drew up outside the cottage where Miranda had spent so many years. Emerging, she took her husband's arm, prey to quakes and fears. "I hope she does not rail at me too much."

"Don't worry, love. She will not take the time from praising me to carp at you. Being an earl has some benefits as well as drawbacks." He raised his hand to the holly-wreath knocker. The rap echoed queerly.

Putting her cupped hands to the window, Miranda peered in. "Nathaniel! Everything is under Holland covers."

"Aye, miss," said a voice, closely followed by the scent of pipe tobacco. Ned Whitman, his bright neckerchief shining in the sun, came around the corner of the house. "If yer lookin' fer Mrs. Polkington, my lady, she's gone."

"Gone?" Miranda echoed. "Gone where?" Had her defection caused her stepmother so much grief and embarrassment that she'd had to leave Trenton?

"Up to the Manor, this last fortnight as ever was." Seeing that he had made a sensation, Whitman smiled around the stem of the pipe. "I thought as that would throw you if ever you came back. Aye, she's moved up to the Manor, with every stitch she owned. This house is to be let. Nice bit o' garden, good roof, dry cellars. And me, as a resident man of all work."

Nathaniel asked, "And what of my sister?"

"Oh, she's there, too, my lord. Never seen two women take on faster, once the two of you had gorn off like that. Back and forth, every day that God sent, gabblin' away like turkey hens."

Arriving at the Manor, Miranda and Nathaniel found every word to be true. Mrs. Polkington stood in the library, reading a book on ornamental gardening to Lady Evelyn, who reclined on a couch within range of the breeze blowing through the open windows. "Prune decisively, and notable results will be achieved. The hedges should stand in seried rows like soldiers on strict parade, while the plants beyond should be arranged according to height, color, and profusion of blossom. See figure A."

Upon the earl's entrance with his new countess, both ladies' eyes flew at once to the third finger of Miranda's left hand. Reassured by the gold she saw there, Lady Evelyn swung her feet to the floor. Very nearly upright, she patted the couch and said, "Come sit by me, Miranda, and tell me all about your wedding trip."

With a glance at her husband, Miranda did so. Having learned to be wary of Lady Evelyn's mode of conversation, her answers were at first somewhat terse. But she found herself the focus of a considerable charm that reminded her of Nathaniel's.

Mrs. Polkington, on the other hand, had immediately asked Nathaniel's advice about her plan for improving the yield of the lower fields. "I never knew I had such a talent for farm management," she said, laughing. Nathaniel politely complimented her. "Oh, I owe it all to dear Lady Evelyn. She's encouraged me to take an interest in the home farm."

"Pish!" Lady Evelyn interjected, hearing this. "Why, if it weren't for you, dearest Caroline, I should still be living the life of a complete invalid. Why, Nathaniel, I got up and walked clear around the herb garden last week, after Caroline pointed out how silly it was to lie about all day."

"I was surprised, Mother, to find you'd given up the house."

Lady Evelyn answered, "Now, that *was* my doing. I couldn't live alone in this great house, and I felt for Caroline, left all alone, too. Not that I blame you for that,

Miranda. Love must have its way, but we two poor old ladies did feel a trifle forgotten. Sharing this feeling, we thought it best to find comfort in each other's companionship, and so Caroline moved up to the Manor."

Nathaniel and Miranda exchanged another glance, each knowing that a good many other feelings must have been shared, including complaints about ungrateful children. Invited to stay as long as they pleased, they went up to change from their traveling attire.

Only later, when Miranda found herself alone with her stepmother, did she ask, "So you enjoy living here, with Lady Evelyn?"

"What could be better? Oh, I don't know that she's the easiest person to jog along with, but once I'd mentioned one or two things that troubled me . . ."

"As in?"

"Oh, minor irritations, hardly worth mentioning really, but we decided from the beginning that we wouldn't hedge about problems but head straight toward a solution. Take my advice, it's a good way to manage your husband, too."

"So you and Lady Evelyn have no quarrels."

"No, no, I find her no trouble at all. All she wanted was rousing up, and I soon saw to that!"

Nathaniel, called into his sister's presence, found that Lady Evelyn had changed her quarters to the second floor. "Caroline persuaded me that the air is healthier up here."

"I understood you to say, before the king's fair, that is, that you thought she was not ladylike."

"You must have misheard me, Nathaniel. She's a trifle robust, that's all. A few rough edges lend a certain cachet to all she says and does. I try to drop little reminders to her, and to demonstrate by my behavior that peaceful words can do more than all the shouting in the world. You might try such a technique with Miranda."

"And what is wrong with Miranda?" Nathaniel asked, his eyebrows rising.

"Why, nothing in the world, dearest. I find her a sweet child, but a trifle fond of hearing herself talk. Now, do tell me all you plan for Morest."

Despite such trying moments, Nathaniel and Miranda enjoyed their stay at the Manor. They kept it brief, though, as she was eager to go on to her new home at Morest.

As they mounted up into the chariot to make that journey, an argument started between Lady Evelyn and Mrs. Polkington.

"Nonsense, Caroline, there has never been an Earl of Morest named Patrick, not in two hundred and fifty years."

"Patrick is a good name. Her father's name was Patrick."

"Yes, yes, it's a fine name for a clergyman, or a scholar, but not for an earl. It must be something that resounds with nobility and—"

"Shouldn't you wait," the present earl asked from the carriage step, "until there is the possibility of a child before arguing over its name?"

His wife laid her hand on his sleeve. "Hush, dear, or they'll start suggesting how we go about managing that."

"Do you think I need suggestions?" He kissed her, and then pounded on the side of the coach. Waving good-bye, they left the two ladies still arguing the question.

"Patrick!"

"Orlando!"

"Pat . . . Orlando?"

A
SUMMER'S
FOLLY

Sarah Eagle

1

"*I* AM UNDONE, COMPLETELY UNDONE. WORDS CANNOT express my anguish," pronounced Miss Thalia Dumont in ringing tones as she draped her lithe form carefully against the doorframe of the morning room. The ruffled elegance of her white muslin dress and her unbound raven hair lent her a fragile air as she raised a languid arm, lightly touching the back of her slender wrist to her forehead. "Woe is me. It's too tragic to speak of, too terrible for this to happen in my young life. I shall go into a decline unable to utter a word of my distress."

A solitary figure in the center of the sitting room was the only witness to Thalia's soliloquy. Eliza Dumont stood behind the Pembroke table and continued to arrange the vase of fresh market flowers before her. Without uttering a word in response, she silently congratulated her cousin on her ability to be so articulate under extreme duress— whatever the cause, real or imagined. Then, dismissing the uncharitable thought, she remembered she meant to speak to her uncle about Thalia's predilection for melodramatic literature of late. Eliza could not understand why a recently engaged young lady at the tender age of eighteen would thrive on such maudlin fare.

At the advanced age of five and twenty, Eliza had always imagined a bride-to-be would dwell on happy thoughts and delight in planning her wedding. The Honorable Mr. Russell Towne, though the younger son of an earl, was a fine catch for Sir Cyril Dumont's youngest daughter—the last of the three to marry. Russell's blond curls and green eyes were a perfect foil for Thalia's raven tresses and dark eyes. Despite Russell's tendency to treat his betrothed like a piece of delicate china, there was nothing to promote the girl's melancholy turn of mind. It was not as though she were a charity case past her first blush of youth with no more than average looks and only a lackluster future as an unpaid companion.

"What is all this moaning and groaning I hear? Can't a man read his morning paper without some sort of female nonsense disturbing his peace?" Sir Cyril blasted as his stout figure came into view, stopping beside his distraught youngest child.

"Oh, Papa, it's too awful, too horrible for words," the girl announced and, much to his disgust, cast herself against his broad chest, crushing his cravat and the *Morning Gazette* in the process.

Eliza purposely kept her eyes trained on the petals and stems in front of her as her agile fingers arranged the blooms, shutting out her uncle's widened gaze that called for her to come to his rescue. After twenty years in the Dumont household, she knew when it was or was not appropriate to intervene whenever her cousins importuned their parents with their personal problems. Since there was no sign of tears from Thalia, this was certainly a minor dilemma denoting a calculated gambit on the young woman's part. Such dry-eyed histrionics aimed at Sir Cyril usually involved money; however, with Aunt Felicity visiting Chidester for Selina's lying-in, there was no one else at the moment for the girl to accost.

"Speak up, child. I can't hear you if you insist on mumbling into my neckcloth," Sir Cyril demanded, extracting his daughter from his chest by grasping her arms and forcibly holding her at arm's length. "What do you have to say for yourself? It took Pepperman a good half hour to tie a Mathematical this morning, and now you've ruined it. What is it, girl?"

"I can't bear even to repeat it in my weakened state!"

Thalia exclaimed in a trembling voice, though finding more than enough strength to wiggle free of her father's hold. She thrust out her hand, showing him a crumpled piece of paper in her fist before flattening it against his waistcoat. "Here, take it from my sight."

The pronouncement caught Eliza's interest; Thalia had finally arrived at the heart of the matter. Dusting off her fingers, Eliza reached down for her spectacles from their primary resting place on a ribbon around her neck. Her cousins teasingly accused her of vanity in forgetting to wear the lenses that corrected her shortsightedness, and Eliza thought it was kinder not to contradict their assumption. Most events in the Dumont household were better observed slightly out of focus. Her refusal to wear her spectacles had nothing to do with the fact that her eyes occasionally appeared a violet color in just the right light.

As she perched the wire frames on her nose, she had a clear view of her cousin dropping with a limp grace onto the gilt-trimmed blue velvet settee. Satisfied that Thalia—now lying full length—was at rest momentarily, Eliza gave her full attention to her uncle. Sir Cyril had not moved from the doorway, still clutching the piece of offending paper that his daughter had forced upon him. With a sigh of resignation Eliza asked as she crossed the room, "What is that in your hand, Uncle?"

"Beg pardon? Oh, oh, this?" He bent to the task of unfolding the missive as his niece waited patiently for her answer. One trait Sir Cyril shared with her father, the late Captain Aldus Dumont, was a short attention span—unless it dealt with horses, the 'Change, or the latest fashion in neckcloths.

"Would you like to read it aloud, Uncle?" Eliza prompted a few minutes later, standing close at hand but unable to read the elaborate handwriting upside down. Once he silently read through what appeared to be a letter, Sir Cyril looked from the paper to his daughter with an expression of complete bewilderment.

"It's an invitation from Towne's mother to spend a few weeks with the family. She's to join them at Laxton's place in Cumbria. Towne will act as her escort on Tuesday week," he explained, absently reaching up to scratch the back of his head while handing the missive to his niece.

Eliza read through the Countess of Laxton's letter, absently wondering how she was going to console poor Pepperman after he saw his hard work on both Sir Cyril's neckcloth and coiffure so wantonly destroyed. Unfortunately, like her uncle she could find nothing in the cordial invitation that could have induced Thalia's present mood. She looked up into her uncle's perplexed face and gave a shrug of her shoulders to signal her own bewilderment.

"Owwwwww, doesn't anyone understand?" Thalia exclaimed in a shrill voice that quickly captured her companions' attention. Giving a sigh of exaggerated endurance, she sat up to explain what had lead to this morning's drama. "I can't travel with Russell on such a journey without Mama. It's just like Selina to have her baby now, so I can't spend a lovely holiday with Russell's family. *I* am Mama's favorite, but she's off in Chidester waiting for some silly baby she's never seen to be born."

"Now, dear, this *is* the first grandchild," Eliza said smoothly, assuming her customary role of mediator with a reluctance that surprised her. Why was she finding her family more tedious than usual of late? For some reason they seemed to have become more scatterbrained and ridiculous as the end of Thalia's second Season had approached and more so since the girl's engagement had been announced. With the approach of the last Dumont marriage, Eliza had a sense of restlessness that was at odds with her normally placid nature.

Still puzzling over the strange, unsettling feelings, she sat down beside her young cousin and placed a comforting arm around her shoulders. "Aunt Felicity would still have gone to Selina if the invitation had arrived before she left.

There would have been an ugly scene that would have left both of you unhappy and fretful."

"But, Eliza, what shall I *do*? You simply don't understand what it is like to be young and in love," her cousin whined, giving no regard to anyone's feelings but her own—as was the habit of her entire family. "What if Russell decides to cry off? He might think I don't want to meet his family. What if his brother cuts him off without a farthing for having such an insensitive betrothed?"

"I'm sure Russell and his brother will understand. You need a chaperon for a journey, and your mother—"

"Yes, a chaperon, and your cousin sitting right there under your nose," Sir Cyril pronounced, cutting ruthlessly into Eliza's soothing words. His face held a smirk of satisfaction at coming up with the solution to the matter. "What fustian. All this sniveling when the remedy was right in front of you, young lady. I'm amazed Towne even offered for such a ninnyhammer."

Thalia was on her feet instantly, clapping her hands as she danced a little jig. After one skipping circle she gave her father a fierce hug. "Oh, Papa, how brilliant! Why didn't I think of Eliza myself? She's already been my chaperon on a few occasions when Mama was indisposed. We'll need to go out immediately—I haven't a thing to wear for a country holiday. Eliza must have some decent dresses as well. She can't possibly wear that horrible brown bag of a dress, even if no one looks at a chaperon."

As Thalia tripped out of the room with her father close at her heels, Eliza slumped back against the settee. No one had *asked* her if she would like to go along. Neither her uncle nor her cousin seemed to think it necessary to inquire if she had an opinion on the matter. Spreading the material of the dreary brown dress between her hands, she asked herself how she felt about the sudden trip. It might not be so terrible, if Thalia meant to treat her to a new dress or two. Though she did not care for the re-dyed dress that

previously belonged to Selina, Eliza had not realized how
drab it truly was until this minute.

A holiday in the country that inspired the likes of
Coleridge and Wordsworth might cure her mysterious
discontent. Or was it so mysterious? she wondered as
she rose to her feet. Perhaps she was tired of her family's
lack of notice after all these years. She was an orphan, thrust
upon them at the age of five by her feckless parent when
her mother had died. As a military man, Aldus Dumont had
his duty, which did not include more than cursory attention
to his drab little child. Once he had her settled with his
brother, he had returned to his career, only visiting every
few years until his death during the ill-fated Walcheren
Expedition.

As Eliza walked up the stairs to fetch her spencer from
her room, she did not pause to look in the gilt mirror
hanging at the turning of the stairs. She knew what she
would find: an ordinary woman of medium height with
medium-colored hair and a medium figure. While her cousins Selina, Penelope, and Thalia were all tall and willowy
with striking raven hair and translucent skin, Eliza had
inherited her looks and temperament from her mother's
family. She was a brown wren living among a bevy of
elegant swans.

Unlike her relatives, Eliza took her time in considering
matters, and nothing seemed to stir her to the passionate
heights her cousins seemed positively to thrive on, including Philip and Albert. While a simple matter of a lost piece
of clothing or a missing invitation could send any one of
her cousins into the boughs, Eliza moved placidly through
life. On most days she kept the Dumont household running
smoothly and without more than two or three crises.

The visit to the Towne family's country house might
prove enlightening, Eliza decided as she absently selected
her outer garments for the shopping expedition. She would
be able to observe if the Dumonts' household was the

norm. The trip would give her time to contemplate her recent melancholy as well. She had a small inheritance from her grandmother and a small pension from her father, certainly not enough to declare her independence. What was she going to do when Thalia left home?

2

"Y OU'D BEST LOOK LIVELY, LAD. A BOY JUST ARRIVED from the village ta announce the arrival o' her ladyship's coach," a gruff voice announced from the doorway to the library. The dark-haired young man he addressed did not move from his position sprawled on the window seat. His tall, lean form clad in an open-necked shirt and leather breeches remained relaxed as he continued to absorb the view of Tarn Hows's blue waters some distance below through the mullioned pattern of the window. A few centuries past, a canny border lord had watched for his enemies' approach at the same spot of the fortified house perched strategically on the rough landscape.

"Are ya goin' ta sit there and let herself find ya sittin' here as pretty as ya please?" the iron-haired man at the door was forced to ask in disgust. He rose to his full six feet of height and looked down his no less imposing nose. "I don't fancy feelin' the sharp side o' her tongue when she discovers I've allowed ya ta live in comfort here for the past fortnight."

"The Countess of Laxton is the last person I want to see at the moment," his companion replied, lazily turning his face toward the door at last to study the older man from beneath heavy-lidded blue eyes and raising one dark winged brow. After a moment's consideration of the grim-faced man regarding him, he shrugged and eased his boot-encased legs to the floor, placing his book and glass of wine on the window seat before getting to his feet.

Stretching indolently, he winced slightly, favoring his right side before he dropped his arms to his side again. "Jenkins, you've forgotten in your retirement that the countess, like all quality, does not travel quickly. Even as we speak, the lady and her party are partaking some refreshment at our friend Mr. Billows's hostelry before scaling the hillside to invade our peace. Have you cleared out my things and taken them to the crofter's hut?"

"Aye, sir. Herself won't be aware o' any trespass, and the servants have been warned about speakin' o' the matter," said Jenkins, his rough-hewn face almost turning to a graven image at being questioned over the matter.

"Very well, I shall take my leave, then, if only to put your mind at rest." The young man sauntered out of the room, whistling off-key as he headed toward the back of the house. The sound of a trumpet blast from the front of the house caused his footsteps to falter. With a look of surprise over his shoulder at the front door, he could distinctly hear the sound of horses' hooves and jingling harnesses. A look of annoyance crossed his narrow face before he turned and loped toward the kitchen. "Blast the woman, why can't she leave me in peace?"

3

"OH, RUSSELL, I'M NOT READY FOR THIS. CAN'T WE go back to the inn and have more of Mrs. Billows's lemonade?" Thalia pleaded, clasping her hands around her fiancé's arm while giving him her most beseeching look. The coach was climbing steadily uphill, twisting and turning along the wooded drive that led to Laxton's Retreat.

"Thalia, dear, there's nothing to be alarmed about. You've met Mother countless times while we were in town," the young man assured her. He smiled indulgently while he patted her small hands where they clutched his arm with a viselike grip. "You're giving your cousin the wrong impression of my family, I'm afraid. Mother isn't such a gorgon, truly, Miss Dumont."

"Yes, I know, Mr. Towne. I met her at Thalia's engagement luncheon and found her very charming," Eliza assured him, trying to squelch her traitorous thoughts. Why had such a nice, levelheaded young man offered for her henwitted cousin? This same thought had come to mind too frequently over the past few days of their journey north.

"Yes, Russell, your mother is a dear, but what about your brother? He was rather formidable that one time we met," Thalia continued, not bothering to worry over Eliza's remarks. "I do so want to make a good impression with him."

Russell shifted in his seat slightly, a frown marring his boyish face momentarily before he cleared his throat. "My brother hasn't come with us on this trip. Ah, he's still

128

recovering from his wounds at Waterloo, don't you know? That's why he wasn't about much this Season. Mama didn't think he should attempt the rigors of such an extended journey." A look of sheer relief covered the young man's narrow face as the coach reached level ground. Giving his companions a sparkling grin, he exclaimed, "Here we are already!"

Young Mr. Towne needs to learn how to dissemble with greater success, Eliza determined as she was helped down from the coach. Until now Thalia's fears about the earl had seemed ludicrous, something Eliza attributed to her cousin's flighty turn of mind. Surely the man had recovered sufficiently from his wounds by now, almost a year after the great battle. Was it significant that Thalia had only met the earl once, and now he had not accompanied his family on holiday? With a slight shake of her head she chided herself for beginning to think like Thalia. Eliza decided there was a perfectly logical reason for the earl's absence and turned her attention to the house.

"House" was not an adequate description for the edifice in front of her. The name Laxton's Retreat had conjured up a cozy setting in her mind's eye, something rustic from one of Mr. Constable's paintings. This structure with its imposing twin tower battlements and uncompromising gray stone facade was an image from the pages of *Waverley* or *Guy Mannering*, not Wordworth's lyric lines that so recently glorified the beauty of the area. Eliza had little time to dwell on the incongruity of spending a summer holiday in a small fortified castle as Russell escorted her and Thalia through the imposing front portal.

"Russell, my dear, here you are at last. I was beginning to think you wouldn't make an appearance until tomorrow," Clarice, Countess of Laxton, exclaimed as the three travelers stepped immediately into a cavernous room with a high oak-beamed ceiling. Though a widow approaching her sixtieth year, Lady Laxton still possessed the golden beauty of her first Season and looked much too young to

have borne three fully grown sons. "We've been so anxious
for the *three* of you to arrive."

"Yes, the *three* of us are here," her son returned before
bending to receive a maternal kiss on his cheek. As Thalia
was granted a similar tribute, Russell's green eyes never
wavering from his mother's identical gaze, he stated rather
loudly, "Laxton took your advice and decided to rusticate
at the home farm after all. We seem to have a large enough
party without his company, however. Mama, you remember
Thalia's cousin, Miss Dumont, I'm sure."

"My dear, how nice of you to accompany your cousin,"
the countess said graciously to her newest guest, though her
welcoming smile did not reach her eyes. "Let me introduce
you to Sir Basil and Lady Witmer-Gow and their daughter
Lisette while Jenkins takes your baggage to your rooms. We
shall all become close friends in our little retreat. Thalia,
dear, you will be sharing a room with your cousin in the
east tower."

The introductions were quickly performed. Sir Basil was
a stout gentleman with a bluff manner while his wife and
daughter were both pleasant and soft-spoken. Eliza was
glad for her new wardrobe as she took a seat next to Miss
Witmer-Gow, who was a tall, statuesque young woman
the same age as Thalia. Between Thalia's dark beauty and
Miss Witmer-Gow's golden radiance, she felt every bit the
spinster chaperon. This was not an auspicious start to the
holiday that she imagined would be the inspiration for her
future.

4

"THAT'S IT. IT'S SO SIMPLE!" ELIZA EXCLAIMED TO THE morning sky and the disinterested trees that surrounded her two days later. The fortress was indeed cramped quarters just as her hostess had said, and this morning she had felt the need for solitude, an escape from her fellow guests. Thalia was still sleeping in the tower room they shared when Eliza had left the battlements behind to explore the surrounding countryside.

Now as she gave into the childish impulse to wade in the dancing stream she had discovered, she had the inspiration she had been waiting for. Thanks to Miss Witmer-Gow's shy questions about the London social scene, Eliza had the answer to her future. Her years of accompanying her cousins could be put to good use. "I shall be a consultant to those poor naive girls during their first Seasons— a lady of independent means. No more catering to Aunt Felicity's whim and fetching her sal volatile at the least provocation."

"A very noble idea. I applaud your enterprise, but how will Aunt Felicity be able to survive without her sal volatile?" asked a polite male voice from behind her.

Eliza spun around on her bare feet, almost losing her balance on a slippery rock as she attempted to keep her limbs properly covered without dampening her skirt. Training her myopic gaze in the direction of the husky voice, she searched the embankment for her unexpected companion. Finally she discerned the distorted outline of a form that was neither a tree nor a shrub. Narrowing her eyes in hopes of sharpening the image, she decided that he was leaning against a tree. "W-Who are you?"

"Randall," the apparition answered simply, never moving from his relaxed position. Though she was not sure, she thought he was laughing. At least, there was a flash of white approximately where his mouth should be. "Who are you? I didn't think there were water nymphs this far north—much too cold in the winter."

"Water ny—" Eliza bit back the rest of her words. His ridiculous statement required no reply. Frantically she wondered how she could retrieve her spectacles without releasing the death grip on the skirt of her slate-blue walking dress. There was simply no way to be self-possessed while standing barefoot in two feet of water. Eliza refused to be defeated, stiffening her back and raising her chin slightly as she asked, "Who exactly *is* Randall?"

"Not fair, wood nymph. You know my name but refuse to tell me yours," he returned easily, apparently prepared to wait until he had the satisfaction of knowing her name.

Now she knew he was laughing, but she was at a loss over what to do next. This impossible encounter was beyond her experience. Though well versed in polite behavior—having lectured all three of her cousins on the matter countless times—she had never had such an unorthodox encounter. None of the gentlemen of her family's acquaintance would ever have placed her in this position. What did one do when confronted by a stranger in the forest—one who may or may not be a lunatic? She was not far from the house and, strangely enough, did not feel threatened by the man, only perplexed.

"Oh, dear, you haven't gone mute on me, have you? Tell me it isn't some curse that steals your voice when you're confronted by a lowly mortal."

"Don't be absurd," she stated in her most repressing voice, because she suddenly had the urge to giggle at his absurdities. "My name is Miss Eliza Dumont. I am staying at Laxton's Retreat. Now, does that satisfy your curiosity, my good man?"

"For the moment." He fell silent, seeming content to watch her still figure in the middle of the stream.

"Good, then you can be on your way," she ordered in a voice she hoped sounded autocratic. Eliza was overly conscious of her lack of bonnet and the haphazard hairstyle she had fashioned earlier. Her mousy brown hair was caught up at the crown of her head with a ribbon, allowing her nondescript tresses to tumble around her shoulders.

To add to her discomfort, the man was standing at precisely the place she had entered the water, where the embankment sloped downward to the water's edge. She would be forced to stand in the water until he moved, unless she wanted to attempt scrambling up the steep fern-covered bank. Her feet were becoming slightly numb in the cool waters that had felt so delightful a few minutes ago. There was no answer or movement from her companion. "I wouldn't want to keep you from your duties, which are . . ."

"Ah, very clever, nym— Miss Dumont. Have no fear, I'm a very respectable, law-abiding gamekeeper, not a poacher as you suspect. Jenkins will certainly vouch for me."

"I never—"

"Tut, tut. I know a young lady should never be too careful," he continued smoothly over her sputtering noises, "and though I hate to ruin our budding friendship, I must ask you to remove yourself from the stream. The fish around here take exception to sharing their home. It makes them skittish. His lordship's guests would be greatly displeased if they found his favorite fishing spot had gone fallow."

She knew she did not have any choice in the matter. The mention of the stream's other inhabitants caused her toes to curl as if something was about to nibble on them. With as much dignity as her flushed cheeks would allow, she walked carefully to the bank. She made sure her ankles remained as discreetly covered as possible, keeping a wary eye on the irritating man.

He straightened from his resting place when she was only a step from dry land. Eliza considered going back to the safety of the stream until she recalled the possibility of scaly companions and decided his assistance was not quite so off-putting. Stepping forward, she was able to drop her hem demurely over her bare feet as he grasped her hand and assisted her final few steps. With her hands no longer occupied, she quickly perched her spectacles on her nose to inspect the intruder.

She almost snatched the wire frames back. Before her stood—or rather leaned, since he had quickly returned to holding up the tree—a tall, darkly handsome man. His short jacket and leather breeches were well worn but of an excellent cut, giving him more the look of an impoverished gentleman than a gamekeeper, in spite of the pouch looped over his shoulder. Though no gentleman of her uncle's set would dare wear such scuffed top boots, Randall wore his shabby apparel with a nonchalance that would be the envy of an aspiring dandy. The breeze ruffled through his dark sable hair as his blue eyes twinkled with suppressed amusement over her inspection.

Lifting one winged brow, he smiled to display glittering white teeth. A crease appeared in his left cheek as he quirked his mouth to the side. "Do I pass inspection?"

"I-I'm s-so s-sorry," Eliza managed, fixing her gaze on the blue-and-white-dotted Belcher handkerchief tied loosely at the open collar of his shirt. In her discomfort she blurted out, "Until now I couldn't see what you looked like. You were rather fuzzy."

"I see," he managed before a whimpering noise close at hand distracted him. Eliza let out her pent-up breath and followed the direction of his gaze to the leather pouch suspended at his side. It's alive, she thought in alarm, then realized something inside was wiggling to get out. She watched in horrified fascination as Randall widened the opening of the pouch and reached inside. A second later a pair of limpid brown eyes regarded her over a wet nose, then another.

"Puppies!" she exclaimed with a sigh of relief, not sure what she had anticipated. The sound of her voice turned the dogs into a wiggly mass of fur and bone as they tried to escape from their master's hands. Their tricolored bodies of white, black, and tan strained to investigate the new world around them.

"Miss Dumont, may I introduce Castor and Pollux, the earl's latest acquisition?" Randall said gravely, then reached forward to allow the pair to sniff delicately at her upraised hand.

"They're adorable. May I hold one?" she asked wistfully. Eliza had always longed for a dog or cat to keep her company, but Aunt Felicity always claimed that house pets made her nervous. She took one of the squirming bodies from his hand with great care, nibbling on her lower lip as she tried to restrain the puppy's enthusiasm for a new acquaintance.

"Miss Dumont, you are now holding what will be the beginning of the earl's kennel, purebred Coniston foxhounds. Castor, pay your respects to the lady," Randall instructed before bending down to let Pollux explore the damp ground at his feet. "Laxton's hounds will be the finest trailing dogs in the county in a year or so."

"Hunting in this rough country? But how can you follow on horse—" Eliza let out a squeak of sound as something cool and wet touched her bare toes. Clutching Castor to her chest, she ventured to look down for her assailant— an inquisitive Pollux. He sat happily back on his haunches and gave a yipping bark, then gazed up at her adoringly as his tongue lolled out the side of his mouth. As Randall's rich laughter enfolded her, Eliza was very conscious of her unladylike appearance once more. Where had she left her shoes and stockings?

"There are dangers lurking in the wood for the unwary, Miss Dumont," her companion stated solemnly, though his eyes continued to sparkle with amusement.

Eliza stepped back quickly, wondering what to do next as he moved closer. Her alarm rapidly turned to chagrin. Randall walked around her to the rock where her missing apparel rested. Not knowing what else to do, she buried her flaming cheeks in the soft fur of the puppy, who promptly licked her nose.

"I think I had best remove my livestock before you have spoiled them for the outdoor life. They aren't accustomed to meeting charming ladies in the woods." He held out her shoes and stockings in exchange for the puppy.

Once the dog was returned to his owner, she snatched her possessions from his hand. "Thank you," she managed to whisper before being struck mute again. What did one say? Only a few moments ago she was confidently going to instruct young ladies on the perils of the Season, and now she had no idea what to say to a common gamekeeper.

"I enjoyed meeting Castor and Pollux, Randall, but I really must go now. The others will be wondering where I am." There, she had managed two entire sentences without stammering. Was it because Randall was preoccupied with returning the puppies to their pouch? She did not linger to discover the answer but turned on her heels and fled into the trees.

Randall watched her hasty retreat with a surprisingly strong sense of regret. Was he getting lonely in his self-imposed exile? Discretion kept him from pursuing the lady, even when she stopped suddenly by a tree a mere five hundred yards away to put on her shoes. He stepped back into the cloaking arm of a nearby pine tree, torn between fascination and amusement, and watched her look furtively over her shoulder to assure herself that she was alone, all the while shoving her slippers on her feet sans stockings. What connection did this unusual young lady have with the countess's party? Surely she was not the latest candidate in the matrimonial stakes the earl's mother produced with great regularity. If so, the countess's taste was improving.

At first he had thought Miss Dumont was a plain little thing, standing forlornly in the middle of the stream in her prim, unadorned blue dress. Then she raised her determined little chin and a purple-blue fire seemed to glitter from her round eyes. She had looked like an indignant water nymph with her lustrous brown hair cascading around her shoulders, the sunlight highlighting traces of red and gold to create a glistening nimbus around her oval face. A delightful mixture of innocent child and proper lady, he decided, and grinned at the memory of her intent look when he handed her Castor's wriggling body.

Perhaps he had been too hasty in leaving before the countess and her guests arrived. A duet of fretful whines interrupted his speculative thoughts. Castor and Pollux had worked themselves to the top of the pouch, both giving him a reproachful look.

"Sorry, my friends, I won't let her get away so easily the next time. For now we'll continue on our way and get you settled in your new home." This seemed to satisfy his companions. Randall returned to his speculation on the presence of Miss Eliza Dumont at Laxton's Retreat.

5

"MOTHER, YOU CAN'T HIRE A RUNNER TO TRACK DOWN A peer of the realm." Russell's impassioned words stopped Eliza where she knelt to remove the pebble in her shoe on her way toward the tower steps. The words echoed off the stone walls and high ceiling since the door to the countess's chamber stood ajar, allowing the conversation inside to easily be overheard. She tried not to listen, moving quietly to avoid being seen in her bedraggled state, but Eliza's curiosity was piqued.

"I'm getting desperate. What could your brother have been thinking? He has barely recovered from his wounds," Lady Laxton returned with some heat. "You don't suppose he has taken a fever and is lying ill somewhere with no one to care for him."

"The doctors declared he was well months ago." Russell's statement was punctuated by a heavy sigh. "The saber wound has healed nicely, and despite the complication, his leg is as good as new without a sign of a limp. No one would suspect it had been broken in two places from his horse rolling on him when it was shot out from under him. Laxton is in perfect health again."

"How would we know if he had a relapse? No one has seen him in almost three weeks. Three weeks? How could he do this to me, his own mother?" the lady persisted, despite her son's assurances. "What am I going to say to the Witmer-Gows? I'm sorry, but my son has disappeared off the face of the earth?"

"Laxton undoubtedly knew that you were bent on producing another prospective bride during this little jaunt. He wasn't fooled by all that talk of discovering the delights of the Lake District." The young man's voice was now indulgently teasing, undoubtedly in hopes of cajoling his mother out of her sulks. "Very few members of the *ton* have a house party at a hunting lodge that was once a reiver's stronghold. Father had this place for years, and you never showed the least interest in it."

With that Eliza decided it was time to continue on her way. She had no business eavesdropping this way, especially on such personal family matters. As she moved away, she heard the countess exclaim, "If your brother had a wife, he wouldn't be pulling such a childish stunt. Such nonsensical behavior for a man approaching his thirtieth birthday when he should be setting up his nursery."

"This has been a very strange morning," Eliza murmured, unable to keep from dwelling over what she had just heard while ascending the winding stone steps to her room. Surely the earl had not run away; he had simply not informed his mother where he had gone. Men were apt to do such inconsiderate things when seeking their pleasures. It was possible Russell knew exactly where his brother had gone, she decided as she recalled his evasive manner in the coach, but he had kept quiet out of a sense of sibling loyalty.

She dismissed the matter easily, now that she knew the earl was not purposely avoiding meeting her cousin. It was none of her concern, though she felt a twinge of sympathy for the sweet, unassuming Miss Witmer-Gow. Did the girl realize the plans Lady Laxton had for her? She was much more suited to someone with Russell's compassionate nature, more so than Thalia. The traitorous thought brought Eliza to her senses. She had no business speculating on the proper bride for anyone in the Towne family, especially the earl.

There were more important matters for her to contemplate than romantic entanglements: her plans for her future.

It would take all her concentration to determine exactly how she was going to approach the matter. She would begin by making a list of her needs—finding a cozy little house for herself, a companion and servants, and the proper connections. So much to anticipate and so little time before she returned home.

"Eliza, *where* have you been?" Thalia's imperative whine assaulted her the moment she stepped into the room. "You can't *imagine* what I've been through this morning. It is just too horrible for words. Why *do* these disasters always happen to me?"

With a resigned sigh, Eliza wondered why she had not lingered in the woods. The bothersome Randall had been a much more amusing companion than Thalia, with her litany of complaints about the drafty room and the maid's clumsiness in breaking her favorite bottle of scent.

6

"WHAT'S SO IMPORTANT ABOUT A CIRCLE OF STONES left behind by some silly old Celts, Russell? I do *not* want to go for a walk down to the shore. Why can't we sit here and admire the view? Eliza seems to have the right idea by bringing her sketchbook," Thalia complained, not caring that she was making a scene. Her cousin noticed that the other ladies who made up the picnic party became extremely interested in the majestic view of the fells across Tarn Hows. This was not Thalia's first complaint.

"That is fine. If you prefer to stay with your cousin, I *will* escort the ladies," Russell stated patiently, his shoulders drooping in a sign of defeat that Eliza understood too well. In the role of host he was manfully trying to deflect his betrothed's growing dissatisfaction. When Sir Basil's gout flared up that morning, Lady Laxton had insisted the others should not cancel the outing. She had charged her son with the responsibility of the picnic while she remained behind to catch up on correspondence and nurse her guest.

"No, Mr. Towne, you really should stay with Miss Dumont," Miss Witmer-Gow declared softly, giving him a timorous smile. She was in exceptional looks, her floral spotted muslin festooned with pink and blue flowers and the matching blue pelisse accentuating her fair skin. Her high-brimmed poke bonnet perfectly framed her heart-shaped face. "Mother and I can take the footman with us. The ground shouldn't be too difficult to navigate."

"I wouldn't think of it," he said hastily and returned her smile. "Mother would be appalled if I was such a poor host. Perhaps Eliza will lend Thalia some of her paper and charcoal to entertain her while we take our ramble."

Before Eliza could agree to the arrangement, Thalia settled the matter. "Oh, very well, I'll *go* on your silly walk." With a sidelong look at Miss Witmer-Gow, she tightened the pink bow of her straw capote that was an exact match for her ruffled jaconet walking dress. Giving Russell a flirtatiously sulky look, she snared his arm and began pulling him along the sloping path down the fell.

As the group proceeded down the hillside, Eliza assured the footman she had everything she needed and settled back in the shade of a larch tree to begin her drawing. After a few minutes she removed her bonnet to allow the afternoon breeze to ruffle through the newly cropped curls she had allowed Lady Laxton's dresser to style that morning. With Thalia joining the others, she would have a half hour or so of peace, though she knew she was going to have to speak to the girl about her appalling manners before the day was through.

For now she could lose herself in her drawing, she decided, settling her spectacles in place and selecting a piece of charcoal from the box beside her. As her hand hovered over the sketchbook propped on her knees, a flash of white out of the corner of her eye caught her attention. When she turned to inspect the object, she smiled involuntarily at the sight of Castor and Pollux moving toward her, sniffing the ground intently. Judging from the animals' haphazard path, she was sure that the puppies were still far from honing their trailing skills.

"Your young friend had best be careful, or one of her companions will push her in the tarn without any further provocation."

Though she should not have been surprised at the sound of Randall's husky voice, Eliza could not help the jerk of her hand that created a long trail of charcoal down the pristine page in front of her. Tipping her head upward, she discovered him standing a few feet to her left, resting his shoulder against a conveniently situated tree trunk. Did the man ever stand upright for longer than a few minutes at a time or have any clothing that did not need mending? How did such a lackadaisical person perform the rigorous outdoor responsibilities of a gamekeeper?

Rather belatedly she remembered that she should be defending Thalia's actions to this stranger. "My cousin is young. She still needs to mature a little and understand the need of catering to others' wishes."

"Your cousin, you say? She'll need to mature rather quickly if she doesn't want to lose young Russell to the soft-spoken young lady," Randall returned, his gaze narrowing as he looked down toward the blue waters sparkling below them. The walking party had made good progress, and though they were now miniature in size, it was clear that Russell was solicitously helping Miss Witmer-Gow and her mother over some treacherous ground with Thalia waiting impatiently ahead of them. "Does she plague you in the same manner?"

Eliza did not question how he knew about the tie between Russell and Thalia because Randall had now turned his sleepy blue gaze back to her. Self-consciously she raised her hand to the fetching topknot that Wilkins had fashioned, overly aware that the wispy curls at her forehead and temples were undoubtedly too young for a lady of her advanced years. Weakly she repeated, "She is still young."

"Ah, so she does play the same game with you," he concluded triumphantly with a nod of satisfaction. "Enough about her. Who is the fetching blonde with the elegant manners? Though she seems innocent enough, her mama has a calculating look that doesn't bode well for your cousin."

His flashing grin was as impudent as his words, but Eliza did not reprimand him immediately. How could she as she watched him amble toward her with a lazy animal grace to stretch himself out on the ground at her feet? A quick glance back at the carriage showed that the footman did not seem disturbed by Randall's presence. Did the gamekeeper make a habit of conversing with the guests at Laxton's Retreat?

Clearing her throat, she strove to bring the conversation back to a more conventional level and stated politely, "The young lady is Miss Witmer-Gow. She and her parents are visiting with the countess and her son as well as my cousin."

"Aren't you a guest?" he asked, the winged brow she found fascinating ascending as he leaned negligently on his elbow and propped his chin in his hand. One raffish lock of sable hair had fallen forward over his forehead, giving him a wicked boyish look.

"I'm Thalia's chaperon," she said curtly, turning back the soiled piece of paper and applying her charcoal to a new sheet. Perhaps if she ignored him, he would go away. He made her feel like a gawky schoolgirl, and she did not like it. Unfortunately her traitorous fingers were unsteady and took on a life of their own, preferring to sketch the tall, lean body on the grass in front of her rather than the intended landscape.

"You look too young to be a chaperon, and I'm sure you don't enjoy it. Relatives should not force others into doing something they dislike. Is that why you were declaring your independence yesterday morning?" he asked softly, as though not wanting to disturb her concentration.

Peering over the top of her spectacles, Eliza was relieved she could not clearly see his cheeky smile. He almost seemed to be annoying her intentionally. Nibbling on her lower lip, she resolved that the man was not going to overset her. For good measure she removed her spectacles, making a pretense of cleaning them with her lace-trimmed handkerchief. "I was merely making plans for after my cousin's marriage. I think it is time for me to leave my uncle's house, now that the last of my cousins is to wed. I have depended on their charity much too long as it is."

"Ah, yes, the sal volatile. Does your aunt treat you any better than the spoiled miss who was ordering you around earlier?"

"You were spying on us? Shouldn't you be attending to your duties?" His negligence of his work was really none of her business, but she was not about to discuss her family with this brash stranger.

"There isn't much to be done beyond exercising my new charges, since the earl isn't in residence," he explained smoothly, nodding his head in the direction of the two puppies that were in the midst of a canine wrestling match. "So, you're going to escape the servile prison of your uncle's household to become an arbiter of young lady's etiquette."

"I don't really think this is any of your concern, Ran— sir." She stiffened her spine, hoping for a quelling posture that would squelch his audacious manner. How did one deflate such a person's pretensions when one didn't know his last name? Or was Randall his last name?

"Nicely done, just how a young lady should handle an importunate gentleman. Did you remove your spectacles so I would become fuzzy again?" he asked with great perception, making Eliza abruptly return the wire frames to their proper place and bringing his challenging grin into sharp focus. "It's such a shame you don't wear them more often, since they frame your purply eyes so well."

"They are violet," she corrected without thinking, then felt the heat rising to her cheeks. She resisted the impulse to snatch her spectacles off her nose because it would only serve to increase his amusement at her expense.

"That is a matter we'll have to discuss later. I hear your friends returning," he informed her, jumping quickly to his feet at the sound of voices drawing near. With a rapid move that startled her, he scooped up Castor and Pollux, then gave her a solemn bow. "*Au revoir*, Eliza."

Diverted by his flawless inflection, Eliza realized he was gone before she had a chance to admonish him for his easy use of her name. Was it common for gamekeepers to speak a foreign language? *Until we meet again.* There was no reason for her heart to skip a beat at the thought of another encounter with the man. He was an ill-mannered lout.

"But, Russell, they *were* just ugly stones."

Thalia's petulant tone brought Eliza to her senses. She carefully folded the sketch she had done of Randall, slipping it out of sight before she returned Miss Witmer-Gow's greeting.

7

"*I* WOULD HAVE PLAYED BETTER THAN *SHE* SINGS," THA-lia hissed in her cousin's ear later that evening. She did not worry that anyone overheard as she glared at Lisette Witmer-Gow, who had agreed to Lady Laxton's coaxing in providing the evening's entertainment. Russell was seated close to the lady, accompanying her on the lute, since—to Thalia's displeasure—there was not a pianoforte to display her only musical talent.

Placing a firm hand on the girl's arm, Eliza leaned over to hiss in her ear, "Thalia, mind your manners. Miss Witmer-Gow has a lovely voice, and Russell has certain duties he must perform as our host."

"Well, I would have," she protested loudly, but her words were lost in the applause of the guests as Miss Witmer-Gow's song ended.

Eliza could see with one look at Thalia's face that a storm was brewing, and she quickly decided how to avert a disaster. As Lady Laxton complimented Miss Witmer-Gow on her performance, Eliza rose to her feet. "Yes, that was love-ly. You will excuse Thalia and me if we retire now, won't you? All that fresh air today seems to have exhausted us."

"But, Eliza—"

"Now, Thalia dear, you know how too much exercise fatigues you and you begin to look peaked," she broke in ruthlessly before the girl could contradict her. With a prac-ticed move, she looped her arm through her cousin's and exerted a steady pressure, all the while smiling pleasantly at the rest of the company. For good measure she directed a sidelong look at the countess, to remind Thalia that she wanted to make a good impression on Russell's family.

In less than two minutes she had her charge out of the room but did not breath a sigh of relief until she had Thalia up the first flight of stairs. Once Eliza felt they were safely out of earshot, she began to speak. "I don't think it such a good idea to be so outspoken when we are in company, my dear. I don't know what's come over you of late, but you are turning into a sniveling child. What has happened to the smiling girl that Russell proposed to?"

"Oh, Mama warned that this would happen. He would begin to look at other women if I wasn't careful!" Thalia exclaimed, giving a genuine sniffle as she groped for her handkerchief.

Eliza prudently led her down the hallway to their tower room, knowing that this was going to be a lengthy ordeal since Thalia was not making a bit of sense. What kind of fustian was her aunt telling the girl? Once they were safely behind the solid oak door to their chamber, Eliza pursued the matter. "What is this nonsense about Russell and other women?"

The young girl dropped forlornly on the bed, her slender shoulders beginning to tremble as silent tears coursed down her face. "Mama warned me that gentlemen need to be reminded constantly of their obligations," she managed in a warbling voice. Thalia was a pretty crier, her nose never growing red or her eyes puffy—which Eliza always envied. "She said that I should make sure I was always first in his consideration. Gentlemen like a lady who needs guidance and protection, someone soft and winsome. Just like Russell said when he proposed—I was a delicate flower that he would always cherish and protect."

"What absolute rot!" her cousin exclaimed before giving in to the laughter that tickled the back of her throat. Thalia had been trying to be some shrewish ninnyhammer due to her flighty mother's imagination and Russell's romantic notions. Not that the girl had far to go from her usual manner, but her attempts had probably had the adverse effect. Instead of feeling protective and loving toward his betrothed, Russell could be having second thoughts.

"It's *not* funny, Eliza. I managed to make a better catch than either Selina or Penelope, and now that Witmer-Gow person is making advances to him," Thalia snapped, jumping up from her perch for the express purpose of stomping her foot in aggravation. "If the earl hadn't gone into hiding to avoid her, she wouldn't be making calf eyes at Russell instead. Well, she can't have him because it took me an entire season to snag him."

"Don't you love Russell?" Her amusement died at the calculating look that had replaced Thalia's woeful expression.

"Eliza, you are so silly at times," her cousin announced, giving a disdainful sniff for good measure. "Love is such an old-fashioned emotion. Position and security are what are important. Selina foolishly married a parson, and Penelope didn't fair much better with a solicitor—all for love. I wasn't going to be caught by such nonsense. Russell may be a younger son, but he has a respectable inheritance from his maternal grandfather and a house of his own."

Eliza dropped into one of the heavily carved chairs positioned near the fire. She did not know what to say to the girl. What she had imagined as a romantic courtship had been a calculated game of one-upmanship on Thalia's part; she had to marry better than her sisters. Poor Russell.

"Miss Pasty-faced Witmer-Gow can set her sights elsewhere," Thalia spat out, seeming to enjoy her diatribe about the innocent young lady downstairs. "No matter what Russell says, his brother *did* run away to avoid the Witmer-Gows' machinations."

"Did Russell say where his brother had gone?" The question was a red herring to draw Thalia's ire away from the innocent young woman, who seemed to be everyone's pawn. Eliza could not think of another subject that would not escalate into a major row. This was not an auspicious moment to point out the error in the girl's logic. In her present mood, Thalia would not take kindly to any criticism of her behavior. Taking another look at Thalia's thunderous face, Eliza knew that the ache beginning between her eyes would only grow worse if she pursued the matter tonight.

"Russell told me some Banbury tale about his mother being overly protective of his brother to allay my suspicions," she declared as she continued to pace around the room. She was warming to her subject, especially since Eliza remained silent. "He says it's because his elder brother drowned on the way to Waterloo, just before his middle brother was wounded. Now Lady Laxton won't let the earl out of her sight, although she is anxious for him to marry. If that isn't the silliest thing I've ever heard. An earl does not need to run away from home."

The words struck a responsive chord in Eliza's mind. Lady Laxton said much the same just yesterday. Pressing her thumb and forefinger to the bridge of her nose, she wondered how she could find out the truth. That would be the only way to detour Thalia from her present disastrous course—find out why the earl was not at Laxton's Retreat. The image of dark hair and smiling blue eyes that came to mind proved to Eliza that she was overtired and needed to sleep on the matter. Randall the impudent gamekeeper was the last person she needed to seek out for assistance.

After a good night's sleep she would consider the matter again and arrive at a viable solution—something sensible that did not include Randall. With a sigh of exasperation she rose slowly to her feet. What had happened to her lovely holiday that would help her plan her future?

8

"THIS GAME CAN'T GO ON MUCH LONGER. THE NEW FOOT-man reported the gamekeeper's rag-mannered behavior ta me yesterday with great affront," Jenkins growled in way of greeting as he approached the stone cottage late the next morning. Randall did not bother to look up from his task of polishing his boots. He remained intent on the task until the older man stood squarely in front of his bench near the door.

"I must start training Castor and Pollux as guard dogs along with tracking so they will bark in warning when unwanted visitors approach," he murmured, giving the frowning, heavily lined face looming over him a speculative look. Jenkins had never been known for his sense of humor, especially when it came to boys, young or old, playing pranks.

"Those dogs have no more wit than you do." The old man sighed, then took a seat on the bench next to his companion. "What were ya thinking o' ta approach one o' the guests? What if she had said something ta the others?"

"I was merely keeping her amused while the others were gone on their ramble and unfortunately didn't manage to get a look at her sketch," he answered easily, smiling into the high-polished surface of the hand-tooled leather in his hand at the determined way the lady had tried to ignore him. "Castor and Pollux took a liking to her the first day they met her, and I simply followed their lead."

"This wasn't the first time?" The prospect seemed to leave Jenkins without another word to say, momentarily, seeming fascinated by the way Randall was buffing his footgear.

"I was curious about who had accompanied the family, and Miss Dumont, while a trifle reluctant, was able to identify all the guests," Randall continued lightly, holding up his boot for inspection. "What do you think? Would it pass Brummell's inspection? Now what has gotten into their maggoty little brains?" he exclaimed at the sound of the puppies whimpering and whining. Both dogs were bobbing up and down behind the fence at the side of the cottage, attempting to jump over it to escape their imprisonment. Glancing in the direction of their line of escape, Randall was at a loss for words—possibly for the first time in his life.

Eliza—as he always thought of her—was standing a few feet away, her slight form cloaked in rose sprig muslin remaining perfectly still as his eyes met hers. The sight of her spectacles dangling from the ribbon around her neck dampened his sudden feeling of elation. She had not sought him out but simply lost her way during her morning walk due to her reluctance to wear her eyeglasses. Involuntarily he stood up and took a few steps forward, uncharacteristically ill at ease and overly conscious of his stocking feet.

"Good morning, Mr. Randall. I hope you don't mind that I came to visit Castor and Pollux," she said softly, never moving from where she stood.

Randall knew his jaw was hanging open, but he could not help himself. He wanted to give out a resounding *Huzzah*; she *had* come to see him. After a moment he was able to recapture his composure, quickly glancing over his shoulder to find that Jenkins had disappeared. The old man might lecture him in private, but he was not about to be caught in a conspiracy with the rascally gamekeeper. Would Eliza think it strange the servant had run off?

"El— Miss Dumont, the pups will be honored to receive you," he finally managed. He hoped she could not see the telltale flush that was burning his cheeks. A man close to his thirtieth birthday did not blush like a callow lad. With no other alternative, he carelessly tossed his boot over his shoulder to join its mate under the bench. He was not about to hop around from one foot to the other pulling on his boots under Eliza's interested gaze.

"Here are the scamps. They ate my best shirt for dinner last evening, so I have put them in confinement," he explained, now in full possession of his self-control. "Perhaps you would like to put on your spectacles to see them better." His suggestion was rewarded by a fulminating look from the lady that accelerated his heartbeat to a triple tattoo.

Eliza bent down to greet the puppies, whose tails were shaking their entire bodies in their excitement over the visitor. He was afforded an excellent view of the crown of her rose-colored poke bonnet. Lost in speculating on how to get her to look at him instead of the silly dogs, he almost did not catch her words.

"Mr. Randall, I have need of some information and think you might be of assistance," she explained very stiffly, her gloved hand occupied with finding the sweet spot behind Castor's left ear, much to Pollux's disgust.

Crossing his arms over his chest, Randall rested his shoulder against the cottage wall. The lady was dressed for a formal afternoon tea and talking like a stiff-rumped matron. What was she up to? Did it have something to do with her plan to leave her family? He was not altogether sure he wanted to help in that endeavor, unable to understand his reluctance. Judging from what he had seen of her cousin's behavior, the rest of the family certainly could not be any better.

When he remained silent, she peeked up at him through the veil of her sooty brown lashes. He extended his hand to assist her to her feet. "Your wish is my command, Miss

Dumont. How can I be of service?"

"Well, it is rather impertinent, but it is important to my cousin's peace of mind," she said quickly, as though she would lose her courage otherwise. "I need to know where the earl has gone. Servants are the most reliable source of information, but I didn't think Jenkins would oblige, and the other servants seem to be fairly new to the household."

"I see," he returned, drawing out each word as he contemplated exactly where this discussion would lead. He did not like it. "Will it ease *your* peace of mind?"

"Yes, very much," she said eagerly, letting the words tumble over each other as she explained her purpose. "You see, Thalia's taken it into her head that the earl has not joined the house party to avoid Miss Witmer-Gow, since his mother is trying to marry him off. So the young lady is making eyes at Russell as a prospective bridegroom instead. It's all nonsense because of the most ludicrous advice from my aunt, but Russell has told Thalia his brother is merely avoiding his mother because she has been overly concerned about his health. And Thalia—"

"I think you should try to take a breath, my dear," Randall broke in, raising his hand for good measure as he straightened to his full height. He thought he understood at least half of her tale. "Why don't we go over to the bench to continue this enlightening conversation? You will put on your charming spectacles and stop talking to my feet."

"Oh, will you be serious," she demanded, suddenly abandoning her stiff manner, but complied with his wish to adjourn to the bench. "I was up half the night listening to Thalia's rantings and ravings on how her life is ruined. I don't know why she is so concerned. She doesn't love the poor boy but seems bent on marrying him. Oh."

He was fascinated by her startled realization of her rash words. He had thought she was in her best looks when angered, but now he had to reconsider as she pressed her hand to her mouth and gave him a wide-eyed look of chagrin. Resisting the temptation to kiss her button nose, he retrieved her spectacles from the end of the ribbon and held them up for her.

"I won't say a word until you put these on," he stated with a slight smile. That did the trick; she forgot her embarrassment in her annoyance.

"Why are you the only person who can make me angry?" she murmured without realizing she had spoken aloud, but perched the offending spectacles on her delicate nose.

"Now, let's see if I can be of help. Yes, the countess would like her son to marry in the near future," he said smoothly, counting off each point on his fingers to make sure he did not forget. "The earl is avoiding his mother, not the young lady. Although he has recovered from his wounds at Waterloo, his mother has not. You see, his older brother died just before battle when his yacht floundered while crossing the channel. She has been determined to cosset the earl to the point of madness without being aware how trying it has been for him." He stopped abruptly and frowned at her. "Why are you so anxious to help the girl? She seems to have little affection for you." He immediately regretted the words. She rose to her feet, seeming ready to depart now that she had her information. How could he entice her stay?

"I don't like conflict, and if I can't find a solution to the matter, there will be an awful scene," she answered succinctly without bothering to prevaricate. "She is still too young to control her emotions. I would like to spare the Witmer-Gows, who seem to be nice people. So, Thalia is my responsibility for now."

"I see," he murmured, stung by her final words. *Responsibility* was a word he had kept tucked in the back of his mind lately. "You're still determined to become a lady of independent means, then?"

"Oh, yes," Eliza stated firmly, a smile of true enjoyment replacing the tiny frown that had furrowed her brow. "If I hadn't set my mind to it before now, this trip has stiffened my resolve. I will have the best of both worlds, mingling with the best of society and going home at night to my own cozy fire. I will instruct the girls, but their parents will have the main responsibility. Now I'd best return to see if Thalia has done any damage in my absence."

Randall could not find any means to detain her longer, much to his regret. After each meeting he was becoming more anxious to see her again. Was he simply becoming bored with his own company, or was it something else? Absently rubbing the healed wound in his side, he wondered if he wanted to examine his emotions too closely. It seemed more dangerous than facing a French calvary charge.

9

ELIZA DESCENDED THE STAIRS WITH SLOW, MEASURED steps, not eager to rejoin the others assembled in the Great Hall for the after-dinner entertainments. She had gone to retrieve Thalia's shawl the minute her cousin mentioned feeling a slight chill. Since the younger woman had been on her best behavior all evening, Eliza did not want to upset the precarious balance. Now, as she reached the bottom step, she hesitated, savoring the momentary solitude while still out of sight of the others.

She squared her shoulders and took a deep breath in preparation of facing the company again. Then the sound of footsteps from the dim recesses of the hallway diverted her attention. The merest peek over the banister had her gaping at the all-too-familiar blurred figure silhouetted by one bright spot of light. Quickly she grabbed for her spectacles and ruthlessly thrust them in place, then blinked as if still unable to believe her focused vision.

It *was* Randall, ambling toward a closed door at the end of the hall. He made no pretense of stealth, as if he had a perfect right to be there. What possessed the man to wander through the house while the countess and her guests were likely to discover him? she thought wildly, casting a watchful eye toward the Great Hall. She relaxed her tensed body slightly when the murmur of conversation continued.

No one had heard his echoing footsteps, she decided in relief, turning to look down the hallway again as Randall continued on his merry way. Under her astonished eyes, he opened the door and disappeared from sight.

Eliza was indecisive about what she should do. Should she warn him of his folly? How did the man expect to remain gainfully employed if he continued to act in such an audacious manner? He had confirmed that the earl was avoiding his mother, so she was in his debt. If he was not able to sense the danger, she felt obliged to warn him.

Almost without realizing it, she began walking toward the closed door. Clutching Thalia's shawl in front her like a shield, she tiptoed closer—having the good sense to practice the stealth that Randall had not. The latch turned silently under her hand, and she peered cautiously around the door as though she expected to be confronted by a ghostly apparition at any moment.

What she found was Randall standing on the far side of the book-lined room before an open cabinet and lifting down a crystal decanter of dark liquid. The man knew no shame. Not only was he courting the danger of discovery, he was sampling the earl's spirits from a hidden store.

"You needn't hover in the doorway, my dear," he said clearly without turning around. "Come in and join me for a glass of wine. The old earl had the presence of mind to lay in an excellent cellar."

Shock more than anything else had her obeying his invitation. She hastily stepped into the dimly lit room and closed the door securely behind her. One of them had to show some sense. He had not even bothered to lower his voice—though she did acknowledge there was not as much of an echo in this room.

Randall turned to face her at the sound of the latch clicking shut. His brilliant smile flashed in the light of the brace of candles on the massive desk beside him. "Good, you decided to stay, so I won't have to drink both glasses of this excellent port—though it wouldn't be much of a hardship."

"Randall, have your wits gone begging?" Eliza shot out suddenly, the words almost forcing themselves from her mouth. "The countess and her guests are only a room away."

"Not to worry, dear Eliza, I only came to borrow a book," he explained guilelessly and began moving toward her.

She took a few steps forward, not wanting to seem as ill at ease as she felt. After all, she was the one on the side of righteousness as an invited guest. Why should she have the irrational feeling of being a rabbit trapped in a snare?

"I usually have the run of the house," he continued, as if reading her mind, trying to justify his actions, all the while moving closer. "I have sampled his lordship's private stock many times."

"This is extremely foolhardy," she stated, now standing almost toe to toe with him and unsure what to do next. Had she come on an empty errand? Perhaps the countess was not as rigid with her servants as the Dumonts were with theirs. Uncle Cyril was always suspecting the butler or the footmen of pilfering his wines and kept a keen eye on the level of every bottle in his household.

Not that it mattered how the countess treated her servants. Eliza's heartbeat seemed to have increased tenfold, and her palms were damp at the thought of discovery at any moment. She had never experienced such emotions before, almost excited and frightened at the same moment. A shiver skated down her spine as she looked up to meet Randall's hooded gaze.

"Randall, you must leave," she urged him, not daring to speak above a whisper.

He only smiled again in answer, holding one of the stemmed glasses under her nose. "I promise to leave when you have finished your wine. I need something to ward off the chill on the solitary walk back to my cottage, and I hate to drink alone."

For an irrational moment she was tempted to snatch the glass from his hand and dash the contents into his face in a fit of pique. She had wasted her concern on a lunatic.

Why else could the man remain so calm under the circumstances? Jenkins or Lady Laxton could find them here at any time. Oh, why *had* she followed him? Even on such short acquaintance, she sensed he was accustomed to flaunting proper behavior. If they were discovered in the dimly lit room pilfering the earl's wine, Randall would be dismissed, no matter how lenient his employer. Her reputation would be marred as well.

Or would it? she wondered dispiritedly. She had always behaved in a proper manner, so undoubtedly no one would look askance at her presence in the room. No one would believe she would do anything unseemly. Like as not they would know this was not an illicit assignation and that she had been playing at being Mrs. Grundy—to no avail.

"Eliza, haven't you ever done anything the least bit naughty in your whole life?" he asked, demonstrating his mind-reading skills once more. A singular winged brow ascended at the query.

Almost defiantly she took the glass that was still hovering in front of her nose. Staring at the top button of his vest, she took a tentative sip. Randall knew his spirits—and so had the old earl. The wine was excellent. Unconsciously she licked her lips, only aware of the gesture when Randall made a strange noise deep in his throat. Confused, she dared to look up.

Though he had struck his habitual nonchalant pose by resting his hip against the desk, his face was devoid of its usual humor. There was an intent expression in his eyes that she did not understand. Her mind went blank, unable to form a coherent thought. So she acted instinctively, raising the glass to her lips and tossing back the contents. Only as the potent liquid slid down her throat did Eliza realize what she had done. Blinking back tears, she repressed the urge to cough. It was bad enough the man had her behaving in such an ill-bred manner.

"Now—" She broke off to clear her dry throat, narrowing her eyes, almost daring him to begin teasing her as he was wont to do. "Now that I have finished my wine, you may keep your promise to leave."

A slight smile curved his lips as he silently regarded her, twirling the stem of his glass between his thumb and fingers. His gaze never wavered from hers as he raised his glass to his lips and—seeming to mimic her actions—drained the glass in a single swallow. Eliza shifted her feet uneasily, then started in surprise as he took her glass from her unresisting grasp. Randall still did not speak as he carefully set both glasses on the desk.

"I'll take my leave as the lady requests," he said softly, the familiar twinkle returning to his blue eyes, "but I demand a forfeit for my sacrifice."

Eliza did not have time for more than a gasp of astonishment before he bent forward to touch his lips gently against hers. Though she knew she should move away, she was spellbound by the warm contact, lowering her lashes to keep the room from spinning around her. Then he was gone.

How long she stood staring down at the empty glasses with her fingers against her trembling lips, Eliza never knew. Suddenly she recollected her surroundings, heat rising to her cheeks at the thought of what had just taken place. For a moment she considered fortifying herself with another glass of port, but shook her head at the ludicrous thought.

Randall was becoming an extremely bad influence, she decided, ruthlessly dismissing the image of his smiling face from her distracted brain. She had to collect herself and return to the Great Hall before they sent someone looking for her.

10

"I'VE BEEN LONGING TO EXPLORE THE MINSTREL'S GAL-lery since we arrived," Miss Witmer-Gow confided at the entrance while she and Eliza waited for the footman to light the archaic torches that lined the supporting wall. The dark balcony had not been visited in a number of years, by guest or servant, judging from its dusty appearance in the strong light. "I'm so glad you agreed to accompany me, Eliza. May I call you Eliza?"

As the girl blushed prettily over the request, Eliza returned her shy smile before linking her arm companionably through the taller girl's. "A rainy afternoon is the perfect time to explore, especially since I took such a short walk this morning. Have you learned anything of the history of our fortress?"

"Father used to come here with Rus— Mr. Towne's father to do some hunting and fishing. He says this was the stronghold of a notorious reiver with a black heart," Lisette whispered to test the echoing effect with satisfactory results. "The man wasn't very political and enjoyed raiding who-ever brought him the most profit, English or Scot—a thor-oughly unsavory neighbor to have."

"Was he a relation to the Towne family?" Eliza asked absently as she began to peruse the pictures hanging on the long wall. Most of them were not very good, even to her amateur eye. By concentrating on the discussion at hand, she kept her traitorous thoughts in check. She would not think about another rogue currently in residence.

"No, the earl bought it after visiting a friend in the area,"
Lisette continued, wandering toward the gallery railing to
inspect the carved figures of the balusters. "Lady Laxton
claims he furnished the place with the ugliest furniture he
could find and transported every painting and decoration
she loathed to ensure she would never want to accompany
him. This was a truly male-oriented household."

"He sounds like an ingenious gentleman, though I suppose the summer months would be the only time she might
have been tempted," Eliza reasoned as she considered the
late earl's method of preserving his solitude. Apparently
his son was of a like mind, judging from his recent disappearance. The Towne men did not seem to like feminine
interference in their lives.

"Indeed, my room has been positively frigid at night. I
think the countess said there was a portrait of her husband
in his younger years up here," Lisette mused, looking down
the row for the particular painting. "She says he looks like
an idiot, very pompous and foolish, fresh out of university.
Ah, here it is in the corner."

Foolish was a pallid word to describe the emotions that
assailed Eliza as she studied the young man in the portrait.
Her body was alternately blazing hot, then chilled to the
bone. Randall bore a striking resemblance to his father;
there was no mistaking the relationship. It seemed as though
the artist had captured the gamekeeper's laughing blue eyes
and challenging grin.

"It's a very good likeness. Lady Laxton is right—he
does look silly." Lisette's laughing comment broke into
Eliza's chaotic thoughts. "He is supposed to take after a
Black Irish rogue who sailed with Sir Francis Drake. The
coloring shows up in each generation."

"Oh, I see," Eliza said inadequately but was amazed that
any sound came out at all. Her entire body seemed numb.
Who was Randall? Only now did she admit with a bitter-
sweet turn of mind that she had enjoyed their encounters
in the woods and last night in the library. The brash game-

keeper brought an unexpected spark to her otherwise dull life. Was he more than that? She found she did not want to consider the more legitimate reason for the resemblance. A poor relation had more in common with the family by-blow. Was that why he had disappeared so abruptly the day of the picnic? So Russell would not see him?

"Well, that seems to be all there is to the minstrel's gallery, doesn't it?" she exclaimed in false brightness. There was no use in making a complete fool of herself. To think she had actually sought out his company twice yesterday. A child would have realized that his speech was too cultured and his clothing, though worn, too well cut for an ordinary gamekeeper. Hot tears stung her eyes as she considered what had taken place in the library last night. She was a fool.

"Yes, it is rather a disappointment," Lisette agreed and fell into step with her companion. "I wonder if Thalia is over her headache by now. I do hope her nap has raised her spirits. Rus— Mr. Towne has been very concerned about her."

Eliza did not comment on either Thalia's or Russell's state of mind. Her own thoughts were in turmoil. Perhaps she should take to her bed for the rest of the visit. That seemed to be the easiest solution. It was much simpler than attempting to ask a gentleman if he was legitimate, and if he was not, what his intentions were.

11

R ANDALL TOOK PLEASURE IN WATCHING ELIZA WITH HER head bent intently over her sketchbook. He decided he liked her best in the blue dress, undoubtedly because he knew how it reflected in her eyes. Fleetingly he wondered why she had only ventured to the promontory a few yards from the house this morning. Her other rambles had taken her farther afield. Was she avoiding him because of a kiss he had been unable to resist?

Since he had left his canine companions at the cottage, she still had not seen him. Were the others still abed, making it safe for him to approach her? Would it be so bad if he was seen? He had tossed and turned all through the long night, his mind preoccupied by a man's responsibilities and obligations, as well as some other more pleasant notions. He was still uncertain about what he planned to do, but he did know that he wanted to talk with Eliza once more before he came to a decision.

"Good morning, fair lady. How do matters stand between our young lovers today?" he inquired, dropping down beside her. Propping himself up with his elbows, he made sure he had a full view of her delightful face. His smile slowly faded as she raised her head to regard him with a level, emotionless stare.

"Good morning, Randall. Everything is fine." She did not smile or even blink before she returned her attention to the paper in front of her.

"That's all? *Everything is fine.*" A chill skimmed down

his spine at her toneless words. What was amiss? Was the simple kiss that he had stolen the cause of her icy tone? He had been wise not to open the conversation by alluding to their brief evening tryst. "I was counting on Thalia having hysterics or Russell making a complete cake of himself."

"No, Thalia has been on her best behavior since yesterday," she commented without bothering to look up, though the implication was clear that others should have followed the same pattern. "As for—Randall, I'm sure you would know more about Russell's behavior than I would."

The chill slowly spread through his entire body. Had he delayed his confession too long already? Was this how sweet Eliza dealt with her anger, turning into an ice maiden? In the past few days he had wanted to strangle her cousin— as well as the rest of her family—for their careless treatment of such a treasure. Were they not aware that his Eliza was worth more than a dozen Thalias?

His Eliza. Strange he had not thought her in quite that way before, but he liked it. How would it sound if he spoke it? Would it cause her to smile or perhaps return the sparks to her lovely eyes? He was not brave enough to take the chance at the moment. Instead he asked, "When do you leave Laxton's Retreat?"

"Three days." She was worrying her lower lip in such an endearing manner that it took him a moment to comprehend her answer.

"Then there is still time for an explosion, I suppose," he determined, trying once more to capture her attention. Perhaps she was simply tired from dealing with her cousin. Was it selfish of him to think he had caused her mood?

"I suppose, and I had best go see if she is awake. We are going to have a long talk this morning about the complexities of the male species," she declared as she rose gracefully to her feet before he could move a muscle.

"We are?" He knew it was not the time for levity, but he was at a loss over what to do next. If she was already angry about an innocent kiss, he did not dare mention it. With a sinking heart he jumped to his feet and watched her gather up her supplies, wondering if she would say another word before she walked away.

She straightened suddenly, her troubled gaze meeting his own. "No, *we* are not. Are you ever serious about anything?"

"Oh, yes, my dear." Unconscious of moving, he had her in his arms before he realized what he intended to do. It was a simple matter of lowering his head to taste the sweetness of her parted lips. He was elated as she responded tentatively, then her soft body stiffened. Without warning her hand was against his chest, pushing him away.

Tears were forming in her beautiful eyes, sparkling diamonds behind the lenses of her spectacles as she stared defiantly up at him. Taking a deep breath, she murmured, "That is the most unkind thing you have ever done."

Randall was stunned at what he had done and the look of mortification on her face. Before he could speak, she ran toward the house as if the devil himself were chasing her. For a long time he remained perfectly still, staring at the doorway where she had disappeared from sight. Only when he finally turned to go did he see the sheet of paper on the ground. Listlessly he bent to pick it up and idly spread it open.

There was a painful ache around his heart as he looked down at his own smiling face. It was a good likeness, or it had been, before his Eliza had drawn two heavy black lines across the page. Would she ever be his Eliza? With a grim set to his mouth Randall headed toward the cottage. He knew what he had to do. Jenkins would be beside himself with pleasure, but how would Eliza receive him when next they met?

12

"If THE WEATHER PROVES FAIR TOMORROW, WE SHOULD see if we can hire a boat for a picnic and explore one of the inlets," Lady Laxton declared to her guests as they assembled after dinner in the great room.

"That would be a lovely idea, Clarice," Lady Witmer-Gow agreed, looking up from her embroidery where she sat near the foursome at the gaming table.

"Not if my dear mama stands up in the boat and dunks everyone into the tarn," stated an amused masculine voice from the entrance to the Great Hall. "We were fortunate the pond at Laxton is only five feet deep. However, Reggie and I got dripping wet and came down with colds just before the summer fete."

"Randall." Eliza's involuntary murmur was drowned out by his mother's squeal of surprise. No one noticed Eliza's lack of surprise or her interest in the new arrival. Russell and Lady Laxton hurried to greet the prodigal son while the others talked among themselves over the sudden appearance of the gentleman.

"My dear boy, why didn't you send word you were coming? Have you eaten? How are you feeling?" Lady Laxton exclaimed while clutching at his arm. She seemed to need the feel of some portion of him to prove that he was actually there.

"Mama, I know how you love surprises. I thought it best not to disrupt dinner and waited to come down until after you were finished," he said easily, walking rapidly toward the group that was gathered around the fire. "I had Jenkins bring me a tray in my room, and I've never felt better in my life."

"Didn't I tell you that he was perfectly all right, Mama?" Russell broke in, giving his brother a hardy slap on the shoulder. "You don't know how good it is to see you, old man."

"Please be less enthusiastic, little brother!" Randall exclaimed and rubbed his shoulder with exaggerated care. "Instead of beating on me, introduce me to these charming ladies."

Eliza kept her head bent over the cards that were spread out on the gaming table in front of her. She heard Thalia's and Lisette's response to the earl's engaging banter. All too soon it was her turn, and she reluctantly looked up to meet Randall's challenging blue gaze.

"Surely, Miss Dumont, you are much too young to be anyone's chaperon," Randall had the audacity to say, as if daring her to speak out about his charade. His flashing grin was in place, but it did not reach his eyes. He watched her very intently as he made a slight bow.

"You are too kind, m'lord," she returned demurely, keeping her gaze centered on the first button of his silk waistcoat. He was devilishly handsome in evening dress, she admitted reluctantly to herself, daring to study him through the veil of her lashes as he spoke briefly to Sir Basil. His tall, lean form was perfectly suited to the dark tailcoat and pantaloons he wore with the same careless manner as his gamekeeper's garb.

"Won't you join us in a game of whist, Lord Laxton?" Thalia asked eagerly in a loud voice, seeming desperate to draw his attention. "Russell was just saying that he was growing bored with the game, so we need another player to be my partner."

Eliza clenched her teeth tightly together as Randall took his brother's place to her right. His foot brushed against hers as he settled in his chair. Was it intentional? She did not dare look up to confirm her suspicions without giving herself away to him and to the others. She misplayed her next card, much to her cousin's delight. How long would she be able to stay in the same room with him before she did something incredibly foolish? she wondered, squelching an uncontrollable urge to run to her bedchamber.

The second time Randall's foot brushed against hers she knew it was intentional, but she gave no sign that she was aware of it. She kept her eyes focused on her cards, not daring to look right or left. Though she knew it was ridiculous, her lips still seemed to tingle from the warmth of his that morning. Calling herself three times a fool now that her worst fears were confirmed, Eliza did her best to keep her mind on nothing but the game.

After a half hour she could no longer stand the strain and quickly excused herself. Her headache was not a fabrication; her temples were throbbing, and her throat ached from holding back misguided tears. She tried to keep her thoughts from wandering, but a small voice deep inside kept asking, Why did he do it? Why did he kiss me twice? Was it another one of his jokes to have a flirtation with a spinsterish chaperon?

Falling listlessly into her bed minutes later, she wondered how she was going to survive the next two days. For such a sensible person she seemed to have been harboring some ridiculous notions. Why would a peer look twice at a plain, poor relation? A dozen unanswered questions swam around in her head as she drifted off to sleep and dreamed fitfully of smiling blue-eyed gentlemen.

13

THE BOOMING CHIMES OF THE CLOCK IN THE LOWER HALL increased the throbbing in Eliza's head the next morning as she descended the stairs. After a fitful night, alternating between wakeful periods of chastising herself and dreaming of grinning gamekeepers wearing coronets, she was not surprised that she had overslept. Perhaps a cup of weak tea and dry toast would ease her queasy stomach as well as her aching head.

"Ah, Miss Dumont, how nice of you to join us." Randall's cheerful voice echoing off the high ceiling of the dining hall made her wince as she crossed the threshold. She considered turning on her heels and returning to her room; however, Thalia's presence made her reconsider. She would not give Ran— Lord Laxton the satisfaction of seeing her discomfort. Fortunately with her cousin in the room she would not be forced to converse with the man.

"I was just telling *dear* Randall what a slugabed everyone seems to be this morning," Thalia announced with a slight edge to her words. She laid a hand on the earl's arm, practically pulling him back into his chair at her side when Eliza took a seat on the opposite side of the table. "The two of us *were* having such a delightful coze with no one else around. Weren't we, Randall?"

"Delightful."

Eliza barely heard his murmured response as she gave a hovering Jenkins her request for a meager breakfast. After one look at the old man's dour but sympathetic expression, she occupied herself with the task of unfolding her linen napkin. Did the butler know of his employer's most audacious acts while he had been impersonating the gamekeeper? Was that why he was overseeing breakfast? Perhaps this was not the first time the gentleman had taken to playacting.

"Oh, dear, I seem to have left my handkerchief in my room!" Thalia exclaimed in tones that implied a far worse tragedy. "Eliza, would you be a dear and run upstairs to fetch it for me?"

Without bothering to consider the matter, Eliza began to rise to her feet, only to be brought up short by the earl's abrupt command. "Sit down, Eliza. Thalia is perfectly capable of running her own errands."

"But, Randall, my cousin is *always* glad to do these little favors for me."

Eliza forgot her own troubles as she watched the pair across the table. Her young cousin's lower lip was thrust out in a mock pout as she batted her eyelashes prettily for the earl. Then the girl was blinking in confusion at the thunderous look on the earl's face. Perhaps for the first time she had discovered a gentleman who was immune to her coquettish manner.

"Your cousin has only just sat down," Randall stated in a clipped tone of voice. "Her breakfast will be cold by the time she returns with your handkerchief. Since you are already finished eating, you can simply go fetch the item yourself."

For a moment Eliza was not sure who looked more mutinous, Thalia or Randall. No one in her memory had ever spoken to the girl in this manner. She knew her cousin was on the verge of a tantrum—something she was very accomplished at—but Thalia was hesitating since she was unsure of her audience's reception. Silently she assessed her host with a wary eye. The sound of cheerful voices from the hallway seemed to herald a diversion from imminent disaster,

Eliza thought with relief. In her present state of mind she was not sure she could cope with Thalia, especially in front of Randall.

The sight of Russell and Lisette's flushed and smiling faces made her quickly reconsider the matter. Thalia turned her attention away from the earl, her dark eyes narrowing dangerously as she watched the couple advance across the room.

"Good morning, all!" Russell exclaimed, giving everyone a jovial salute. He directed a benign smile at his brother before he assisted Lisette into the chair next to Eliza. "What a glorious morning for a ride. I've worked up quite an appetite. Jenkins promised me trout this morning. Can I tempt you, Lisette?"

"No, thank you, Russell," she declined prettily, sitting down next to Eliza. Her cheeks deepened in color as she raised her lashes to meet his grin with a shy smile. "I would prefer tea with some of Mrs. Beaton's scones and preserves."

"Ah, yes. She told Mama that you had wheedled the recipe from her yesterday," Russell remarked, turning toward the sideboard to do as she bid.

"Russell, *I* would like to sample some trout." Thalia's shrill demand stopped the young man in midstride after he had taken two steps.

He regarded his fiancée with a puzzled look, almost as if he had not realized she was present until that moment. "Oh, Thalia, I thought you didn't care for fish."

"I haven't tasted trout before," she stated, directing a look across the table at her cousin as if daring her to contradict the blatant lie. "While you were out cavorting on those smelly old horses, Randall has been telling me about the splendid catch from his early morning angling. So I really must reward his efforts."

"Don't trouble yourself on my account, Thalia, if you don't care for fish. Trout can be an acquired taste," the earl broke in, raising his brow in a commanding manner and cocking his head slightly in Thalia's direction. Russell looked almost crestfallen, as if his brother had betrayed him in some manner.

"Oh, but, Randall, that would be so poor-spirited of me," Thalia returned sharply, seeming to forget which brother she was addressing. "I may not be as hearty and daring as Miss Witmer-Gow to go riding *alone* with a young man, but I think I have the nerve to taste trout."

Lisette's gasp of surprise at the venomous words was heard only by Eliza as Russell made a fatal mistake in handling his fiancée. "Thalia, what kind of nonsense are you spouting this time? Don't be an idiot."

"Nonsense? This time? Idiot?" she shot back, tossing her napkin onto the table and jumping to her feet. In her anger she forgot that the others were present, including the earl, to whom she had been giving such solicitous attention only a few minutes earlier. "What do you mean? *You* are the one who went off with another woman this morning. Did she cozen you into thinking she might be a better wife than I because she can ride some silly old horse?"

"Thalia, how could you—" Eliza began, but she was cut off by Russell's fretful words.

"Lisette, I'm very sorry that Thalia has childishly turned her temper on an innocent person."

"You're apologizing to *her*?" Thalia shrieked, her dark eyes flashing as her fiancé walked away from her to the lady in question. Her face was flushed with barely suppressed rage, her mouth a thin line of displeasure.

Eliza was in a quandary about what to do. She might set off the final explosion if she said a single word to her cousin, but if she did not, she was not sure what would happen next. Helplessly she looked across the table at Randall, hoping that he would assert his authority to settle the matter.

She barely heard Russell's soothing words to the white-faced Lisette, who was bravely holding back her tears. Randall was leaning back in his chair observing the scene before him as if watching a play. He actually had the audacity to smile. Suddenly she remembered her comments to him when she had foolishly thought he was the game-keeper. If she did not know better, she would think he had manipulated the situation to have Russell break his engagement.

"I will not stand for this," Thalia announced before advancing around the table, heading directly for her fiancé and the hapless Lisette. There was murder in her eyes as she raised her arms, clenching and unclenching her fingers with each step closer to her quarry.

"Thalia!" Eliza practically shouted and shot to her feet. She intercepted her cousin a mere foot from Lisette's chair, taking the younger woman's arm in a firm grasp. By shaking her none too gently, she was able to bring Thalia to her senses.

"What did I tell you, Eliza," she practically whimpered, tears flooding her eyes as if on cue.

"Thalia, please don't—"

"Not now, Lisette," Eliza interpolated gently, knowing anything the young woman said or did at this point would be useless. If the situation was to be saved, she had to remove her cousin from the scene before her temper took hold once more. "Thalia and I will go upstairs to refresh ourselves while the rest of you finish your breakfast. She needs some peace and quiet to restore her usual good humor."

"But, Eliza—" Thalia protested, drawing out her cousin's name in an undignified whine.

"Please, not another word, young lady, until we reach our room," Eliza instructed in her most repressive voice, leading the now weeping young lady toward the door. As they crossed the threshold, she could not resist looking back over her shoulder at Randall.

His smile was gone now as his brother took the chair that Eliza had abandoned so precipitously. He never noticed, his brooding look trained solely on two figures in the doorway. Eliza found she was on the verge of tears herself as she returned his regard. She turned back to her cousin, trying ruthlessly not to feel sorry for the man. He had gotten his just deserts by trying to manipulate others people's lives, she decided, wondering why she was not happier over the matter.

14

"YOU ARE AN IMBECILE, ELIZA DUMONT," SHE REMARKED
flatly to the nearby trees rustling under the cool afternoon
breeze as she sat beside the bubbling stream that had begun
her descent into idiocy. After hours of trying to console
Thalia, she had been given a respite when the girl cried
herself to sleep. Though she should be trying to think of
a way to remedy this morning's disaster, Eliza found she
was thinking about her own troubles.

Taking the coward's way out, she had left the house to
avoid Lady Laxton and her guests. How she hated scenes.
Surely this was the last place anyone would come looking
for her. Diffidently she tossed pebbles into the shimmering
water. She should be planning her departure from the
Dumont household as soon as she returned home, but
somehow the idea had lost its appeal. Albeit the prospect
of dealing with Thalia and her aunt if Russell cried off was
not encouraging.

"You seem bent on destroying my favorite fishing spot."

She did not want to look around. It was undoubtedly
a figment of her wistful fantasies. The blur of a small
white, black, and tan body appeared next to her on the
embankment, then another. She did not need to put on her
spectacles to recognize Castor and Pollux. This was not a
dream.

"I suppose I was right that first day. You are a wood
nymph under the spell of an evil witch," he continued
conversationally, stretching his lean body out on the ground

next to her. He was close enough for her to discern he was still outfitted as a proper gentleman from his top boots to his intricately tied cravat.

"You have a very active imagination, Ran— Lord Laxton," she murmured, her fingers nervously playing with the dark green fringe of the shawl that covered her green-and-white-striped jaconet morning dress. Foolishly she had left her bonnet behind in her haste to leave the house, and she missed the shield the wide brim would have provided.

"I was simply trying to ascertain if you would speak to me. Last night you seemed determined to ignore me now that I am myself again. And this morning . . ." He allowed his words to drift away, sitting upright and bringing his face level with hers. "A gentleman needs to know if he is going to receive an answer when he pays his addresses to a lady."

Involuntarily Eliza turned her head, startled to discover that his distracting blue eyes were only a few inches from her own. She did not need her spectacles to see his determined expression. Unable to withstand the intensity of his gaze, she looked away toward the stream, where the puppies were timorously exploring new territory at the water's edge. "I thank you for your consideration, sir, but I don't think it is necessary," she managed in a remarkably calm voice. It was not every day a nondescript, poor relation received a proposal from a peer. "No one but Jenkins and the footman know about our meetings, which were perfectly innocent. You have no obligation to me."

"Eliza, you should know by now that conventions mean very little to me," he replied with a snort of derision. "That has been a point of conflict between my mother and me for months. It wasn't simply her bothersome coddling that made me leave for a few weeks of respite. I am *not* making an offer because I may have compromised you. What a hen-witted idea."

"Yes, I can see you do hold me in great affection," she shot back dryly, beginning to feel the ice around her heart melt as aggravation took its place. First he had deceived her, and now he was calling her names. The man had no manners whatsoever.

"Dammit, Eliza, I've never done this before!" he exclaimed, taking possession of her hand to stop her nervous fidgeting. "I was never supposed to become the earl. Reggie was the one who was groomed to follow my father. Russell and I teased him unmercifully as we were growing up about all the pomp and nuisances that came with the title. Mama has always despaired over my lack of proper respect for my position. You'll discover we'll be spending more time in the country tending to the serious matters of the tenants' needs than we will doing the pretty in town." He paused for a moment, as if gauging her reaction, and sighed when she did not speak. "Oh, we will go to London. I will be taking my seat in the House, but that will supersede any fancy dress balls or visits to the opera."

"Sir, there really isn't any need to continue this charade," she protested in spite of the rapid beating of her heart and a shortness of breath. "I have my own plans, you know. All my life I've done what everyone expected of a poor relation, quietly doing my duty. For the first time in my life, I'm going to do what I choose."

"Tell me what you really want, sweet Eliza," he murmured, his breath warm against her cheek. "Tell me that you would rather be shepherding spoiled young ladies from one stuffy ball to another. I may not be the biggest prize on the marriage market—though your cousin did find me fascinating momentarily—but I know marriage to me would be much more entertaining. Wouldn't you rather share a life with me than dance to the attendance of all those strangers? Never mind what anyone else would think or say, tell me what *you* want."

Afterward she was never sure what prompted her action, his laughing tone or possibly the comment about Thalia. Randall always had the most curious effect on her. Before she had a chance to consider what she was doing, she turned to him and framed his narrow face in her hands. Then she realized the impropriety of what she intended; however, Randall did not give her a chance to pull back. As his arms snaked around her waist, he fell back among the ferns and groundcover, pulling her down with him.

His warm mouth claimed hers, and Eliza felt it would be undignified to struggle. Though it was not entirely proper, she felt obliged to return the pressure of his lips. A lady in her social position never knew when the opportunity might arise again. All too soon Randall moved to his side, gently settling her on the ground beside him.

"Now, I'm only going to ask this once more," he stated in a fierce growl, gently brushing a wisp of her hair away from her temple. "Will you marry me, love of my life?"

"Love? Y-you love me?" she asked breathlessly, wondering if she was dreaming after all.

"Yes, you peagoose. I love you!" he exclaimed, giving an exasperated sigh before he brushed a kiss on the tip of her nose. "Where are your spectacles?" Grasping the ribbon, he nudged the wire frames into place and stated, "I want your full, focused attention on me. I, Randall Aloysius Francis George Towne, love Eliza Dumont, who is the most beautiful woman in the world to wear spectacles. I plan to buy you hundreds of pairs to match every gown you own."

"Oh, Randall, only a man besotted with love could make such an outlandish statement. You should really be paying your addresses to someone suitable like Miss Witmer-Gow—"

"*Eliza*," he growled impatiently, cutting into her protestations.

"Yes, I, Eliza Henriette Dumont, agree to marry Randall Aloysius Francis George Towne before he comes to his senses."

After that she had little time to say anything else; she was assaulted by the most delightful feelings as Randall sealed her acceptance in a satisfactory manner. Her last rational thought for quite some time was that marriage to Randall would be vastly entertaining.

Some time later, when Randall found that they both needed to breathe, Eliza discovered the real world quickly came back into focus. Adjusting her spectacles, she cast her newly betrothed a teasing look. "Randall, I know that this isn't the most romantic suggestion, but could we go back to the house and find a cozy place by the fire? The ground is damp, and Castor and Pollux are feeding on my ankles."

He immediately sprang to his feet, taking the puppies to task for nibbling on Eliza's tender skin. Encircling his Eliza in his arms, he declared, "That is why our marriage will be such a success. You are much more practical than I, my love, and will temper my impulses."

Placing a daring kiss on his chin, she smiled up at him before they turned down the path toward Laxton's Retreat. "I'm counting on you to teach me to be more frivolous. Before I forget all my sensibility, however, what are we going to do about Thalia and Russell?"

"Don't worry your pretty head over the matter," Randall assured her, whistling to Castor and Pollux as they began to wander astray. "After he sees what true love is like, I'm sure things will come about. Now, I have more important matters to occupy my mind than my brother and your cousin." He demonstrated by nuzzling the soft curve of her neck.

"Yes, dear," Eliza agreed, laying her head against his shoulder. "We need to plan our honeymoon. Wouldn't it be delightful to have Laxton's Retreat all to ourselves?"

TIDES
of
LOVE

———

Melinda Pryce

"*I* REALLY NEED TO STOP!" ALFRED WHINED AS HE bounced up and down on the purple velvet seat cushion of the elegant carriage.

Louisa Hamlin felt that she, too, would not mind a brief respite in their travels. But the Red Lion Inn in the village of Hand Cross, which they were now approaching, was as crowded as all the other inns had been.

I don't blame them for stopping, Louisa thought as her empty stomach rumbled its protest. Even at this distance she could smell the tempting aroma of the freshly baked gingerbread that the innkeeper in the doorway was busily distributing from his wicker basket.

Passengers of the Brighton coaches paused at almost every inn on their journey to the sea to partake of whatever local specialty the innkeepers had to offer. Of course, the passengers had little choice in the matter, as the coachmen were all tipped handsomely by each innkeeper to stop at his particular establishment.

Louisa sympathetically eyed the son of her late cousin, Stephen Hamlin, Lord Duville. She and Alfred, like the passengers, had little choice in this matter, either. But unlike the coachmen, Alfred's mother had no intention of stopping until they had reached their destination.

"Mama, if I don't stop soon, something *terrible* will happen!" Alfred warned.

Louisa's heart sank when Lady Duville replied, "Oh, Alfred, can you not wait just a bit longer?"

"No!" he wailed and drummed his feet against the seat.

"Just wait until we arrive at our own nice house in Brighton," her ladyship suggested. "We're almost there."

"No!" His round little face screwed up in a terrible grimace.

"You don't *really* want to use the wretched facilities at a public inn, do you?"

"Yes!"

"Oh, Nanny, can you not do *something* to distract the child?" Lady Duville demanded testily of the fresh-faced lass seated opposite Louisa.

"I think he needs less distracting and more relieving," Nanny answered bluntly.

"We've already wasted too much time," Lady Duville complained. "At this rate, by the time we reach Brighton, 'twill be Christmas and Prinny will have returned to London."

"Beatrice, surely a brief stop would do no harm—and perhaps 'twill do some good," Louisa interceded. "After all, Brighton will still be there, no matter when we arrive."

"So will Lord Lanford," Nanny grumbled, ostensibly under her breath but actually quite audibly.

Again the ubiquitous Lord Lanford! Louisa thought.

She had never made the gentleman's acquaintance. She was merely the impoverished, orphaned cousin of the late— and briefly lamented, at least on her ladyship's part—Lord Duville. Louisa had neither the wherewithal nor the desire to aspire to the lofty circles in which her cousin and his wife had traveled.

Still, she felt she knew Lord Lanford quite well from Lady Duville's constant chatter of the man and his sterling attributes.

"Ah, those celestial blue eyes! Never did even the heavens aspire to such a hue!" Lady Duville would exclaim upon returning from some ball or soirée where his lordship had been. "Ah, those flaxen curls! Like a veritable Apollo, or some Viking warrior bound for Valhalla! 'Tis all without

artifice, too," her ladyship quickly pointed out. "No foppish curling irons nor crimping papers for Marcus! And
those wide shoulders, that broad chest, that flat stomach,
and those lean hips!"

Upon reaching this point in Lady Duville's laudatory
itemization, Louisa always hoped that her cousin's widow
would have the discretion not to reveal that his lordship's
manly figure was also without artifice and that he needed no
buckram padding to enhance his jacket—or his trousers!

Thank heavens, Lady Duville always stopped.

In point of fact, Louisa was heartily sick of hearing Lady
Duville rave about the man. She was highly skeptical that
any mere mortal could be as devastatingly handsome as her
ladyship made him out to be.

Yet, here she was, Louisa mused, along with Alfred and
Nanny, torn from their comfortable Mayfair town house and
hurtling themselves headlong down the Brighton Road—at
peril to life and limb, and not even stopping for a moment's
comfort—just because Lord Lanford had accompanied the
Prince Regent to Brighton for the summer and Lady Duville
could not bear to have him gone.

*Poor Cousin Stephen was hardly cold in the ground when
Beatrice set her cap for Lord Lanford, and she has pursued
him the better part of a year without success,* Louisa mused.
She released an inaudible sigh. *Still, in this, as in everything
else, Beatrice will allow nothing to prevent her from eventually succeeding.*

Louisa smiled to herself as the inspiration came upon her.

"Beatrice," she said, a bit more loudly than usual in order
to be heard over Alfred's pitiful wail. "Perhaps you should
stop and walk about a bit to exercise your legs. After all,
you've been traveling in these cramped quarters for over
three hours. You would not want Lord Lanford to see you
descend from your carriage, hobbling about like some aged
crone actually come to Brighton for a cure."

"Indeed not!" Lady Duville decided. She leaned forward
a bit.

Louisa leaned forward, too, the better to hear her lady-ship over Alfred's sustained lament.

"His lordship believes me to be only four and twenty, although in reality I am . . . well, just a bit older," Lady Duville reluctantly conceded. " 'Twould never do to have him discover . . . or even to suspect otherwise!"

Pounding upon the roof of the carriage with the tip of her parasol, she ordered the coachman to halt.

Alfred was out the door before the horses had completely stopped.

"No, no, leave that," Lady Duville scolded.

Louisa placed the extremely modish, not to mention expensive, bonnet upon the dresser, adjusting the primrose-colored ribbons so that they hung as flat as when she had first packed them in the bandbox.

"Shall I attend to something else?" Louisa asked as she glanced about the spacious bedchamber that Lady Duville had claimed as her own. Judging from the quantity of baggage, Louisa fully believed they had not merely let the house on St. James Street for the summer but were to reside here for the remainder of their natural lives.

"No. The first thing I must do," Lady Duville informed her, "is stop at the lending library and inscribe my name in the register."

For the first time since Lady Duville had initiated this wild trek, Louisa's spirits revived.

After her mother died when she was eighteen, Louisa and her father usually passed their evenings reading to each other in their cozy sitting room. Upon his death two years ago, Louisa had been forced to leave their little cottage in the Cotswold to live with her cousin and his wife and child in their town house in London. Her cousin's meager library could not compare to her father's well-stocked shelves. Louisa eagerly anticipated some new reading material.

"I vow, Louisa," Lady Duville complained as they left the house and made their way along St. James Street. "You needn't look quite so elated. 'Tis not natural for a lady to read so much. Although at seven and twenty—"

"Five and twenty," Louisa corrected, although she knew as surely as night follows day that Lady Duville would persist in adding several years to Louisa's age—and in subtracting from her own several more.

"At five and twenty, there's not much else left for you to do but read, is there?" Lady Duville continued.

Louisa supposed there were quite a few things of which she was still capable. Oh, how she loved to dance at the country assembly balls! If only, she thought wistfully, Lady Duville would allow her to accompany her to a ball.

But Louisa was well aware of the futility of arguing with her ladyship, so she merely shrugged and remarked, "Oh, I'm not ready to let the coffin maker take my measure yet."

"Still and all, you'll ruin your eyesight with reading over much," Lady Duville continued to scold. "And then of what use will you be to me?"

Louisa turned away, hoping to shut out Lady Duville's tiresome harangue. She stopped to examine the buildings across the street.

"Oh, what are you gaping at?" Lady Duville called back peevishly. She tapped her foot impatiently against the brick walk. " 'Tis only Raggett's, a subscription club where gentlemen come to gamble. 'Tis of no concern to you. Now, do stop dawdling. I vow, you're as irritating as Alfred!"

Louisa hurried to catch up to Lady Duville. The constant breeze from the sea was refreshing. Indeed, it led Louisa to agree heartily with the sages of a generation ago who touted breathing the ozone at Brighton a highly efficacious cure.

Then a sudden gust of wind caught Louisa's bonnet. In spite of the lavender ribbons, which she thought she had tied securely under her chin, the bonnet flipped backward off her head. Thankful that no one but Lady Duville had witnessed her embarrassment, Louisa quickly retrieved her runaway bonnet. She clapped it firmly down upon her dark curls and tied the ribbons more securely beneath her chin. Still, she kept one hand on the crown, just to be safe, as she hurried along.

"Why such a rush to reach the library?" Louisa asked breathlessly as they turned the corner. "I never thought you overly concerned with reading."

"Reading?" Lady Duville repeated mockingly. "Who cares a fig for reading? Unless it is the *Fashionable Chronicles* to see who has come to town. And who gives a fig who is in town? Unless it be Marcus."

Louisa could make no reply in the face of such irrefutable logic.

"Begging your pardon, Beatrice," Louisa said as they walked along. "Did we not just pass an excellent-looking library?"

Lady Duville glanced back to her left to inspect the colonnaded building that Louisa indicated.

"Perhaps," she conceded as she continued on. "I would not know. The library we shall subscribe to is there, across the Steine." She waved her hand toward the south, across a broad expanse of grassland surrounded by a wide brick walk and enclosed by a white wooden fence. "Bowen's is ever so much to be preferred."

Louisa looked from one building to the other. For the life of her, she could see no outward reason to patronize one over the other.

" 'Tis even farther away from our house," Louisa noted. "How can it be preferred . . . ?"

"You have not been listening to a single one of my plans!" Lady Duville accused. "Marcus subscribes to Bowen's."

Louisa nodded her complete comprehension. How could she have been so obtuse!

"I say, do have a care," the elegantly attired gentleman who sat under the colonnade in front of Bowen's protested as Lady Duville fairly brushed his newspaper from his hands as she passed.

Louisa, head lowered, her face flushed with embarrass-

ment, apologized. She also apologized to several ladies who
were too engrossed in watching others stroll up and down
the Steine to beware of Lady Duville. Louisa knew from
experience that her ladyship's attention was upon reaching
her intended destination—not upon whom she offended.

Louisa continued making apologies for them both as
Lady Duville's unstoppable progress brought them into
Bowen's. They bypassed persons who were gossiping, persons who were playing cards at several tables arranged
for their convenience, as well as a few people who were
actually reading.

"Still I do not see him!" Lady Duville whispered crossly
into Louisa's ear. "Ah, well, Marcus *is* here. I see his name
there in the register. Sooner or later I *will* encounter him."
She signed her name in the book with a grand flourish. "Pay
Mr. Forth my guinea, Louisa."

Louisa rifled through her reticule for the small kid leather
purse of coins that she carried at her ladyship's request.
She produced the shiny new guinea and presented it to the
rather nondescript gentleman to whom Lady Duville had
referred.

Lady Duville nudged Louisa in the side and said, "You
must pay, too."

With a small sound of apology, Louisa began to withdraw
another guinea from the purse.

"No, no!" Lady Duville exclaimed in a hoarse whisper.
"Not *my* money."

"I had supposed you would be paying, Beatrice," Louisa
whispered softly. After all, she reasoned, coming to Brighton
was Lady Duville's idea.

Lady Duville glared at her. "Well, *I* am not going to be
the one reading the books here, am I?"

'Twas useless to protest. Louisa replaced the leather
purse and fumbled through her reticule for her own small,
homemade purse.

A guinea would severely deplete what was left of this
quarter's allowance. With a surge of panic she worried,

what if Lady Duville should begin to require her to contribute her share of the rent as well?

She truly saw no need to pay to enlist the services of
the Master of Ceremonies, as she highly doubted that she
would be seeking introductions to important personages,
or needing Mr. Forth's advice upon precedence or settling
quarrels. Still, she *did* intend to make use of the library.

Louisa signed the register and relinquished the precious
coin.

Marcus Kendall, Lord Lanford, was losing at hazard again.
Still, he barely managed to stifle his yawn. It mattered little
to him. If he lost one day, he would only win again the
next. Even in its uncertainties, his life was quite predict-
able.

He would dine at the Pavilion with the Prince Regent
and his cronies tonight, as he had so many other nights.
He would listen to His Highness expound with endless
enthusiasm upon Nash's latest plans for the renovation of
the already ornate building.

He would dine upon food that, not only by its composi-
tion but by its very overabundance, was designed to produce
severe dyspepsia even in persons who boasted the stoutest
of constitutions.

Even the company, while certainly not dull, would still
be the same. Most of those who circulated about the Prince
Regent in London inevitably followed him down to Brighton
at one time or another.

Thank heavens there was one who would be missing from
the company this evening, Lord Lanford thought with relief.
He was fairly certain he had made good his escape from
London without Lady Duville being any the wiser—at least
for the time being.

Lady Duville was still wearing mourning for her late husband when she began paying Lord Lanford more attention
than their slight acquaintance warranted. He knew for a
certainty she had wheedled, bribed, and even threatened one

poor *parvenue* with social ostracism just for an invitation to any affair she discovered he was attending. Somehow, Lady Duville always managed to track him!

Imagine! he silently grumbled to himself as he picked up and discarded the playing cards. *The Marquess of Lanford sneaking out of London like any common thief.*

However, given the fact that his pursuer was more ingenious and persistent than any Bow Street Runner, Lord Lanford forgave himself this seeming cowardice. Any time spent away from Lady Duville was a distinct relief.

'Twas not that she was a perfect horror. If the truth be owned, her fair curls, large blue eyes, and slim little figure were rather pretty, in a conventional sort of way. 'Twas simply that, beyond a mere speaking acquaintance, Lady Duville held no attraction for him whatsoever.

Being the gentleman that I am, Lord Lanford modestly admitted, *I can scarcely tell the woman to go to the devil.* Still, how else could he rid himself of her unwanted—and of late increasingly irritating—attentions?

"Oh, I say! I've won again!" the young man seated to Lord Lanford's right exclaimed. He reached out his gangling arms to scoop up the coins stacked in the center of the table.

Lord Lanford regarded him with a certain degree of detached amusement. While his gaming partners at Raggett's varied from day to day, inevitably, year in and year out, one encountered the same type of fool.

In referring to his current gaming adversary as a veritable "pink" of the *ton*, Lord Lanford believed himself much closer to truth than to metaphor. Too much brandy too late last night and again too early this morning had rendered the young man's nose a most roseate shade.

The fellow's hands shook as he gathered his winnings, sending several coins to the floor. When he bent over to retrieve them, he tumbled off the chair and sprawled across the floor, giggling uncontrollably.

"Well," Lord Lanford said, glancing about at his companions who remained upright. There was a slight, mocking lift of his eyebrow. "I suppose that puts an end to this game."

The other, more sober, gamesters readily agreed. The plump fellow from Edinburgh left, announcing his intention to dine. Lord Lanford's friend Lord Mattling merely folded his cards, laid them on the table, and sat regarding the young man scornfully.

Lord Lanford knelt down, resting one arm across his knee. He gently tapped the young man on the shoulder to gain his attention.

"A word to the wise, sir—although in your case, that remains to be seen. Take your winnings, settle your accounts here, and retire to your country estate," he suggested quietly.

'Twas common knowledge the young man's estate was mortgaged to the hilt to provide the funds to support his frivolous carousings. His winnings made a mere scratch in Lord Lanford's extensive fortune. But if the fool sobered up enough to realize not to gamble it all away the next day, his winnings might allow him to leave Brighton with his creditors satisfied, and run his estate properly just one more year.

But the stupid fellow continued to lay there and laugh.

Lord Lanford pressed his fine lips together more tightly and regarded the young man with a mixture of disgust and pity. He had tried to help him, but if the fool could not follow good advice, well, there was little he could do. Lord Lanford rose with a sigh. He was as bored with fools as he was with everything else.

He turned abruptly on his heel and strode to the window, which overlooked St. James Street.

"Oh, damn it all to hell!" Lord Lanford muttered aloud in spite of himself.

"Never known you to be put out by a bit of a loss, Lanford," Lord Mattling remarked as he came up behind him. "Much less that it should cause you to swear like Letty Lade."

"No, 'tis not that, Rollo," Lord Lanford said. The scowl never left his face.

Lord Mattling followed Lord Lanford's line of sight out the window. "Ho, ho!" he exclaimed with a wicked laugh. "She has found you."

Lord Lanford grimaced as he watched Lady Duville's trim figure bustling along St. James Street.

"Just when you thought yourself rid of her," Lord Mattling said, a facetious smirk widening his narrow face.

Lord Lanford made no reply. At the moment he was far too angry to risk speaking.

"Well, your outburst was quite understandable," Lord Mattling forgave him. "The woman could cause a saint to curse, much less cause ordinary sinners such as you or I to lose our customary cool demeanor."

Lord Mattling peered farther out the window. "But I do not recognize the unfortunate creature Lady Duville is dragging along behind her. Who is she?"

Lord Lanford, himself, was just wondering the same thing. Ever so slightly—so that no one present could ever aver that they had seen Lord Lanford display an undue interest in anything—he inched his way closer to the window. He turned his head imperceptibly so that he could watch the ladies.

As always, Lady Duville appeared quite the vibrantly hued iris in her cream-colored muslin gown and vivid purple satin spencer. She completely eclipsed this . . . He searched for an appropriate comparison. Yes, Lord Lanford at last determined from the color of her gown and her retiring, almost subservient demeanor—this shy little violet.

He watched her making her way down the sidewalk. Although she trod upon mere baked clay, Lord Lanford felt as if he were watching her make her way through pastures of newly blossomed wildflowers.

He felt the anger that seethed within him slowly ebb away, leaving him with a strange sense of peace. Just watching her, he was seized with the unaccustomed urge to smile.

"I say, wake up, Lanford," Lord Mattling chided him, intruding unwelcomed into his silent observation of the unknown lady. "I asked who she could be."

" 'Tis rather difficult to tell when her face is obscured by that ridiculous bonnet." The lady's bonnet was a good bit older and a great deal cheaper than Lady Duville's stylish headwear, he estimated.

"Lady Duville would certainly not have brought a friend to Brighton with her," Lord Mattling reasoned. "In the first place, she would never deign to be seen with anyone so lacking in style. In the second place, she would never admit any potential competition where *you* are concerned."

Lord Lanford decided to ignore his friend's reference to any possible connection between himself and Lady Duville. Silently he could not help but marvel that any lady would allow herself to be seen in public wearing so hideous a bonnet.

Could this be Alfred's nanny? Lord Lanford wondered. No, she was a lady, of that he was certain. She had a delicate grace that made her good breeding clearly evident, in spite of the poor quality of her clothing. The longer he watched her, the more Lord Lanford wondered how he *ever* could have mistaken her for a servant. But who was she?

Perhaps a paid companion? An impoverished relation, living on Lady Duville's rather dubious charity? If that was the case, he pitied the lady all the more for whatever dire circumstances had reduced her to constant association with Lady Duville.

Much to his surprise, he found himself releasing a sigh that held just a touch of unaccustomed wistfulness. Lord Lanford watched her, speculating. He stopped himself abruptly. No. The lady's identity did not signify, he told himself, especially if discovering it meant associating with Lady Duville in the process.

He intended to turn away from the window, to join Lord

Mattling in a glass of port or perhaps find another card game, but for some reason which he hesitated to examine further, he remained, gazing out the window, just a little longer.

A sudden gust of wind tore the bonnet from the unfortunate lady's head, revealing to Lord Lanford's fascinated gaze her tousled raven curls, her creamy skin slightly blushed from the breeze and the exertion of her hurried walk, and her almond-shaped azure eyes.

She was no green girl, Lord Lanford could tell that much even from this distance. She was no wretched crone, either. Her slim nose and softly rounded chin imparted a certain agelessness to her face.

She made a dive for the runaway bonnet, sending her dark curls into further disarray. Surely a lady of her age should be wary of appearing a hoyden. Yet her action seemed somehow charmingly innocent.

She retrieved the bonnet quickly. She was an agile little nymph, Lord Lanford thought, allowing himself the barest hint of a grin. He recalled other ladies of his acquaintance who would never deign to do anything for themselves if they could get someone else to do it for them.

The unknown lady clamped the bonnet down upon her head. Yet, even after tying the ribbons securely under her chin, she felt the apparent need to cling to it still. What a strange mixture of impulse and caution she was.

She was not the most beautiful woman he had ever seen. She was far from the best attired. Yet there was a freshness about her that Lord Lanford found intriguing.

As Marquess of Lanford, he had a veritable surfeit of the finest of everything. Not many things piqued his interest or curiosity anymore—until he saw this lady.

The devil take Beatrice! Even the prospects of associating with her again would not prevent Lord Lanford from discovering her mysterious companion's identity. She was the first person who had made him want to smile—to genuinely smile—in a long, long time.

*   *   *

Lady Duville was so intent upon locating Lord Lanford *immediately* that they had left the library before Louisa could even glance at the shelves, much less make any selection. They walked the entire circuit of the Steine, past the Pavilion to the east, past the blue- and buff-painted houses to the north—even though their journey took them on a complete circuit of the Steine when they need only have retraced their steps to return home. Who knew but that they might not encounter Lord Lanford as he was exiting the Pavilion?

Louisa highly doubted that they would. From everything she had heard of his lordship, she did not think a gentleman of his refinement would be seen near what was, to her mind, such a monstrosity as the Pavilion—unless it was under the cover of darkness!

Alas! Lady Duville was greatly disappointed when Lord Lanford was nowhere to be found. When they returned, she retired to her room with a headache.

After her own meager belongings were quickly unpacked, Louisa again looked in on her ladyship. From the resonant snoring emanating from the room, Louisa could tell that she was peacefully asleep.

Nanny came up behind Louisa and whispered, "I've left his little lordship napping in the housemaid's care. I'm off to see the town." She grinned mischievously at Louisa. "Come with me!"

Louisa hesitated. How could she run off enjoying herself when she still had duties here that must be attended to? She glanced back at Lady Duville's recumbent, and noisy, figure.

Nanny waved at her ladyship with a gesture of dismissal. "Oh, she's dead to the world—at least until dinner." When Louisa still hesitated, Nanny reminded her, "We'll be going past the library."

"Reading can be a truly edifying pastime," Louisa remarked in order to assuage her guilt. Quickly she retrieved her bonnet.

Nanny was an infinitely more pleasant companion for a stroll, as she seemed to enjoy dawdling about, observing the passing people, and peering into the bowed shop windows almost as much as Louisa did. When they entered Bowen's, Nanny busied herself with gossiping with other nannies and abigails who were waiting until their ladyships' businesses were concluded. Louisa was free to find her own entertainment.

As she headed for one of the bookshelves, Louisa noted a gentleman who stood over the very same register that had recently cost her so dearly merely to sign. He stood with his back to the door, conversing with Mr. Forth. He was apparently searching for something, as Louisa could clearly see him moving his finger down the pages until he came to the particular registry he sought.

The gentleman was tall, with exceptionally broad shoulders. His fair hair waved softly over the back of his head. She could not see his face, yet Louisa had the oddest notion that she had met the man before.

Impossible, she chided herself. *You've spent your entire life quietly in the country. Wherever could you have made the acquaintance of so fine a gentleman?*

Trying very hard to dismiss the unidentified gentleman from her thoughts, Louisa returned to the original reason for this excursion—the bookshelves. Still, she could not shake the overwhelming sensation that the gentleman had not left the library—and that he was watching her.

Why would he be watching me? I am no Incomparable, whose charms no man can resist. With mounting panic she speculated, *Merciful heavens! Despite his gentlemanly attire, could he be some sort of procurer, a man who lures innocent young women off to a life of sin and degradation in the sordid dens of iniquity in London?* Suddenly, she stopped and scolded herself, *Oh, Louisa! Do find a pleasant travel volume—and stop reading those blasted Gothic novels!*

She made a bit more of an effort to concentrate on the

contents of the shelves, and a great deal more of an effort *not* to think of the unidentified man. The contents of the bookcase did nothing to assist Louisa in her efforts. Most of the volumes were rather tedious tomes. The ones that did interest her, she had already read.

All the while she searched the shelves for some innocuous tale, Louisa believed she could still feel the gentleman's eyes, watching her every move. She was aware of someone approaching from behind.

'Tis that same gentleman, following you. . . . She firmly put a halt to her deranged ramblings. *Oh, poor Louisa. Beatrice is succeeding in driving you insane!*

The gentleman stood beside and slightly behind her. Merciful heavens! Did he not realize that standing so close without a proper introduction was bordering on rude?

She wanted to turn and look at him, just to satisfy her curiosity as to who was this insolent fellow. But she had the eeriest sensation that if she did, she should see him not studying the bookshelves at all, but regarding her with every bit as much curiosity as she felt about him. Therefore, in order to be safe—and certainly not to appear as impudent as he—she devoted a great deal more attention than necessary to the bookcase and inconspicuously inched away. It was impossible to ignore the fact that the gentleman inched his way along the bookshelf right beside her.

At last! This momentous find could even take her mind off the mysterious gentleman by her side. She had been hoping to read the next novel by the anonymous author of *Waverley*. And here it was, *Guy Mannering*, just waiting for her in Brighton! She would take the book and be gone from Bowen's—and from this gentleman.

As she extended her arm for the book, his long arm reached out and a sun-browned hand seized it before she did.

Oh, blast! she silently wailed. *One might expect reading to be an appropriate pastime for an impoverished spinster such as I, but one would certainly think a stylish gentleman*

*could find better things to do in Brighton than to read—
especially the book I wanted.*

Louisa whirled about too quickly to mask the disappointment on her face.

"Oh, I beg your pardon, miss. Did you also want this
book?" the gentleman asked.

Suddenly her expression changed from disappointment to
surprised recognition. She managed to refrain from gasping
aloud. She had never met him, but she knew him in an
instant.

*Oh, merciful heavens! It is him. It must be Lord Lanford.
Who else could fit the description I have heard time and time
again?* With a sudden flush that rose from her breast, up her
throat, and across her cheeks, Louisa realized, *Beatrice has
been correct all along!*

Who else but Lord Lanford could be endowed with such
waving blond hair? Louisa was also quite certain that it
was without the aid of curling irons and papers that the
soft strands of fair hair fell across his smooth wide brow
and around his small ears.

Who else could have shoulders that broad? And, just
as Beatrice had described, so evidently without the need
of padding. With a concentrated effort, Louisa resisted
the lascivious impulse to glance down to the man's tight
trousers—just to see if Beatrice might have been correct in
that respect, too.

She looked up quickly into the gentleman's eyes instead.
Oh, why did I do that? she silently demanded of herself.
It would have been better if she *had* followed that first,
prurient impulse. Then she merely would have looked and
been gone.

Lord Lanford's eyes *were* every bit as blue as the sky,
with the slightest deepening of color about the outer edges
of the iris, just like the hint of a storm looming on the
horizon on an April morning. Just as one watched the sky
to see what the day would bring, Louisa could not tear her
gaze from Lord Lanford's eyes.

"Excuse me. Did you also want to borrow this book?" the gentleman repeated, snapping Louisa from her boorish inspection.

She flushed and lowered her eyes to the apparent safety of the book, which he held in front of his waist.

Oh, blast! she wailed inwardly. *Could he not hold that wretched book elsewhere?* She managed to pull her eyes up again to meet his.

"Yes," she answered. She made the tiniest swallow to ease her suddenly dry throat. "I have not read it yet . . . I had rather hoped . . . I did so enjoy reading *Waverley.* . . ." She began to regret loosening her throat, as now she could not keep herself from babbling on like the veriest ninnyhammer.

"I, too, enjoyed *Waverley,*" Lord Lanford graciously picked up the foundering conversation. "The author has quite a talent for writing exciting scenes."

Louisa nodded her agreement. "I most enjoy the wonderful characters he creates."

Oh, Louisa! If your dear departed mother could see you now, she silently chided herself. *Conversing in public, unchaperoned, with a gentleman you do not even know— actually.*

Lord Lanford smiled. "Then I must defer to milady's wishes." Bowing, he offered her the book.

As she took it from his hand, his fingers brushed against hers. They were warm and smooth, she decided, in spite of their sun-browned appearance.

"I hope you enjoy the book," he told her. "Brighton is a small town. Perhaps we shall meet again."

"Perhaps," Louisa managed to answer.

With another bow Lord Lanford backed away and was gone.

She watched him turn and leave the library. She was seized with the tremendous impulse to hurry after him, to return the book to him—any excuse to be with him again. She even considered, for a very brief moment, importuning

Mr. Forth to effect an introduction. After all, she'd paid a guinea for the privilege. What a terrible lightskirt she should appear if she did! Blast the conventions that prevented her!

Blast my own silly conceit, too, she scolded herself. *As if the Marquess of Lanford should ever permit an introduction to a little nobody such as I.*

In all the time in which Lady Duville had been pursuing him, not once had Louisa encountered Lord Lanford. He had never called at their town house in Mayfair, and she had never been invited anywhere his lordship might be. Silently, and just a bit sadly, she decided it was highly unlikely that she should ever encounter him again, unless it be at his and Beatrice's wedding—*if* Beatrice invited her.

Louisa looked down at the book in her hands. Lord Lanford was not only devastatingly handsome, he was also extremely kind. Imagine the Marquess of Lanford relinquishing to her a book that he wanted to read, merely because she wanted to read it, too!

She held the book close to her breast. In reality it was not any warmer than usual because of him touching it. Perhaps it was just she who felt that way after having met him. Slowly she moved the book out to a suitable distance, just in case others were watching her somewhat peculiar behavior.

Small wonder that Beatrice is so taken with his lordship, Louisa now admitted. *If he has this effect on a sensible lady such as myself, imagine the palpitations that he must cause a shatter-brained ninnyhammer like her!*

After the rigors of travel and the disappointment of not encountering Lord Lanford immediately, Lady Duville was not quite herself again until noon of the following day— for which Louisa was extremely grateful. She had an entire evening and morning in which to enjoy the peace and solitude that contributed to her complete absorption with the novel.

Well, perhaps not complete. There were more than a few moments when memories of curling blond hair, and a pair of intensely blue eyes, and a strong, warm hand brushing against hers, insisted upon intruding into the tale she read.

That was when she wandered down to the kitchen to find something on which to nibble—a biscuit or a piece of cheese—anything to get her mind off Lord Lanford.

"Oh, this will never do!" Louisa wailed as she ate her fifth biscuit—on this foray alone.

Her family's modest circumstances had prevented her from indulging in the rich sweets that she loved, allowing her to maintain her slimness. Beatrice's household was run with considerably more abundance, but her ladyship's slim figure had set a rigid example that Louisa had been determined to follow. She knew with dismal certainty, however, that if Lord Lanford continued to intrude into her thoughts, and if she continued to seek distraction with biscuits and chocolates, she stood in grave danger of attaining the proportions of the Prince Regent himself.

Louisa wisely refrained from seeking diversion with a sixth biscuit and returned to her room to continue the tale of *Guy Mannering.* She hoped that Lord Lanford would stay out of her thoughts, and yet, she was also hopelessly certain that he would not.

When Lady Duville finally arose at noon, she plunged with a vengeance into her plans to find and ensnare the hapless Lord Lanford. Reclining upon the sofa, she perused the morning's post.

"No." Her ladyship flipped the cream-colored card out of her hand. She was concentrating on the next invitation in the pile and was heedless of where she sent the first. Nevertheless, the invitation landed at Louisa's feet. "No. No. No." She flipped several more in rapid succession.

Louisa stooped to retrieve them from the floor.

"Send them our regrets," Lady Duville ordered.

"*Our* regrets?" Louisa repeated. She thought petulantly, *They are not* my *regrets. I have never been invited to a one of these affairs.* She felt rather hurt and just a bit sorry for herself.

Lady Duville ceased her shuffling of the little cards and turned to Louisa. "Well, you *do* have the finest hand," she said by way of excusing herself from the tedious task.

Louisa looked through the cards at the names of the people whom Lady Duville had rejected.

"Lord and Lady Summerville, Lord and Lady Abernathy, Sir Harry and Lady Montford . . ." Louisa looked up from such an imposing list. "Whyever should you decline?" Louisa quickly stopped. She was the veriest fool of the world if she could not deduce this puzzle. "Because Lord Lanford will not be attending these affairs," she finished. Feeling a bit peevish, and therefore a bit more bold than usual, she asked, "Which one *will* his lordship attend?"

Suddenly much more animated as the conversation turned to his lordship, Lady Duville raised her languid form from the sofa.

"I have reliable information from Nanny, who has been talking with Lord Lanford's valet's sister, who is nanny to the Uppingtons, who occupy the house next door to the Teasels," her ladyship said, revealing her sources of information, "that Lord Lanford will attend the dinner that Sir Joshua and Lady Teasel are giving this evening in their new house on the Marine Parade."

Lady Duville turned again to the assortment of invitations. "I vow," she muttered as she flipped through the cards, "if there is not an invitation from the Teasels to their dinner party, I shall personally tell everyone I know that Daisy Teasel stuffs her bodice with cotton wool." She shuffled through more cards. Suddenly she crowed with triumph and held aloft a single card. "Well, Daisy Teasel is safe for the nonce."

And poor Lord Lanford is not, Louisa thought, with growing pity for the gentleman who had been kind enough to relinquish *Guy Mannering* to her.

"Well, isn't this the strangest thing!" her ladyship exclaimed, examining the invitation more closely.

"What is so strange?"

"*You* are invited!"

"I?" Louisa, quite forgetting decorum, fairly squealed. She rushed to Lady Duville's side.

Her ladyship turned the invitation over and over, as if by magic, turning it would cause it to say something different each time.

Louisa peeked over Lady Duville's shoulder. When her ladyship stopped turning the card about, Louisa managed to read aloud the handwritten note on the bottom. "Do bring your charming companion."

"Why, that's ridiculous!" Her Ladyship said. "They don't even know you. Whyever should they think you charming?"

Louisa was far too excited to take umbrage at Lady Duville's careless remark. But her excitement vanished as quickly as it had appeared.

"We *are* going, aren't we?" she asked, just a bit fearful that Lady Duville might experience one of those sudden changes of mind to which she was so prone.

"Well, of course," Lady Duville answered. "Marcus will be there."

Louisa sighed with relief. How could she have doubted for a moment?

Lady Duville gave Louisa a scathing look up and down. "And I suppose you'll do no harm."

As Louisa sat silently at the long dining table, she recalled Lady Duville's words. True, she had managed to do no harm thus far this evening—although she doubted that she could continue her good behavior much longer.

The gentleman to her left—Lord Mattling, she believed they had called him—was interested only in recounting tales of his escapades at the green baize tables. Never having had much enthusiasm for games of chance, Louisa was at a loss for conversation. Unfortunately, the gentleman was not and continued his stories, requiring from Louisa only a smiling nod or a sympathetic shake of the head—depending upon which was most appropriate at the moment.

In spite of his faults Lord Mattling was much to be preferred over Mr. Blake, the gentleman to her right. If the man placed his pudgy, greasy hand on her knee one more time, instead of just quietly moving her leg farther away, Louisa vowed to herself she would stab the offending hand with her fork. Surreptitiously appraising the plump, pale, and rather flaccid Mr. Blake, she debated whether 'twould be appropriate to use the fork for fish or for pork.

In point of fact, she should not be sitting between these two gentlemen at all. The place cards had indicated that she should be *there*, in the seat across the table, beside Lord Lanford. She glanced up wistfully from her plate to see Lady Duville firmly ensconced in that chair, chattering so incessantly to his lordship that she scarcely had time to eat.

Small wonder she keeps her marvelous figure, Louisa thought with the slightest twinge of jealousy—and her ladyship's figure was only a small part of the cause for such feelings.

Upon viewing the seating arrangement, her ladyship had called Louisa aside and harassed her so unmercifully that Louisa eventually agreed to exchange seats—but, oh! she would much rather be sitting beside Lord Lanford.

It did not bother her—much—that his lordship had merely acknowledged their earlier introduction with a pleasant, "How do you do, Miss Hamlin? How very nice that you could join us this evening." That short remark had been accompanied by a gleaming smile and a piercing look from his extraordinarily blue eyes, but she truly could not expect his lordship to acknowledge their previous encounter any further. At any rate, Lady Duville had so monopolized his lordship's time in the brief interlude between their arrival and the service of dinner that he scarcely had the opportunity to converse with anyone else, much less anyone as insignificant as she.

Louisa was doing her best to maintain an expression

appropriate to Lord Mattling's conversation. She was more engrossed in watching Lord Lanford. His lordship appeared to exhibit greater interest in the roasted ham and Madeira sauce on his plate than in anything that Lady Duville said.

Louisa frowned with puzzlement. Could it be that Lord Lanford was not as taken with Beatrice as she was with him? No, Louisa decided, her speculation was overly optimistic—and decidedly improbable.

Suddenly Lord Lanford looked up from his plate directly into Louisa's eyes.

Louisa drew in a quick breath. She could not chew, she could not swallow, she could not even blink, much less look politely away. How embarrassing to have his lordship catch her staring at him! Yet, in spite of her embarrassment, she found she rather enjoyed watching the candlelight flicker in his lordship's gleaming eyes.

Suddenly his eyes softened and took on an inquiring look as they searched her face. Whyever should he look at her that way? Whatever could his lordship want of her when he could so readily have the inimitable Beatrice?

Louisa watched as his lordship moved his head ever so slightly in the voluble Lady Duville's direction. Then he rolled his eyes upward and grimaced. She sputtered and grabbed for her serviette, holding it before her mouth to hide her giggle. Lord Mattling offered her a goblet of water. Mr. Blake leaned over her solicitously, but Louisa could tell he was more interested in the contents of her bodice than the state of her health. Lady Duville directed a dagger-eyed glare at her.

Lord Lanford's brows were drawn close together as he watched her recover. But there was also a secret merriment in his blue eyes that he shared with her and her alone.

She had no idea that anyone as dignified as his lordship could ever be so mischievous. As much as she wanted to, Louisa found it very difficult to look at Lord Lanford again throughout the meal—and even more difficult not to.

Lord Lanford wished Miss Hamlin would raise her lovely azure eyes to him again. Lady Duville's boorish rearrangement of the seating had angered him at first—especially when he had gone to so much trouble to persuade Lady Teasel to include Miss Hamlin among the guests, and to accept his suggestion for a proper seating arrangement. Still and all, 'twas just the sort of behavior he might have expected from Lady Duville.

In fact, it had not turned out so dreadful after all. Even though he did not now have the opportunity he sought to converse with Miss Hamlin, he was enjoying just watching her from across the candlelit table.

If only she would look at him. Oh, the things he wished to tell her with his eyes—and perhaps later, to elaborate upon verbally.

Ah, well, 'twas still interesting just to watch her, especially when she did not know she was being observed.

Miss Hamlin raised the silver fork to her full, pink lips. How soft her lips appeared, how pliant to the touch. Lord Lanford drew in a deep breath. Oh, how he would love to prove to himself that her lips truly felt that soft and pliant against his own.

Lord Lanford's glance drifted to his friend, seated to Miss Hamlin's left. As usual, Mattling was chattering incessantly—most probably, if he knew his friend, about his gambling. Lord Lanford smiled at the ill-disguised expression of complete disinterest in Miss Hamlin's azure eyes. However, it was her futile attempts to appear engrossed in the conversation that made him want to laugh aloud.

More sophisticated ladies relished tales of Mattling's escapades at the green baize. A few could probably top some of his boastful stories. What *did* pique this lady's interest, he wondered, besides reading?

Lord Lanford was also carefully eyeing the gentleman to Miss Hamlin's right but with less amusement. He could not see what the man was about under the table, but considering Blake's reputation and Miss Hamlin's reaction, he evidently was not keeping his hands to himself.

A more experienced lady might have put a halt to his advances with a crushing verbal set-down—or even have accepted his licentious overtures. Lord Lanford's lips twitched as he watched Miss Hamlin continue to inch quietly away from Blake each time he drew closer to her. He wondered how long before she slid off the chair completely and landed upon the floor—or in Mattling's lap, the lucky sot.

Miss Hamlin was such an innocent, Lord Lanford lamented. How could she know how to protect herself against the likes of Blake?

He contemplated hurtling his dinner knife across the table, skewering the blackguard. No, he reconsidered. 'Twould only ruin everyone's appetite and Lady Teasel's tablecloth. He did decide to appoint himself Miss Hamlin's guardian against Blake's advances.

The ladies rose and withdrew, leaving the gentlemen to their port. Even though, for some unexplained reason, the invitation had specified that Louisa was invited to this affair, she found her hostess, and every other lady there, far too preoccupied with their gossips about their own personal circle ever to admit her into their conversations.

After a while Louisa had seen every watercolor hanging on each wall and had examined every snuffbox on every side table and each Meissen figurine on the mantelpiece. Unnoticed, she wandered out of the drawing room and down a short corridor. To her right, an open doorway led to a darkened room.

Her proper upbringing would have prevented her from entering there unbidden, but the sight through the window enticed her. The moon, not quite at its full, shone not only in the evening sky but reflected in bits and pieces on the dark surface of the water below.

Louisa moved slowly across the room to the window. She rested her hands upon the windowsill and gazed silently out over the sea.

"Ah, so there you are," the deep voice came to her from across the room.

Oh, surely, 'tis not my lecherous dinner partner! Louisa felt a sudden chill of fear as she realized just how alone she was.

She turned quickly to the gentleman who approached her through the darkness. His blond hair seemed almost as white as the moon, while his blue eyes had turned the deep indigo of the sky.

She felt much safer knowing it was Lord Lanford—and yet, at the same time, she felt oddly disconcerted. Still, she managed to give him a relieved smile.

She watched his tall figure advance upon her through the darkness. He certainly did not appear as threatening as her awful dinner partner. Still, there was an almost palpable power in his stride as he came to the window. Louisa could almost feel a challenge—or an invitation—in his stance as he stopped beside her.

"I wondered where you had gone," he said. His voice was as soft as the moonlit darkness surrounding them. It caused her throat to contract in an automatic swallow and her heart to beat inordinately faster.

"They were all talking . . . I came here . . . I didn't think anyone would miss me. . . ." Louisa had always, quite modestly, assumed herself to be a reasonably intelligent, reasonably articulate lady. Why, oh, why, in Lord Lanford's presence did she persist in turning into a babbling idiot?

"*I* missed you," he told her.

If there was an appropriate answer, Louisa was certain she would manage to babble it out as incoherently as she had everything else. As she could not think of any response, she decided 'twas better to remain silent and be thought a fool than to speak and remove all his lordship's doubts.

"I was rather hoping you would enjoy yourself here this evening," he told her.

"You were . . . why would you . . . ?" Oh, there she was, babbling again!

"A lady should have better things to do in Brighton than read," he told her softly.

How odd that she had recently been thinking the very same thing about him—and in less kindly tones.

"Therefore, I prevailed upon my old friends to invite—"

"You asked them to include me? I don't understand. Why?"

"I already told you, Miss Hamlin, I thought a lady as lovely as you are might find more interesting things to do in Brighton than sit reading alone."

In spite of her nervousness and confusion, Louisa began to smile. She even managed to speak without faltering. "Thank you, my lord. The food was delicious and the company . . ."

Lord Lanford shook his head and gestured toward her. "Yet, here I find you, again in some solitary pursuit." He gave her a censorious scowl—yet there was a playfulness behind his deep blue eyes that caused Louisa to grin sheepishly up at him even in the face of his scolding.

He rested his hand upon the sill behind her. He was so close she could at last discern the black pupil from the deep blue iris of his eyes.

He really should not stand this close, Louisa thought. *I really should move away.* Yet she found herself not only powerless but downright averse to moving.

"Did you not find the company interesting?" he asked.

"I am afraid it was *they* who did not find *me* interesting," she admitted reluctantly. "Of course, I can hardly blame them. I am so sorry—"

"There is no need to apologize. 'Tis their own lack of perception," Lord Lanford whispered to her. Even in the darkness she could see his eyes traveling down her body, and then, quite unashamed of his bold perusal, up again to meet her eyes.

His lordship's flattering words and piercing gaze, the very nearness of him, worried Louisa.

I should be extremely disappointed to discover Lord

Lanford was as libidinous as that awful Mr. Blake, she thought with a small sigh. Still and all, when she considered the wonderful shoulders and deep blue eyes of this man who had twice now attempted to make her stay in Brighton more enjoyable, she could not prevent herself from thinking, *Well, perhaps I should not mind at that— but* only *with Lord Lanford.*

Shocked by her own licentious thoughts, Louisa tore her gaze from Lord Lanford's and turned to look out the window.

"What do you find so fascinating to lure you away from such scintillating company and bring you here?" he asked. There were tiny lines at the corners of his eyes and the edges of his mouth caused by his smile.

" 'Tis not in here," she said, her voice quaking with nervousness. She could feel his eyes still resting upon her— quite an unsettling sensation. To distract his attention from her, she raised her hand and indicated the shining moon and its broken reflection upon the sea. "Out there."

" 'Tis merely the moon." With a small chuckle Lord Lanford asked, "Have you never seen the moon?"

"Not like this," she said, shaking her head. "I have seen the moon reflected on a river or lake, but never on anything so . . . so big."

Lord Lanford looked at her more intently. "Have you never seen the sea?" His voice sounded incredulous. "Have you lived your entire life on this island and never seen the sea?"

"All my life I lived with my parents in the Cotswold. 'Tis a bit difficult to view the sea from over the hills," she reminded him with a grin.

"Miss Louisa Hamlin of the Cotswold," Lord Lanford said slowly.

He spoke, Louisa thought, almost as if by repeating her name he would gain some magical power over her. Indeed, as she watched him in the moonlight, she believed he truly did.

She returned to her silver and indigo view. "And 'tis not the sea, precisely," she said. She tried to use her most detached, instructive tone in order to calm the thundering of her heart. " 'Tis the English Channel."

"My, my, Miss Hamlin, you certainly know a lot about it for never having seen it before," Lord Lanford said with a chuckle. "But do you mean to say that you have come to Brighton, this most famous of seaside towns, and your first glimpse of the sea is at night, through someone else's window?"

"Lady Duville is not much of a one for sea vistas," Louisa admitted.

"Then I must do something to remedy your lack," he said. "I'm certain I can convince Lady Duville that a dip in the sea would be quite the thing."

Louisa wisely refrained from remarking that she was certain Lord Lanford could convince Lady Duville that painting her nose bright blue was quite the thing. Instead, she merely replied, " 'Twould be most entertaining. Thank you, my lord. And thank you for arranging to have me included. . . ."

"Why are you thanking me for something which you evidently are not enjoying?"

Indeed, to enjoy a party, she believed, one must be included in the festivities. As she had been rather ignored by everyone—except the odious Mr. Blake—she had not completely enjoyed the party—until now. But she thought she had at least managed to hide her disappointment.

"Oh, my lord, what a wretched ingrate you must think me!"

"Quite the contrary. I consider myself a poor guest if I fail my host so miserably by neglecting the entertainment of another guest." He extended his arm to her. "Come, Miss Hamlin. Enjoy the remainder of the evening with me."

If she were able to spend the remainder of the evening with Lord Lanford, Louisa believed she would enjoy this party immensely.

She drew in a deep breath and lifted her hand to slip it through the crook of his arm. His body was warm as her hand brushed against him. She could feel his muscles, large and strong, beneath the fabric of his sleeve.

He led her down the corridor, back to the drawing room.

"I have found our missing guest," Lord Lanford declared to those assembled there.

"Oh, Louisa, were you missing?" Lady Duville asked. She raised her fine eyebrows in shock, but Louisa could detect no sign of surprise in her blue eyes. "I had not noticed."

"Apparently Miss Hamlin became so absorbed in looking at all the impressive paintings here that she wandered off and became lost," Lord Lanford offered an explanation for Louisa.

"Indeed?" exclaimed Mr. Blake. His beady little eyes flickered over her with as much hunger as a man who had never seen a dinner table. "I should be pleased to show you some additional paintings, Miss Hamlin."

"Perhaps later," Lord Lanford said, dismissing the obnoxious man.

He gently steered Louisa toward an elderly lady seated upon a sofa. He indicated that she should be seated. As there was only room for two, Lord Lanford remained standing beside her.

Louisa was glad to have him standing so close, so protectively over her. She felt much safer having him near.

"Aunt Betsey," Lord Lanford said just a bit more loudly than one would speak in ordinary conversation.

The elderly lady started and looked up at Louisa with eyes the identical color of Lord Lanford's.

"Might I present Miss Hamlin?" Turning to Louisa, he explained, "My aunt, Mrs. McGowan. Aunt Betsey, Miss Hamlin is from the Cotswold—"

"What town?" Mrs. McGowan asked, cutting her nephew off in midsentence. Before Louisa could reply, she continued, "Do you know the Hammerleas? Pleasant enough brood, although with a penchant for overimbibing, as I recall." She fixed Louisa with a rheumy stare. "Wouldn't be your mother's people by any chance, would they?"

Louisa shook her head. "No, Mrs. McGowan. My mother was a Northville."

"Northville. Northville," Mrs. McGowan repeated, then demanded, "Not one of the Swindon Northvilles?"

Louisa made a small gulp, fearful that Lord Lanford's outspoken aunt should reveal something unsavory about the Swindon Northvilles. "Yes, Mrs. McGowan," she said at last.

Mrs. McGowan began to chuckle. Louisa began to fear the worst family gossip was about to be disclosed.

"My first beau was Hamilton Northville," Mrs. McGowan said. "Oh, how he could dance!"

"Are you fond of dancing, Miss Hamlin?" Lord Lanford asked.

"Oh, indeed," Louisa began, but before she could answer, Mrs. McGowan sharply demanded, "Wouldn't know Hamilton Northville, would you?"

"My mother's brother was Hamilton Northville," Louisa admitted.

Lord Lanford watched with amusement and something that he felt, strangely enough, he would call affection, as Louisa's azure eyes became more animated when she began to speak of her family. How she must miss them, living as she did with the self-preoccupied Beatrice.

"Your uncle? You don't say! Devilishly good-looking man!" Mrs. McGowan exclaimed. "Damned pity I didn't marry him."

Lady Teasel, suddenly very interested in her hitherto inconspicuous guest, insinuated herself between Lord Lanford and Louisa. "Why, Louisa dear—your name *is* Louisa, is it not?"

Louisa nodded.

Despite the lack of space, Lady Teasel then managed to squeeze her broad derriere into the small place between Louisa and Mrs. McGowan. "You little minx, why did you not tell us you were related to Hamilton Northville? Mrs. Northville gave the most splendid house parties! Or so I hear. I vow, I'd have sold my Aunt Hannah's false teeth for an invitation to one of her parties."

Other ladies, who had heretofore decided that Louisa was beneath their notice, also crowded about her, pushing Lord Lanford into the background.

Louisa had been grateful for his lordship's tall, protective form standing beside her. How she wished he were beside her now to shelter her from this unexpected onslaught. Louisa was accustomed to being ignored. 'Twas an unusual— and not altogether unpleasant feeling—to be the center of attention. Although she could not see him through the crush of ladies gathered about her, she felt very grateful to Lord Lanford for all his efforts on her behalf.

Lord Lanford regretted that he could no longer see Miss Hamlin through the throng. She was so beautiful when she was smiling.

Lady Duville was at the outskirts of the circle of ladies. Slowly she moved to Lord Lanford's side.

"It was so kind of you to see that Louisa is entertained elsewhere," Lady Duville said, pressing her arm against his, "so that you and I might . . . converse, alone at last."

Lord Lanford shook his head. He shifted his weight so that he moved away from her.

Lady Duville's expression changed to a petulant little pout. "At any rate, now I needn't be burdened with attempting to find some amusement for her this evening. These country-bred girls can be *so* tedious, don't you think?"

"No, I do not think Miss Hamlin tedious at all," Lord Lanford said. "And I never thought *you* would allow yourself to be burdened by *anyone*. Now I must find our host. Pray excuse me."

Much later that evening, as she strolled homeward, accompanied by an extremely petulant Lady Duville, Louisa decided that she had enjoyed herself at the dinner party after all, and she owed all her thanks to Lord Lanford.

*   *   *

The wagon was painted a cheerful red and blue. Nevertheless, Louisa was quite apprehensive. She was much more accustomed to changing her clothes in her bedchamber. What if the wind should catch the door and blow it open, exposing her for all the world to see?

The long flannel shift with the drawstring-tied neck into which she changed for bathing did nothing to alleviate her embarrassment. Looking down, she knew perfectly well that when this loose, white garment got wet, it would cling to her, shamelessly revealing more than just the outline of her figure.

Worse yet was the knowledge that incorrigible young men—and other men, not so young but equally incorrigible—were seated upon the cliffs above with spyglasses, watching the ladies bathe.

As if her discomfort and embarrassment were not enough, she must also be scared out of her wits. Not only must she suffer the bumpy ride into the water in the darkness of the enclosed wagon, but then the wagon must be turned about so that the horse faced the shore and the door opened out onto the water. There was no means of escaping the wagon except to plunge into the sea!

When she finally summoned her courage to enter the water, Louisa was grateful for the support of the strapping fisherman's daughter who was her dipper. The water was cold and tasted of salt—and it wouldn't stop moving back and forth! She supposed the wretched taste was from the medicinal benefits in the water, but for the life of her, she could see precious little benefit to her health in drowning.

Louisa was even more grateful when her dipper helped her out of the water shortly after her entrance. She knew that Lord Lanford was very generously paying for this entire outing for her, Lady Duville, and little Alfred. She felt extremely guilty wasting his lordship's money by not staying in the water for the full amount of time. However,

Louisa was growing exceedingly weary in the water, and the robust young dipper had already received her fee for her assistance and would not be cheated.

She changed into dry clothing inside the wagon, then climbed the wooden stairs to the hill where Lady Duville sat—very warm, very comfortable, and very dry—overlooking the water and the pebbly beach below.

"Well, Louisa, aren't you just the image of glowing health!" Lady Duville remarked.

Lord Lanford and Alfred were also there. His lordship's fair hair was still damp from his own dip, and was even curlier than when dry. As he stood there, with the sky behind him, Louisa believed that his eyes could not possibly be any more intensely blue.

Louisa wiped one remaining drip from a dark, bedraggled curl. *Oh, why must his lordship see me this way? 'Tis bad enough to be scared and wet and cold. Is looking like a drowned rat the final insult the Brighton folk have planned for those who dared invade and upset their once peaceful little fishing village?*

" 'Twas capital fun, Louisa!" Alfred whooped. He pranced about so that Nanny had difficulty wrapping him in the large blanket to protect him from the constant breeze. "Oh, please, Mama, may we do it again? Please! I'd like to go on my own, without that bothersome wagon."

"That all depends on Lord Lanford, Alfred dear," Lady Duville replied, gazing adoringly at her son's kind benefactor.

Lord Lanford had agreed to take Alfred to where the gentlemen bathed, farther west of the area near Russell House, where the ladies disported themselves in the waves.

Louisa was glad to hear that at least Alfred had a splendid time.

"I had quite a task extracting young Lord Duville from the water," Lord Lanford admitted. "The other bathees who were waiting for the bathing wagons were rather perturbed."

"Oh, Alfred, you must learn to obey Lord Lanford," Lady Duville gently chided her son.

"Well, whatever for?" Alfred demanded petulantly. "He's a 'm'lord' just like me—and not my papa, anyway." Then, as if reconsidering Lord Lanford's recent kindnesses, he amended, "Even if he *is* very nice." He turned back to his mother. "Oh, please say we may do it again."

"Well, of course you may, my pet," Lady Duville replied. Louisa grimaced at her ladyship's agreeableness. Beatrice had been sitting there quite comfortably. *She* had not worn that horrid smock. *She* had not been drenched in cold, salty water.

"I have not heard *you* make any request to repeat our outing," Lord Lanford said to Louisa.

"And you shall not, my lord," Louisa answered, so quickly that she could only regret not being able to call back her hasty words. She drew in a deep breath and held it. She felt the veriest churl for again disliking something that Lord Lanford had obviously gone to the trouble of planning for her. "I . . . I would not presume . . ."

"Shall we come again tomorrow then?" he asked.

"Oh, yes! Yes!" Alfred cried enthusiastically.

"I am not certain . . . what Lady Duville's plans are . . . for herself, or for me," Louisa stammered as she quickly glanced in her ladyship's direction.

Lady Duville was frowning darkly. Louisa knew full well that the glare of the sun was not the cause of her unhappy expression.

"Miss Hamlin, I get the distinct impression that you are not fond of bathing," Lord Lanford said.

"I . . . I prefer to do my bathing in a large tin tub," Louisa answered with a weak grin. She hoped his lordship would appreciate her jest and not think her too ungrateful for this outing.

"I am sure you do it splendidly, too," he said. His voice seemed inordinately deep.

Once again his blue eyes swept her body with the same

searing glance he had given her in the darkened room at the Teasels'. Louisa swallowed with difficulty. She felt as exposed and vulnerable to his perusal as if she were still in that damp white flannel gown. She found herself rather wishing that she were.

"I am sorry you do not enjoy bathing as much as the rest of us," he said. "You must give me another chance to find something that will please you."

How wonderful that his lordship should still be concerned that she enjoy herself while she was here! Louisa thought. And that he should make not one but two attempts. Yet she was too befuddled by his glance and his tone of voice to answer immediately.

"Surely Brighton is not so small nor so remote that there is not one thing in this town which you like," Lord Lanford said.

Louisa looked into Lord Lanford's eyes. Dare she tell him that as long as he remained in Brighton, there would always be one thing here that pleased her? His lordship would be shocked by her impertinence! And that very night Lady Duville would surely murder her while she slept!

Lord Lanford still waited for her decision. Alfred had begun to fidget. Lady Duville watched her with an increasingly narrowing gaze, which bode ill. Louisa had best reply with some innocuous pastime—and quickly, too.

"I . . . I do love to dance, my lord," she admitted. With sudden inspiration she continued, "I recall hearing my parents speak of the dances at the Assembly Rooms. How elegant they were, how pleasant the dancing, when they visited here once many years ago. . . ."

Lady Duville gave a scornful laugh. She turned to Lord Lanford, and with a shrug of her shoulders, she demanded, "Well, what can one expect from a country-bred spinster?"

Before Lord Lanford could reply, Lady Duville continued, "Louisa, you silly old thing! The *ton* does not attend the Assembly Rooms—unless they wish to advertise to the world that their pockets are to let. The *ton* attends

parties in private homes. Unless, of course, they go to the
Assembly Rooms for special receptions for Prinny or other
important people. Or," she added with a wicked giggle,
"to see which of their acquaintances have been reduced to
attending the Assembly Rooms."

"Oh, I did not realize . . . I am so sorry." Louisa knew
her face was as red as the bathing wagon from which she
had recently emerged. She wished at this moment that she
could return to that wagon, plunge beneath the salty waves,
and never reappear.

"The Assembly Rooms it is, then," Lord Lanford pronounced.

"Oh, but really, Marcus—" Lady Duville began to protest.

"No." Lord Lanford stopped her with a raised hand and
an emphatic shake of his head. "I have promised." He
turned to smile at Louisa. "If that is what Miss Hamlin
wishes, then that is what she shall have."

Louisa was astounded. Never had she witnessed anyone oppose Beatrice! Except that one time Alfred had so
insisted upon a pet dog, and for that he had spent the week
in the Nursery on bread and milk. Now Lord Lanford was
boldly contradicting Lady Duville, and there was not a thing
she could do about it. Most marvelous of all to Louisa was
the fact that he was doing it for her!

He gave Lady Duville a haughty stare. "I trust being in
the company of the Marquess of Lanford will ensure your
not being thought completely devoid of all important social
connections."

Louisa didn't care a fig that Lady Duville had pronounced
the balls at the Assembly Rooms quite *outré* for the
ton. Louisa didn't care a fig for the *ton*, either. *She*
thought the Assembly Rooms behind the Old Ship Inn were
wonderful.

Lord Lanford offered her his arm to escort her across
the room, the better to see the large portrait of a portly

old gentleman with a kindly looking face and long white curls, and a brown suit with a row of brass buttons down the front.

"Small wonder the *ton* no longer attends these affairs," Lady Duville remarked peevishly as she followed them, "if that is all the better he could dress."

"Whose portrait is it?" Louisa asked.

"The illustrious Dr. Russell," Lord Lanford explained. " 'Twas he who was responsible for encouraging so many persons to bathe in the waters here—not to mention encouraging them to drink what might possibly be one of the vilest concoctions ever devised."

"What is that?" Louisa asked, grinning. 'Twas not that the gentleman in the portrait appeared inordinately amusing, nor the fact that Lord Lanford had said anything particularly witty. 'Twas the fact that she was with Lord Lanford that made Louisa feel like smiling.

"Oh, who gives a tinker's dam what it was as long as we no longer need drink it," Lady Duville muttered.

Ignoring Lady Duville, Lord Lanford replied, "Sea water and milk."

Louisa made a suitably revolted face.

"My sentiments exactly," Lord Lanford agreed with a laugh.

"I believe I could use a glass of punch," Lady Duville interrupted. "Surely nothing here could taste as dreadful as Dr. Russell's beverage."

"We shall see," Lord Lanford replied. With a bow his lordship departed in search of the punch, leaving Louisa to listen to Lady Duville's incessant, petty complaints.

There were more people here than at any of the country assemblies that Louisa and her parents had attended. However, she had no idea who they were, and Lady Duville patently refused to acknowledge anyone. One gangly gentleman with threadbare cuffs came to beg a dance of Louisa, but Lady Duville rudely told the fellow to begone.

"You may not care what others think of you," Lady

Duville said to Louisa. "In fact, most likely, they do not think of you at all. But I'll not have anyone saying they saw Lady Duville enjoying herself here!"

"Oh, Beatrice," Louisa reassured her, "no one would *ever* accuse you of *that*!"

Lord Lanford approached, bearing a glass of punch in each hand. He offered one to Lady Duville and one to Louisa. The evening was quite warm, and Louisa was glad to have it.

Just as Lady Duville began to sip hers, the orchestra struck up a quadrille. Lady Duville shoved her glass into Louisa's hand so quickly that Louisa fairly choked on her mouthful and barely missed spilling the rosy liquid down the front of her one remaining ball gown.

"Why, yes, Marcus, I should love to dance," Lady Duville said, taking Lord Lanford's arm.

Louisa shook her head. Indeed, her dotage must be not merely creeping up on her but advancing by leaps and bounds, she decided. She had not heard his lordship request a dance of Lady Duville. Nevertheless, Lord Lanford did escort her ladyship to the dance floor, leaving Louisa with a glass of unfinished punch in each hand and no one with whom to converse.

What an interminable dance! It seemed to Louisa a full hour passed while Lord Lanford and Lady Duville danced. She knew it was not actually that long. It was, however, just long enough for the obnoxious Mr. Blake to find her in spite of the crowd.

"You must come dance, Louisa," he said. "Surely, a lady as charming as yourself must be a graceful dancer."

"I cannot dance," Louisa excused herself. "I'm . . . I'm minding the punch for Lady Duville. 'Tis quite delicious. Why don't you go and get some for yourself?"

"There are other things I would prefer." Mr. Blake draped his arm over her shoulder, extending his hand so far down that it nearly rested upon her breast.

'Twas bad enough he called her by her given name without so much as a by-your-leave. 'Twas even worse when he draped his flaccid arm over her with such familiarity.

Even if she were charitable enough to discount the fact that the rooms were warm and that Mr. Blake had been dancing vigorously all evening, Louisa could tell the wretched odor of his body was due not to too much exercise but to not enough soap and water.

"One cannot always have what one wants," Louisa informed him. She tried to give her shoulder a shrug to dislodge Mr. Blake's offending hand, but her motion only succeeded in giving him the opportunity to move his hand farther down.

If Louisa had not been burdened with a glass of punch in each hand, she would have slapped the insolent fellow's face.

"Miss Hamlin!" Lord Lanford exclaimed, coming up to her. "I believe you have had your fill of . . . punch." His lordship's pale blue eyes stared icily at Mr. Blake.

"I shall be quite happy if I never see . . . a glass of punch again," Louisa agreed. She shot Mr. Blake a glance that she hoped expressed all the contempt in which she held him.

Lord Lanford took both bothersome glasses from her hands and bestowed them upon a passing footman. He offered Louisa his arm. "I promised you a dance, did I not?"

"Well, *actually*, you only promised to *bring* her to these wretched Assembly Rooms," Lady Duville reminded him sharply.

"What a wonderful memory you have," Lord Lanford said. "For myself, I am glad my memory is so deficient that I believe I promised Miss Hamlin a dance. I shall keep this promise as well."

"What am I to do the meanwhile?" Lady Duville demanded. She pouted prettily, yet her eyes glared coldly at Louisa.

"You, too, may dance," Lord Lanford told her.

Lady Duville glanced scornfully about the room, then glared pointedly at Mr. Blake. She gave her blond curls a

shake and snorted quite indelicately. "There is *no one* here
with whom I would deign—"

"Then you may wait—quietly, if that is possible," Lord
Lanford said. He turned to Louisa and smiled. His smile
was gentle, inviting her to draw nearer to feel his warmth.
Willingly she went with him to the dance floor.

The orchestra began a waltz. Lord Lanford extended his
arm for Louisa to lay her hand atop his. He placed his other
arm about her, barely touching her back.

She looked up into his eyes. He smiled down upon her.
Louisa had the oddest notion that they should be doing
something besides dancing right now.

Lord Lanford shook himself from his entrancement and
began to lead her in the three small steps that carried them
about the room.

"So, Miss Hamlin from the Cotswold," he said, "you *do*
know how to waltz."

"Just because we live in the country, my lord, we are not
all wretched rustics, devoid of all of the social graces," she
informed him with a grin.

"Indeed not. I should say you were extraordinarily graceful. I see now why you claim to love dancing."

Her heart beat so fast that Louisa found it nearly impossible to make her feet keep time with the differing beat of
the music. She felt extraordinarily bewildered and clumsy
in his warm embrace. He drew her closer to him with each
step. While each corresponding step of hers backed her
away from him, the distance between them grew smaller
as the dance progressed. Louisa knew full well it was not
only his lordship's persistence that brought him closer to
her, but her own attraction to him that prevented her from
completely backing away.

Quite improper, she scolded herself. But she would not
listen. All she cared about was that for a few brief moments
Lord Lanford held her in his arms.

She realized that in a few days in Brighton she had found
what she had never found before—not in the two years she

had spent living with her cousin in London, not in all the three and twenty previous years in the Cotswold. She had found the man she loved.

Unfortunately, she was also dismally afraid that Lord Lanford did not love her. He was merely being polite. How could he have any real interest in her when he was so completely under the spell of Lady Duville? Wasn't he? Why else would he spend all this time with them, finding amusements for her as he had for little Alfred.

She despaired that the memory of these few happy moments would have to last her the rest of her life, and for that reason she tried to savor them all the more.

"Miss Hamlin, have I at last managed to find something that pleases you?" Lord Lanford said.

Barely able to breathe, Louisa found it even more difficult to answer. At last she managed to say, "Oh, yes. Indeed you are . . . you have," she quickly corrected herself.

She winced at her embarrassment, yet Lord Lanford appeared not to make notice.

"Everything you have done so far has pleased me," she told him quietly. She did not know whence she summoned the courage to speak to him thus, but she knew she must tell him how she felt.

"I do not think I have," he said. Louisa's heart plummeted as Lord Lanford frowned at her. But when she saw the playful light in his eyes, her heart lightened again. "I am certain you are not overly fond of bathing."

"That does not signify," she told him with a laugh. Then she even summoned the courage to insist, "You *have* pleased me, my lord."

"How so?"

"Because . . . because you *tried* to please me," she admitted.

Again Lord Lanford frowned, but this time from puzzlement.

Louisa shook her head. "Do not ask me to explain further. I cannot. I only know it does not matter if you succeeded or failed, but that you cared enough to make the attempt."

As the waltz ended, Louisa found herself not in front of a waiting Lady Duville, but on the other side of the room, before a set of doors that opened onto a small garden.

" 'Tis quite warm," Lord Lanford said. "Shall we take a stroll?"

Louisa gave only the briefest consideration to Lady Duville. *Oh, fie on Beatrice! Many is the time she left me,* she decided, and accompanied Lord Lanford into the moonlit evening.

"A pity we cannot see the sea from here," Lord Lanford said as he lifted his face to the dark night sky. "The moon is at the full. What a sight that must be upon the waves."

Louisa was not looking at the moon. She was studying Lord Lanford's firm profile, sharply etched against the starry sky. She realized that she could not stand here staring at him all night—as much as she might want to. She *must* say *something*.

"Why does the moon seem larger by the water?" she asked, turning to its silvery circle in the sky.

Lord Lanford chuckled. Then, very slowly, he turned to her and said, "Perhaps the salt water and the sea air render the moon much bolder than it customarily is."

"Perhaps," Louisa agreed. She looked from the moon back into Lord Lanford's eyes.

"Perhaps 'tis not only the moon which is made bolder," he continued, moving to stand directly before her.

He looked down into her eyes with the same inquiring look he had worn the previous night at dinner. Louisa had no question now. She knew perfectly well what his inquiry was. She also knew perfectly well what her answer was going to be.

"Louisa."

"My lord . . ."

"My name is Marcus."

"Marcus," she repeated.

"I have wanted to say your name, Louisa. And to hear you call me by mine."

He placed both hands on her arms. His hands were warm against her bare skin. Slowly he moved one hand up over her shoulder until it rested about her neck, while his thumb moved softly across the little hollow at the base of her throat.

"Louisa." His voice was deep and seemed to shake with bridled passion.

He took one step nearer. His hand glided from her throat to her chin. With the gentlest pressure he lifted her chin until her lips were within mere inches of his own.

Slowly—so slowly that Louisa's breasts ached—Marcus lowered his lips to hers.

His lips touched hers gently, then lingered, the pressure increasing until his arms had enveloped her completely within his strong embrace. His lips wandered to kiss the corners of her mouth, the hollow of her cheek, and the soft spot beneath her jaw in front of her ear. She shivered with the pleasure of his touch. She could hear his breath coming in short gasps as he sought to control himself. Her own ragged breath echoed in her ears as she willingly responded to him.

"My, my, Louisa, keeping secrets?" Lady Duville's voice cut sharply into the private world that Louisa and Lord Lanford had created about themselves.

Lord Lanford looked up from their embrace but did not release his hold of Louisa. 'Twas she who pulled away from him.

Lady Duville glanced from Lord Lanford to Louisa, then to Lord Lanford again. Slowly she tapped her fan against the palm of her hand as she inserted herself like a barrier between them.

"Could *this* be a new step which the fashionable people of the Cotswold have added to the waltz? Louisa, how kind of you to teach his lordship. And, Marcus," she added acidly, "what an apt pupil you make." She grabbed the small finger of Louisa's hand. "We shall discuss this at home."

Twisting Louisa's finger sharply, Lady Duville compelled her to follow as she made her way swiftly through the Assembly Rooms. Before Lord Lanford could stop her, she forced Louisa out into the now increasingly chill night air and dragged her all the way home.

Lord Lanford stood in the doorway, watching Louisa's retreating figure. Following her now would only exacerbate matters. Lady Duville was in no state to listen to reason— and the reasons that he would give for his behavior would only anger her more.

He would call tomorrow, Lord Lanford decided, when, in the light of day, clear heads would prevail.

Louisa lay in bed the next morning, rubbing her sore finger. She truly had expected a stronger retribution from Lady Duville last night. She had even taken the unaccustomed precaution of locking her bedchamber door—just in case. But her ladyship had merely retired to her own bedchamber in an extraordinary fit of pique. Still, Louisa knew her too well to think that this was the end of it.

What would happen to her? Louisa wondered. Lady Duville could not stop her income. No matter how small it might be, it was hers and hers alone—a bequest from her father.

Could Lady Duville evict her? Legally, Louisa was under the protection of Lord Duville—little Alfred. But who knew what Lady Duville might trick the little fellow into doing? Louisa supposed that she might find a small cottage and live out her remaining days in genteel poverty.

Worse still, Louisa supposed, Lady Duville might insist that Louisa remain in her household—and make of her life a living hell. Louisa decided she might as well begin seeking a cottage to let. She would rather leave of her own volition than be sent packing like a disgraced stepchild.

Then again, perhaps she need not be seeking a new home alone. Louisa's thoughts drew her onward, in another completely different, and infinitely more pleasant direction.

Lord Lanford—Marcus, she corrected herself—would be making her a part of his life.

He had looked at her and held her in a way that left very little doubt as to his feelings about her. He had kissed her in a manner that removed any of her remaining doubts.

Oh, how could Marcus George Kendall, fifth Marquess of Lanford, Viscount Triplingham, Baron Kendleton, take plain Miss Louisa Virginia Hamlin to wife? she asked herself. Well, hadn't Lady Duville been just plain Beatrice Seaforth—no, she reconsidered. Beatrice had never been "just plain" anything. Still, Louisa decided, she would not be the first miss to marry a marquess, nor would she be the last. On the other hand, these developments would *not* sit well with Beatrice at all!

The thought that Marcus cared for her gave Louisa a depth of courage that she had never before possessed. She arose. She could not hide abed any longer. Sooner or later she would have to confront Lady Duville.

Confronting Beatrice would not be pleasant. The prospect of doing so on an empty stomach was even more terrifying. Louisa hoped that she could at least go down for a quiet, solitary breakfast, and that her ladyship would have her chocolate brought to her room.

Unfortunately, Beatrice was exiting her bedchamber just as Louisa left hers.

Louisa leaned against the wall behind her, as if she could sink into it for invisibility. She was quite prepared for the worst. But Lady Duville smiled sweetly at her. Oh, dear. Something was *very* amiss. Louisa felt the soft hair on the back of her neck tingle with apprehension.

With great relief Louisa saw Nanny bringing a freshly scrubbed Alfred down from the nursery for his breakfast. Perhaps, she hoped, Lady Duville would refrain from doing mayhem if there were witnesses.

"Come, Louisa, dear," Lady Duville said pleasantly. "Let us have breakfast and discuss our plans for the day."

Lady Duville gripped the banister with one hand and took

Louisa's elbow with the other. Louisa ran her hand down the wall for support as they began to descend the narrow and precariously steep staircase. Nanny and Alfred followed.

Waldo, the small stuffed dog that Louisa had made Alfred from scraps of an old brown velvet cloak when Lady Duville adamantly refused to allow him to have a live pet, went tumbling down the stairs ahead of them.

Nanny made a dive for Waldo, interposing herself between Lady Duville and Louisa, just as her ladyship gave her hip a forceful nudge in Louisa's direction.

Nanny went sprawling down the staircase and landed in a heap at the bottom. Horrified, everyone rushed to her aid.

At last Nanny managed to sit up. "Oow, that was a terrible tumble!" she mumbled, holding her head as if to still its mad swirling.

"Oh, Nanny, are you all right?" Louisa cried, kneeling beside her.

"Of course I am," she said. "I'm a hardy girl, and a good thing, too. Why, just think, Miss Louisa, if I hadn't made a grab for Waldo, it might have been you what fell when her ladyship tripped."

Louisa pressed her lips tightly together. Tripped indeed! But how could she ever prove otherwise?

"Come now, Nanny," Lady Duville quickly intervened. "Let us remove you to a nice comfortable chair where you may recuperate, instead of cluttering up the hallway."

Alfred immediately seized one of Nanny's arms to assist her to rise. "Don't worry. I'll take care of you, Nanny," he reassured her.

The plump girl laughed. "Oh, m'little lord, I know you're on your way to being big and strong, but I'll need more help than that to get me on my feet."

Louisa knelt at Nanny's other side.

"Oow!" Nanny yelped in pain as she rose. "My ankle! It didn't hurt until I stepped on it."

Louisa and the footman who had come running at the

noise assisted Nanny to the sofa. The physician was summoned. 'Twas not broken, was the verdict of the thin, bespectacled little man. 'Twas merely a bad sprain. Nevertheless, Nanny must not use it for several weeks.

"Whatever will his little lordship do?" Nanny worried as they assisted her up to her room.

"Oh, do not concern yourself with that, Nanny." Turning a smile to Louisa, Lady Duville said, "Louisa will be more than happy to care for Alfred while Nanny recuperates. Won't you?"

Louisa knew this was not a question. Nevertheless, she would willingly care for the little boy, no matter what the circumstances were that occasioned this. Whether she or Nanny had been injured was immaterial; the fact that Louisa would now be occupied with Alfred—away from Lord Lanford—was what mattered to Lady Duville.

Louisa smiled to herself. All Lady Duville's machinations were for naught. Marcus would seek her out. She knew he would! Oh, he had not said he loved her. With Lady Duville interrupting them in that abrupt fashion, he hadn't the time. But Louisa knew Marcus loved her as much as she loved him—and he *would* be with her again.

Louisa saw to it that Nanny was comfortable. Then she tucked Alfred into bed. At last, she settled into the chair in her small bedchamber anticipating that this evening, just like the three previous evenings, would be very quiet and very long.

Ah, well, she thought with a wistful sigh, *at least now I shall be able to finish reading* Guy Mannering.

But try as she might, she could not concentrate. Each time she began, it was not long before her fingers were slowly wandering over the binding where his lordship had touched it, and her thoughts were wandering to Lord Lanford. But was Lord Lanford thinking of her?

Of late, she had begun to think not. Surely he would have called on her by now. But he had not even bothered to send round flowers or a brief note. Could she have been mistaken regarding Lord Lanford's feelings for her?

Such dismal thoughts drew her attention to the delicious little biscuits, which were waiting in the cupboard in the kitchen, and whose sole purpose on this earth was to offer her comfort. They had never failed to do so heretofore.

Before Louisa could rise to get the biscuits, the tapping on her bedchamber door signaled Lady Duville's flamboyant entrance. Her first words this evening, as they had been the past three evenings, were "How was Alfred?" This was quite a change. Usually Lady Duville launched immediately into her praises for Lord Lanford, without giving poor Alfred much thought at all.

Lately, Louisa had begun to think, rather uncharitably, that Lady Duville only did this to further impress upon Louisa that her ladyship had been somewhere with Lord Lanford—and Louisa had *not*.

"Very well behaved, as always," Louisa answered, as she always did. "Although I think he is becoming bored playing in the garden. He would like to go bathing again—or at least for a walk about the—"

"Perhaps later," Lady Duville said vaguely. "He needs to stay home now. He got very wet while bathing. I should not want him to venture out and take cold."

"I think there's precious little chance of Alfred taking cold in August," Louisa remarked. "Especially since he *has* dried out completely by now."

"It is so good of you to be concerned for little Alfred while Nanny recuperates." Lady Duville gave Louisa's hand a condescending pat. "A pity you missed the Massinghams' musicale—although why they should have invited you when they do not even know you is beyond me. You did not make *that* much of an impression on them at the Teasels'. Well, to own the truth, I never would have believed Lily Massingham could sing that well. Of course, Marcus claims he dislikes singing." She leaned closer to Louisa and whispered confidentially, "Well, the man needn't sing a note when he looks like *that*! And he is so devoted to me! In fact, *very* soon I expect to be Lady Lanford."

Louisa had always taken Lady Duville's chatter about Lord Lanford with a grain of salt. But now she had actually met him. Now she knew what his eyes looked like in the sunshine and in the deep blue of the night. She knew what it felt like to rest her hand on his broad shoulders, and to have his strong arms embrace her. She could still feel his lips on hers. She could not bear to think that Lady Duville also knew these sensations—far better than she! Louisa closed the book with a snap.

"Did his lordship make no mention of me?" she summoned the courage to ask.

Lady Duville laughed—a strident laugh, which caused Louisa's ears to ache.

"Whyever should he ask after . . . Oh, dear!" Lady Duville raised her hand gracefully to cover her mouth as if she had said something she had not intended.

Louisa harbored no delusions that Lady Duville had not intended every word she uttered.

Lady Duville regarded Louisa with infinite compassion and patted her shoulder consolingly. "Oh, you poor, deluded little fool. You truly believed he had fallen in love with you, didn't you?"

Louisa merely nodded. She was afraid to speak, as if the sudden trembling in her throat would reveal her rapidly burgeoning doubts.

Lady Duville clasped both of Louisa's hands. She peered intently into her eyes.

"Now, my dear," her ladyship said, in tones which one might use in explaining an extraordinarily complicated matter to an extraordinarily obtuse child. "Marcus is a sophisticated man of the world, and you—well, to own the truth, you're merely a country spinster—and a dreadfully naive one at that. But there are some things which every lady simply *must* understand about men."

Louisa opened her mouth to protest, but Lady Duville held up her hand to stop her.

"Men cannot . . . well, quite frankly, Louisa, they cannot keep their hands—or certain other parts of their anatomy—to themselves. Do you understand?"

Louisa shook her head. Of course she understood what Lady Duville was trying so indelicately to explain. And no, she did not believe such a thing about Lord Lanford, not for one minute.

"But he acted as if—"

"They *all* do," Lady Duville interrupted with a small chuckle. "You really must forgive Marcus. After all, *I* have forgiven him that little *divertissement* with you. He was *so* abjectly penitent to me, claiming it meant nothing to him. Heat of the moment and all that—you *do* understand?"

Louisa was still shaking her head.

"After all, he is but a man, my dear," Lady Duville continued, "and in truth, it did *not* mean anything to him. So you see, Louisa, you really musn't think anything of it, either—now that you know how men—*all men*—are."

Indeed, if Louisa had not known before, she knew now. Lord Lanford had not paid a visit nor sent round a note for the simple reason that he did not think her significant enough to warrant even a fare-thee-well.

Louisa stared into the cold, empty fireplace. She knew Lady Duville's true reason for coming here tonight. She had come here to break her heart.

"But, Louisa," Alfred protested, "I *hate* to go shopping!"

"Well, we're not actually shopping," Louisa explained, "since I have no money to buy anything. Can't we pretend we're searching the contents of the shop windows for contraband?"

In spite of Lady Duville's refusal to allow Alfred out, Louisa was determined—she was taking him anyway. The poor little fellow could not stay indoors forever. Her ladyship was occupied elsewhere today—probably with Lord Lanford, Louisa thought bitterly as she fought down the twisted knot in her stomach. Louisa and Alfred could go out for a stroll about Brighton, and Lady Duville would never be the wiser.

"Do you know what I'd *truly* like?" Without waiting for Louisa to respond, he continued, "I'd like to go into the water again. Oh, please!"

"But I have no money to pay your bather." Louisa did not even know how much one offered the strong men who assisted others into and out of the water and made certain they did not drown in the interim.

"Oh, I can always get some money from Nanny," Alfred said confidently.

Louisa looked up into the clear sky. "It looks as if it will rain," she said without much conviction. "We cannot go bathing in the rain."

"Whyever not? We'll already be wet."

Louisa grinned. Nevertheless, she was forced to admit, "You know how I dislike bathing, Alfred."

"Get one of the footmen to come with me," Alfred suggested.

As trustworthy as the footmen were, Louisa still did not think she wanted to shirk her own duties by entrusting her cousin's only son into their care. Not to mention the fact that news of their forbidden outing would then most definitely get back to her ladyship.

Sensing her hesitation, Alfred screwed his little mouth into a frown. "I wish we could get Lord Lanford to come again. I had lots of fun with him. But Mama keeps him all to herself now."

Louisa sighed and looked off to the horizon again. She was not looking to see what the weather would bring, but to hide from Alfred the tears that welled up in her eyes.

If Beatrice had managed to keep his lordship to herself,

Louisa thought bitterly, *I should not now be nursing a broken heart*.

Louisa grimaced. She truly was not being fair to Lady Duville. Could any one woman, even a woman as beautiful as Beatrice, hold a man like Lord Lanford?

Louisa sighed. Considering what Lady Duville had told her, neither could she hold Lord Lanford responsible. After all, he was merely a man, with certain baser instincts which he was wont to follow. Louisa herself had been all too trusting, all too willing to follow his lead. In truth, her aching heart was entirely her own fault.

"Oh, please, Louisa," Alfred pleaded. "I've no one else to play with but you."

Louisa sniffed and blinked back her tears. She set her lips firmly together and lifted her head. Alfred was correct.

She might be feeling sorry for herself because she had lost the man she loved. But poor little Alfred still had Lady Duville for a mother and rightly deserved the greater pity. Just because Louisa was miserable was no reason to keep Alfred from enjoying himself.

With the back of her hand, Louisa harshly brushed away her remaining tears. What was done, was done. She'd waste no more tears on the likes of Marcus Kendall.

"I'd truly like to go without that blasted wagon," Alfred said.

"I do not think the bathers and dippers would like that one bit," Louisa told him. "They already cast rather harsh glances to the few people who know how to swim and do not need their assistance."

"Well, then, we'll go elsewhere," Alfred pronounced with an emphatic nod of his blond head.

"Where?"

"You're the grown lady. *You* should know these things."

Louisa grinned at Alfred's implicit faith in adults. Sadly she reflected that even as a "grown lady," she still had precious little knowledge of the ways of the world.

"We could always go that way farther," he said, pointing to the west.

Although people were continually planning and building rows of new houses along new streets, squares, and crescents, there were few structures as yet beyond Russell Square. A bit farther west, before they encountered the town of Hove, a small stretch of deserted beach might be found to accommodate Alfred's wish for a dip unencumbered by wagons and other bathees.

"We could hire a donkey cart," Louisa suggested, at last catching some of Alfred's enthusiasm.

"Louisa, can you really drive one of those things?" Alfred looked skeptical.

Louisa gave him a confident smile. "Sometimes there *are* advantages to being a country-bred miss."

"Oh, Marcus, didn't you enjoy the Massinghams' musicale?" Lady Duville asked as they strolled along the Steine.

She clung to his arm as if she would float up into the sky if she let him loose. As a matter of fact, Lord Lanford rather wished she would.

He was bored with yet another circuit of the Steine. He knew every red brick and white fence post and blade of green grass there—and he heartily disliked them all.

Lord Lanford suppressed the sigh that rose in his chest. 'Twould never do to have Lady Duville see it. She would think he was sighing for her like some lovesick swain. What an extraordinary imagination the lady had!

No, he had not enjoyed himself at the Massinghams' musicale. Lily Massingham could sing passably well. Her accompanist was skilled enough. Even the refreshments had been better than the Massinghams' usual fare. Still, had been something very important lacking there. He knew what was missing was Louisa.

"I am looking forward to this evening at the theater, Marcus," Lady Duville continued, oblivious to his lack of a reply. "Aren't you?"

Lord Lanford gave a noncommittal shrug. Perhaps if he shrugged a bit harder, he could dislodge Lady Duville's grip on his arm. The woman was fairly cutting off his circulation!

He frowned. Why should he look forward to the theater? Were the actors going to do anything out of the ordinary? 'Twas not that their performances were inadequate. 'Twas simply that he'd seen them all. He had no wish to see them again.

Well, perhaps he would not mind going, if only—Lord Lanford pressed his lips more tightly together—if only Louisa were going to be there, too.

He missed Louisa. Even in the short space of these past few days, he knew that his life was not the same when she was not there.

Blast him for his own stupidity! Why hadn't he realized that the lady, for however many years she may have spent on this earth, was still as innocent as any miss fresh from the schoolroom? Why had he lured her to the garden? Why had he held her so seductively? Why had he kissed her so lustfully? Oh, why hadn't he been able to control himself, to wait just a bit longer to express his feelings, instead of frightening the poor girl away!

He had tried to call upon her the very next afternoon, but Lady Duville had told him that Louisa had been so embarrassed by her compromised position that she had immediately packed her things and left with the morning coach.

He wanted to follow her. His own chaise and pair were infinitely faster than the lumbering Brighton coach, regardless of its highly touted speed. But Lady Duville had laid a restraining hand on his arm. Peering earnestly into his eyes, she had delivered the devastating message. Louisa's last words as she left had been that she hoped never again to lay eyes on the lascivious Lord Lanford.

As they continued their stroll, he silently cursed Lady Duville's wretchedly bad timing. If she had not interrupted them, he would have been able to express to Louisa the full extent of his feelings for her. He could have told her how much he loved her. He would have had time to propose marriage.

"Lord and Lady Thomerson are giving a masquerade Wednesday next," Lady Duville was still rambling on. "I was planning on attending as Columbine, and I thought perhaps you would make an extraordinarily attractive Harlequin. . . ."

"I think not," Lord Lanford interrupted.

"Think . . . not . . . ?" she repeated. She blinked as if surprised that he should disagree. Quickly she recovered. "Oh, well, perhaps you would prefer—"

"No, I would not," he responded abruptly. "As a matter of fact, I do not think I will be attending after all."

"Ah, well," Lady Duville finally conceded. "I have not expended too much on the costume. There is no need to go if you would prefer to spend a quiet evening"—she brushed her full breasts seductively against him—"just the two of us."

Lord Lanford grimaced. Lady Duville's head was as hard and dense as the bricks upon which they trod.

"You know, Marcus," Lady Duville said, obviously oblivious to Lord Lanford's cold indifference, "I have been giving a great deal of thought lately to the inordinate amount of time that you and I have been spending together, in London and in Brighton. Surely, you cannot deny the fact that we have been seen together almost every day."

"No, Beatrice," Lord Lanford replied wearily. "No one could deny that." He wondered how many persons knew that their proximity was due to Lady Duville's persistence in seeking him out and not due to any desire on *his* part to be with the lady.

"And surely, you cannot deny that we have been enjoying each other's company." Lady Duville fluttered her long, dark lashes at him.

Lord Lanford pursed his lips. How could he explain to her that he had never enjoyed her company—until he had arranged for her to bring Louisa?

"Marcus," she wheedled, "you know that the *ton* talks about people who spend a great deal of time together."

"The *ton* also talks about people who have *not* spent a lot of time together," Lord Lanford answered disinterestedly. "Indeed, they talk about people who have no knowledge of each other whatsoever."

Lady Duville laughed, but it was a hollow little laugh, as if she had a foreboding that his lordship was not thinking along the same lines as she. Her face grew increasingly pink and her eyes grew wide with apprehension.

Suddenly she pulled him to a halt on the brick walk. She drew herself up imperiously.

"Marcus, I shan't mince words. I think in all fairness to my reputation, it behooves you to speak for my hand in marriage."

There! She had said it. Lady Duville held her breath.

Lord Lanford held his breath, too, trying to decide how to be tactful. At length he said, "Beatrice, let us discuss this elsewhere." He glanced meaningfully at the other people who were staring at them with open curiosity as they passed. "Somewhere more private."

Immediately Lady Duville's blue eyes began to shine.

Oh, blast! He never should have phrased it quite that way.

"On second thought, Beatrice, let us remain here. But let us at least continue to walk so as not to clutter up the path."

He attempted to disengage her hands from about his arm. 'Twas a difficult task as he fairly had to pry her clutching fingers off his sleeve.

"Beatrice, I am sorry," he said as gently as he possibly could. "I cannot marry you. I am not in love with you."

"Ha, love!" she replied with a bitter laugh. "One needn't be in love to marry. Do you think I loved Stephen?"

"No," Lord Lanford answered quite simply. He harbored no delusions regarding Lady Duville's capacity for tender feelings for anyone but herself.

"But you think you are in love with *Louisa*?" she accused. She released his arm as if it were on fire. Rapidly she stepped away from him.

"I . . ." Why did he hesitate? He knew he had been in love with Louisa almost from the first moment he had seen her. But he would not tell Lady Duville. Louisa must be the first to know.

"Indeed, you are—or at least you *think* you are," Lady Duville accused. "Well, go then!" she ordered, angrily waving him away. "Go try to find her—*if* you can, and *if* she will see you."

"I shall." Turning abruptly on his heel, he strode away. "If I have to scour every town and hamlet in England, I *will* find her."

Louisa sat on the pebbly beach, her parasol shading her from the sun. Alfred had quickly stripped off his shoes and stockings and headed directly for the playful waves that lapped at the water's edge.

"Come in, Louisa!" he invited. "The water is much warmer here, truly!"

He kicked at the water, sending up fans of salty spray in her direction. Louisa was glad she had the foresight to stay well out of Alfred's range.

"I doubt the waves are any warmer or any more gentle here than anywhere else along the coast of Britain," Louisa told him. "I think I shall sit and watch you."

"Oh, *do* come in!" he pleaded.

Louisa thought Alfred did look as if he could use a playmate. She cautiously glanced about her. The beach was deserted. If she ventured in, who would know besides Alfred?

She removed her shoes. Turning her back to Alfred, she untied her stocking garters as well. Abandoning her parasol, and lifting her skirt slightly, Louisa joined the little boy at the water's edge.

Warmed by the sun, the shallow water truly was not as

cold as it was where the wagon had deposited her farther out. As a matter of fact, Louisa enjoyed the feel of the gentle waves lapping at her ankles and between her bare toes.

Soon the hem of her white muslin gown was drenched and dragging in the waves. Heedless of convention, she lifted her skirt and knotted it at knee height. Unencumbered, she began to follow Alfred's example, kicking at the water to send up plumes of spray.

Alfred was right. This was much more fun without the wagon and the dippers. Louisa did not even mind when one misstep sent her headlong into the water. Laughing, she rolled over to sit in the waves lapping about her bottom. Alfred whooped with glee as, splashing through the waves, he ran to her rescue, doing far more harm than good in his attempt to keep her dry.

"Pack my things, Winston," Lord Lanford ordered his valet as he burst into his town house.

But Winston was not quick enough. Giving his valet instructions to follow in the chaise, Lord Lanford mounted his horse and left.

He pressed his horse to a gallop as he rode out of Brighton, hoping that the vigorous activity would take the edge off his anger. He glowered at each passing inch of terrain ahead of him that separated him from Louisa.

If only he knew where to begin. He could go to Swindon to inquire after her mother's people. If that failed, he would question Lord Duville's solicitor. Surely, Louisa would notify the solicitor of her new direction so that he could continue to send her allowance each quarter. Somewhere, somehow, he *would* find her again.

Suddenly excited shouts in the distance diverted Lord Lanford's intense concentration. He pulled his horse to a halt.

He immediately recognized the pair cavorting on the beach below—how could he not know her? But what on earth were Louisa and Alfred doing in the waves? Whatever it was, it looked deucedly good fun!

He dismounted. They were apparently so absorbed in their aquatic activities that they did not even notice his approach.

Upon spotting him, Alfred cried, "Lord Lanford! Come join us!"

He did not need further coaxing. Pausing only long enough to strip off his finely cut jacket and his well-polished boots— so his valet would not suffer an attack of the apoplexy—Lord Lanford dashed into the water. Alfred squealed with delight and led his lordship a merry chase through the waves.

Louisa watched Lord Lanford. The splashing water drenched his trousers and accentuated the rippling muscles of his long legs as they carried him easily across the beach.

Just as Lord Lanford was about to catch Alfred, the little boy quickly turned about, bent down, and sent a spray of sea water splashing up into his lordship's face. Drenched, the pair took off again, laughing.

Louisa would never have expected to see the Marquess of Lanford frolicking in the waves like a seven-year-old boy. Whatever his terrible reputation with the ladies, Louisa was forced to admit, he *was* kind to children.

Not to mention *awfully* attractive, she thought with a shiver that came not from the cold water but from deep within. His wet lawn shirt molded to his broad chest muscles and billowed out behind him as he ran against the wind. His shirt had come open at the neck, revealing the fine wisps of darker but still definitely blond hair that rose in curling tendrils up the firm expanse of his chest. Louisa dared not look to see what the wet trousers revealed!

Watching him, Louisa forgot how angry she was with the man. She eagerly anticipated when he and Alfred would next pass her as they darted down the beach.

This time Alfred did not run past her but circled about, clutching at her skirts as he placed her between himself and the pursuing Lord Lanford.

Lord Lanford collided directly with Louisa. He grasped her firmly against him so that she would not fall.

Her clothes were wet and chilly. His lordship's body was warm against her cold skin. She could see his pulse pounding in his throat. She realized that her own damp clothing clung to her body, the fine muslin revealing far more than the dipper's flannel shift ever would have.

Louisa felt the saturated fabric of her bodice pulling tautly over her breasts. There was little she could do to cover her lowcut bodice. She tried to bend down to reach the knot in her skirt, to undo it, to let it fall over her exposed legs, but Lord Lanford refused to release her.

"What are you doing here?" he asked. "I thought you—"

"I am surprised that you thought of me at all," she said tartly. She scooped up the sodden mass of fabric of her skirt. Not daring to look into Lord Lanford's eyes, she picked angrily at the wet knot, which refused to be undone.

"Not think of you!" he repeated incredulously. "You are all I have thought about."

"Excuse me if I disbelieve you, my lord," she said. She was so befuddled by his nearness that she could no longer decide whether she wanted to turn and run or to continue picking at this blasted, stubborn knot. "You never even bothered to call—"

"I did call," he insisted, wrapping his arm more firmly about her so that she would not try to escape him. "The very next day. But Beatrice said you had left . . . that you did not want to see me again."

"Beatrice said . . . ?" Louisa let the knot drop from her suddenly numb fingers.

"I was on my way to find you—wherever you had gone."

"Find me?"

Lord Lanford *had* wanted her—*still* wanted her. Louisa felt her heart begin to warm inside her chilled body. Still, there were puzzles and wounded feelings as yet unresolved in her mind.

"Why should you be looking for me when you intend to marry Beatrice?" she asked. She wished she hadn't dropped that blasted knot. It would have served as something for her nervous fingers to fidget with.

"I have no intention—" Suddenly Lord Lanford looked down at the small hands clutching Louisa's waist. He peeked around behind her. "Alfred, my good fellow, why don't you see to my horse? He's a fine bit o' blood, and I think you'd find him interesting."

Alfred clung to Louisa's skirt. "Oh, I think 'tis rather interesting here."

Lord Lanford threw him a playful scowl. Alfred laughed out loud and took off at a run up the beach.

"Louisa!" Lord Lanford spoke her name forcefully. He tried to draw her to him, the better to recall the intensity of the previous moment. "Please believe me when I tell you I have no intention of marrying Beatrice."

"Oh, you horrid cad!" she exclaimed, renewing her attempt to pull away from him. "Are you just dallying with her, too?"

"I *never* dallied with Beatrice! I don't even *like* Beatrice."

"Well, that's not what *she* told me."

"Did Beatrice tell you we were to be wed? That you were a mere dalliance for me?" Lord Lanford asked.

Louisa nodded.

"She told me that you had left Brighton, that you told her to tell me that you never wanted to see me again," he explained. "Is this true, Louisa?"

"No," she admitted.

"Then I think if I were you, I would not put much stock in anything Beatrice says."

"But—"

"Whom do you believe?" he asked, drawing her closer to him. He ran his hand up and down, warming the chill, damp muslin that covered her back. "Beatrice or me?"

Louisa shivered with unexpected warmth.

"I came all the way out here searching for you," he

reminded her. His blue eyes looked down upon her with the familiar longing. "What more must I do to convince you?"

Slowly his lips met hers. He tasted of sunshine and salt water. Louisa savored the flavor of him as his lips continued to caress hers.

"We have only been apart three days, and I have missed you more than anyone else in my life," he murmured into her ear. "I love you, Louisa."

"I've been so miserable without you," Louisa said. "I love you, too, Marcus."

"I have loved you since the first day I sought you out in Bowen's," Lord Lanford told her. "Since the first time I saw the wind blow that wretched bonnet from your head in front of Raggett's."

Louisa's hands flew up to cover her face. "Oh, horrors! Did you see *that*?"

Very softly he said, "I think that is when I fell in love with you."

Louisa looked up at him inquiringly. "Did you truly go to all that trouble at Bowen's and at the Teasels' just to meet me?"

Lord Lanford nodded. "I think you are well worth the trouble."

He swayed her gently to the side, the better to cradle her head in the crook of his arm, the better to tilt her face up to meet his. Louisa lifted her arms and entwined them about Marcus's neck. He kissed her again.

"Say you will marry me, Louisa. Say that we will never again be away from each other—not even for three short days."

"I will not let you out of my sight," she promised him. "Not for one moment."